A FOOL FOR A CLIENT

A FOOL FOR A CLIENT

David Kessler

Hodder & Stoughton

First published in Great Britain in 1997
by Hodder and Stoughton
A division of Hodder Headline PLC

A CIP catalogue record for this title is available
from the British Library

ISBN 0 340 68899 8

Typeset by Hewer Text Composition Services, Edinburgh
Printed and bound in Great Britain by
Mackays of Chatham PLC, Chatham, Kent.

Hodder and Stoughton
A division of Hodder Headline PLC
338 Euston Road
London NW1 3BH

This book is dedicated to my late mother who encouraged my intellectual curiosity and creativity from my earliest childhood, and to my father, who was my pillar of cloud by day and my pillar of fire by night.

Acknowledgments

The author wishes to express his gratitude to those who helped him bring this book into the light of day, both with the research that went into it and the process of getting it published. Firstly I must express a deep debt of gratitude to Bob Burka and Dan Segal, both of whom welcomed me into their homes as a guest when I was just starting out as a writer and patiently answered my sometimes naïve questions about American law. I would also like to thank Martin Adelman, who read an earlier draft of the manuscript and gave me detailed advice on New York criminal law and practice as well as supplying me with a copy of his excellent monograph on the law pertaining to *pro se* defence. I must stress that although these people gave me excellent and detailed advice, I decided to take literary licence on a number of points and that accordingly any remaining errors or inaccuracies are the responsibility of the author alone.

Finally I would like to thank my agent, Jane Conway-Gordan, who believed in me, encouraged me and led me through the painful but worthwhile transition from an enthusiastic aspiring writer to a successful published one. It has been a rewarding process.

'If you're planning to dig a grave, dig two.'

Ancient Chinese proverb

'Anyone who conducts his own defence has a fool for a client.'

Legal aphorism

1

'Your Honour,' Justine Levy's voice rang out confidently, 'this isn't any sort of legal grey area. Under the Sixth Amendment I have the right to conduct my own defence.'

There wasn't a vacant seat in the courtroom, either for spectators or journalists. Only the jury box remained empty. From his vantage point on the bench, the judge surveyed the swaying heads and shoulders that blended in with each other like a stormy sea in tumultuous motion. Crowds like this were unusual for what was nothing more than a pre-trial motions hearing. But the charge was murder, and the case had captured the attention of the mass media, and thus the public. Fact had become blended with speculation in an endless stream of reportage that had been splashed across the pages of the press from coast to coast. The judge knew that a lot of people were going to try to use this case for publicity. He hoped that he would be able to prevent the proceedings from degenerating into a circus.

'The right to proceed *pro se* was affirmed by the State Supreme Court in the McIntyre decision and upheld in the US Supreme Court in Faretta versus California.'

Justine was addressing the judge, the Honourable Justice

Harold Wise. She was speaking in a forceful but not impassioned tone that would have held him spellbound had he not consciously told himself: *She's just another defendant.* As Justine presented her brief argument, Justice Wise, a quietly dignified man in his mid-fifties, sat there in patient silence. He was a patrician figure with an upright posture and proud bearing. His hair, still full and thick, had lost every trace of the light brown that it had possessed in his youth, and was now a solid dark grey, almost like a storm cloud. But its shade made him look all the more distinguished. He wore his robes with an air of confidence, as if they had been tailored to fit his body, and he looked at people with eyes that were firmly focused but not intimidating.

He noticed that unlike inexperienced lawyers, many of whom tend to play to the jury even when there is no jury present, this girl, amateur though she was, did not gesticulate or raise her voice. She stood still, her arms at her sides, almost like a soldier standing to attention, giving free rein to a voice that rang out with an echoing timbre. But the most striking feature was that she stood before him alone with no lawyer at her side and no papers or notes before her.

'I must disagree with the defendant,' the prosecutor said in a voice that the judge noted was uncharacteristically timid.

At the prosecution table stood Daniel Abrams, a man in his mid-forties whose neat dark hair, well-cut suit and commanding height couldn't quite distract the judge's attention from the beads of perspiration that stood out on his forehead. Throughout Justine's short speech, Abrams had remained on the edge of his chair, poised to rise. Now, standing in the centre spotlight, he looked as if he were suffering from stage fright. This seemed strange to the judge. Abrams was an experienced lawyer and should long since have been rendered immune to this kind of nervousness by practice and maturity.

Flanked by a female aide in her early thirties to his right and a young man in his twenties to his left, he looked like a leading actor on opening night, afraid of forgetting his lines.

'The court may rule that the defendant is not mentally competent to conduct her own defence,' Abrams continued.

'Not without declaring me unfit to stand trial,' Justine

retorted. 'If I'm sane enough to stand trial, I'm sane enough to conduct my own defence.'

'Your source for that?' the judge enquired. His tone was mildly pedagogic, as if he were testing her.

'People versus Davis, New York, 1979.'

The judge knew that any partisan display would be professionally improper. But he couldn't resist the urge to smile approvingly at Justine's intellect and the thoroughness of her preparation.

'I see you've done your homework, Miss Levy.'

The Assistant District Attorney surreptitiously loosened his necktie. The judge knew what was on his mind. The job of Deputy District Attorney was coming up for grabs and Abrams had to come over before the public as a man of fighting spirit in order to stay in the running. It was widely known in legal circles that Abrams was in line for the number-two slot, but the DA wouldn't like it if Abrams conceded even a *mildly* significant point without offering at least a token show of resistance. The judge, who was no stranger to the political shenanigans of the legal profession, could guess that this whole charade was part of Abram's strategy for pushing his name to the top of the DA's shortlist.

But the judge sensed that Abrams had a more personal motive. If Justine Levy won on this point then in a sense she would 'win' with the public regardless of the verdict. Conducting her own defence was bound to create sympathy for her, and the outcome of court cases often hinges more on the sympathies or anger of the jury than on the raw facts of the evidence. The news media were already playing up the Murphy extradition case, although it was by no means certain that the two cases were connected. The last thing any politically ambitious prosecutor would want was for a young, pretty female defendant to come over as a crusading heroine fighting off the powerful machinery of a monstrous and unjust legal system.

With a lawyer in her corner, it might be possible to secure a plea bargain, thereby saving the state the expense of a trial and obtaining from the girl a public admission that she had done wrong and was not the courageous crusader that she was being portrayed as. On the other hand, the judge knew that the case was a potential feather in the DA's cap for his *own* political ambitions as well as those of his protégé, and they were probably as loath to accept a plea bargain as to drop the case altogether.

'It's times like this,' said the judge wearily, 'that make me yearn for the good old days before the Gideon decision.'

It was the Supreme Court's ruling in Gideon versus Wainwright which held that in even mildly serious cases, the right to a lawyer, at least at the trial phase of the proceedings, was a claim right and not just a liberty: that is, a right that the subject could demand be fulfilled at the taxpayer's expense.

'All right,' the judge continued. 'Let's not have any more of this bickering in open court. I'll see you both in my chambers. The court stands in recess for twenty minutes.'

It was unusual for the judge to hold an *in camera* meeting with the defendant, for fear of accusations of cooking up a deal that denied the defendant's right to a fair trial, plea bargains always being unofficial. But in this case he had no choice. He wanted to resolve the matter quietly, and take the sensationalism out of the case. From the point of view of the law, the decision was very simple. But the attention of the press had turned a simple legal problem into a complex political one. And he didn't want the trial to carry on with this kind of showmanship and playing to the crowds. He just wanted it to proceed smoothly.

Two minutes later Justine Levy and Daniel Abrams were shuffling awkwardly into the judge's large, blue-carpeted chambers. An uneasy quiet settled over the room as they took their seats at ninety degrees to one another, facing the judge across a polished rosewood desk. But the electric tension that had hung in the air since they started their trek down the labyrinth of corridors steadily intensified with each passing second. Justine looked around at the lustrous wooden panelling and the massive leather-bound volumes that surrounded her. Black shadows danced across the law books as birds fluttered back and forth before the window.

Ignoring the eyes of the judge and the ADA, Justine turned to look out through the window on the fourth side of the room. It offered a panoramic view of the city. She swallowed a lump in her throat, as a fleeting memory came and went.

Half a minute ticked by while the judge stared at Justine. Her height was only a few inches above average, but he could see immediately the enormous power pent up within her. Most women would have regarded her as plump, but to men she was a Grecian goddess, cast from the same mould as the classic statues. Even from afar one could see the straight, broad back of a rock climber, the powerful shoulders of a swimmer and the long, well-toned but not muscular legs of a runner. But her image could never have been preserved in marble or bronze. For Justine Levy had the quality of something firm yet constantly in motion. Only kinetic sculpture could have captured her essence. She was a robot with a face of ivory and a body of tempered steel.

Apart from her smooth complexion, her eyes were nature's major concession to her femininity. They were wide, inset deeply in large orbits, looking out at the world like the trusting, curious eyes of a child, until a change of mood made them narrow down into feline slits that neither sought nor offered comfort.

But the feature that stood out most was her hair. It was neither ginger nor gold, but rather a true deep red.

Red like wine or red like the sunset? Justice Wise wondered.

He remembered his college days, when he still had the youthful tenacity that he now saw in Justine. He had majored in philosophy and he had always been impressed by the symbolism of Nietzsche's metaphysics.

Apollo versus Dionysus.

He somehow sensed, by Justine's posture and steady gaze, that she was very much an Apollonian in character, rational and sober.

Perhaps that's what this case is really about.

Then he remembered that the colour red also symbolized blood. But he dismissed the thought from his mind. He realized in that instant, that he didn't *want* Justine to be guilty. He wondered if any male juror could look at her and see the case any more objectively.

But that was the system. He had seen rapists walk because

prosecutors couldn't prove lack of consent, or because the victim faltered or wavered in the wrong place under cross-examination. He had looked on helplessly while overworked ADAs allowed muggers to plea-bargain a knifepoint robbery down to petty larceny. He remembered letting expediency run its course as armed robbers were allowed to swallow the gun. At times he had been reduced to standing on the sidelines as harried prosecutors allowed seedy little tenth-rate shysters to bully them into watering down near-fatal stabbings into simple assault, using the ultimate threat: to go to trial and force the understaffed DA's office to spend time and money proving to a jury what both sides knew to be the truth.

Whom am I to start complaining now?

He looked away from Justine's face to the file that rested before him. Twenty-three years old, it said. *Old enough to vote*, he thought. *Old enough to drink . . . almost old enough to become a Congresswoman . . . Old enough to be married and with a couple of kids*. At twenty-eight, his own daughter had three. But this girl – this woman – who sat before him seemed older in some ways, as if she had seen things from which a woman of *any* age should be protected. *Or perhaps I'm just being old-fashioned.*

'All right, Dan, now that we're out of the public eye perhaps you'll tell me why you're so dead set against her conducting her own defence?'

'Cards on the table?'

'Like the Cincinatti Kid.'

'Quite frankly I don't think it's going to make a shit-bit of difference one way or the other. I've got a solid case and I'm going for murder all the way. But when it's all over I don't want some smartass reporter re-opening the case on a crusading ego trip and making it look like she was railroaded to jail without a fair trial.'

He was cut down by the sceptical look on the judge's face.

'So it's just your reputation you're worried about.'

'Not *my* reputation, Hal. The reputation of the DA's office.'

'Good answer!' replied the judge, slapping the desk with

mock enthusiasm. 'You missed your vocation, Dan. You should have been a politician.'

'No, I mean it! If people stop respecting the law enforcement authorities—'

'Can it, Dan! Save the speeches for the jury.'

Justice Wise turned to Justine, who was now looking at him with new-found respect.

'And what about you, young lady? Do you really think you're competent to conduct your own defence?'

'I do, Your Honour,' she answered calmly.

'I suppose you've seen a few episodes of *L.A. Law* and some *Perry Mason* reruns and you think you know it all. An objection here and there, a calm opening statement and an impassioned, fiery speech at the end.'

There wasn't a hint of sarcasm in his voice. It was more as if he were trying to sound chummy, as if he were reluctantly trying to convince an old friend to abandon a futile course of action.

'No, Your Honour. I'm a little more sophisticated than that. Although I think you're doing *Perry Mason* an injustice.'

The judge rested his elbows on the desk and interlocked his fingers. He noticed that she never wavered in her politeness even though the element of defiance intruded into her words as well as her tone.

'Well, let's see, then. Do you know about peremptory challenges, motions for change of venue owing to pre-trial publicity, the exclusionary rule and Miranda rights?'

He looked at her smugly as if to say: *You're out of your depth*.

'Anyone who watches TV knows about the Miranda rule. It's so well known it's practically obsolete. But all this is irrelevant.'

A coughing fit broke in Abram's throat, punctuating Justine's reply like a string of exclamation marks drawn violently at the end of an unexpected sentence. The judge looked at Justine with an expressionless, stony stare while he waited for Abrams to bring the thunderous outburst under control. For a few seconds after the crimson-faced ADA had stifled his agony, there was a stunned silence as Justine's words sunk in all round.

'Why is it irrelevant, Miss Levy?' asked the judge slowly.

'Because I don't intend to argue over technicalities.'

She leaned forward, resting her elbows on the desk. It was an innocent, subconscious gesture, but it drew back the sleeves of her white silk blouse, offering a tantalizing glimpse of her ivory forearms. There was no doubt in the judge's mind that she was completely self-assured. But from where, he wondered, did her self-confidence come? From the moral rectitude of innocence? Or from a misplaced faith in the capacity of a beautiful woman to manipulate the men around her?

'You see, Your Honour,' her voice rolled on with relentless smoothness, 'I *know* that I can quibble over whether the chain of custody over physical evidence was broken, or whether an exhibit not explicitly named in the search warrant can be introduced, but I'm damned if I will. The last thing I want is to give the jury the impression that I've got no case and no answer to the charges and that my only hope of saving my skin is to gag the prosecution.'

'Let's not exaggerate, Miss Levy,' said the ADA sharply, almost spitting out his righteous indignation. 'It's only your freedom that's at stake, not your life. Unlike your victim.'

'There's no call for that, Dan,' the judge chided.

Justine half turned and leaned back, meeting Abrams's eyes briefly.

'Oh, it's all right, Your Honour. If he thinks it, he's got the right to say it. I just hope that when he's through presenting his case, he'll close his mouth and open his mind.' Then, looking Abrams straight in the eyes with that uncompromising, piercing stare, she added quietly: 'I see you have a strong sense of justice. I like that. I have a strong sense of justice too.'

It was just a few simple words, spoken in a calm and measured tone. But to the others in the room it rang out with all the rage and thunder of a threat. The judge wondered if Sean Murphy had heard that threat before, or perhaps *failed* to hear it.

'Miss Levy,' the judge's voice came out of the drawn-out silence, 'when you say that you're not going to quibble over technicalities, does that mean you're going to argue your case in terms of the *facts*?'

Justine smiled and nodded.

'That's right, Your Honour . . . *all* the facts.'

The tone of her reply was almost sprightly, and the judge heard a touch of juvenile defiance in it.

So the woman is playing the girl with me.

'All right, I've heard enough,' he said as he rose. 'Let's go back inside.'

Abrams leapt to his feet. Justine leaned forward and rose from her chair. As she did so, the judge looked at her expectantly, as if anticipating an enquiry. But it was Abrams whose impatience got the better of him.

'What have you decided?'

The judge raised a hand, pointing to the door.

'Wait and see,' he said, taking a sadistic pleasure in the prosecutor's discomfort.

Whatever the judge's misgivings about the case, Justine Levy had stirred something within him, something that he couldn't define. He had long ago become blasé about his job, and he wouldn't have believed that a defendant could move him in the way that Justine had. He had seen sympathetic defendants who had pulled on his heart-strings before, like the mothers and lovers who were guilty of the 'crime' of euthanasia. But they were still just routine cases, and with plea bargaining and a certain amount of judicial discretion he had been able to handle them as humanely as the system allowed. But Justine's case was different. He didn't know the truth or the reasons for anything that might have happened, he just knew that he was glad to have met her and sorry for her, even though there was nothing in her manner that cried out for sympathy.

Be careful, he told himself. *Don't get involved.* But he knew that there was no way a judge could avoid getting involved. The danger was Justine. She was not a crybaby, nor a gum-chewing slut, nor an aggressive old hen. She wasn't any sort of stereotype . . . she wasn't anyone or anything that he recognized. But he knew that if he had to choose the company of another person now, whether for a few hours or for the rest of his life, he would have chosen Justine. It was a dangerous feeling, and he didn't feel any safer for recognizing it.

*   *   *

Tension still hung in the air when they returned to the courtroom.

In the press benches, the artists were busily at work, most of them sketching Justine. Although the judge's decision was to be a watershed, it was Justine who was the centre of attention. It was Justine whose vigorous oratory had stood out and whose quiet defiance had set her apart from those other rare cases of attractive women accused of murder. She was no demure defendant. She was the red-headed spitfire who knew not the meaning of the word fear and didn't trouble to hide the fact.

So the press artists drew Justine in what was to become a classic pose and her symbol throughout this trial: standing proudly, almost like a warrior on a voyage of conquest, or a business tycoon who had just taken over a rival corporation. The image conveyed a sense of arrogance. Since she had first been arrested, arrogance had seemed to be her hallmark.

The door behind the bench opened to admit Justine and Abrams, sending a murmur of anticipation through the court as they took up their places. The courtroom was no longer as full as it had been when they left it. But it soon filled out as the reporters returned from the pay-phones and the spectators with weak bladders heard the word that wafted through the building to the effect that the hearing was about to resume. All eyes were on Justine, except those of the press artists which periodically darted back to their sketches to get the details right.

After about half a minute, the door opened again and the bailiff intoned his admonition to all those present to stand. When the judge took his place and everyone was seated he held the attention of every man and woman in the courtroom. He coughed to clear his throat, and peered around reprimandingly to quell the murmuring that still lingered after his entrance. It was stifled within seconds and replaced by a silence that seemed to warn of an impending storm.

'The law on this subject is very clear,' he said slowly. 'In the case of People versus McIntyre it was ruled by the New York Court of Appeals that the option to proceed *pro se* could be invoked as a matter of right as long as three criteria were met. The first was that the exercise of the right be unequivocal and timely. The second was that the defendant make a knowing and informed waiver of the right to counsel. And the third was that the defendant should not have engaged in, and should continue for the duration of the trial to refrain from engaging in, conduct which disrupts the proceedings.

'Regarding the first requirement, it was ruled in McIntyre itself that the request is timely if it is made before the jury has been impanelled. Moreover I think that not even the prosecutor would deny that the defendant's efforts to invoke the right have been unequivocal.'

A smattering of nervous laughter trickled down from the spectators.

'Putting the second requirement aside for the moment and moving on to the third, it cannot be said that the defendant has done anything to obstruct or impede the proceedings. Nor can it be said that she has engaged in disruptive or obstreperous conduct. She has certainly been forceful and vigorous in her assertion of her right to proceed *pro se*. But her arguments have at all times been couched in polite terms and she has shown unwavering respect for the dignity of the court. Therefore she has passed this test of the right to conduct her own defence.'

Abrams slumped back in his seat, defeated. The merest flicker of a smile appeared momentarily on Justine's face. But it vanished as quickly as it appeared, leaving not a single telltale sign for anyone in the courtroom to notice.

'This only leaves the requirement of a knowing and intelligent waiver of the right to legal counsel. State law mandates that when a defendant insists on conducting his own defence, the trial court should conduct a "searching inquiry" on record to ensure that the waiver of the right to counsel is made voluntarily and with eyes open. Accordingly, Miss Levy, I am going to ask you a few questions which you must answer for the record either yes or no or in your own words if you feel that clarification is needed.

'First of all are you aware of the fact that by not being represented by a lawyer you are giving up a valuable source of information and knowledge as to matters of law, possible defences, rules of evidence and procedure that may be invoked at your discretion and rights that are only advantageous if invoked in particular ways, such as the right to challenge jurors?'

'Yes, Your Honour,' replied Justine calmly.

'Are you aware that as a lay person conducting your own defence there is always a danger that you might make a statement or ask a question or perform an action or omission damaging to yourself or to your case, and that a qualified lawyer would be less likely to make such errors and if he did make such an error would provide you with grounds to appeal because of counsel's professional incompetence?'

'Yes, Your Honour.'

Again the voice was calm and the tone respectful. There was not a hint of off-handedness or impatience in her reply.

'Are you also aware of the seriousness of the charges and that you stand in jeopardy of a long sentence if convicted?'

'I am, Your Honour.'

'And are you further aware that you are bound by the same rules of procedure as any qualified legal counsel and the same rules of evidence?'

'Yes, Your Honour.'

'Do you understand, Miss Levy, that in the event you should find yourself in difficulty of any kind, the court is under no obligation to render assistance to you, save by upholding the rules of evidence and procedure, nor can it take over defence chores for you or advise you on when to invoke specific rights.'

'I understand, Your Honour.'

'Is your motive for wanting to conduct your own defence due to financial limitations, Miss Levy? Is it that you desire an attorney but cannot afford one? Are you aware of the fact that if this is the problem then a lawyer can be appointed by the court at no expense to yourself?'

'There is no financial impediment to my hiring a lawyer, Your Honour. I have ample financial resources to pay for a lawyer and I am aware of my Sixth Amendment right to legal counsel, but I do not want one.'

'Finally, having said all that, Miss Levy, I can only advise you in the strongest possible terms that it is in your best interests to employ the services of qualified legal counsel and I urge you to reconsider your decision to conduct your own defence in the light of all that I have said. Will you reconsider, Miss Levy?'

'No, Your Honour.'

'In that case I must rule that the defendant's waiver of the right to legal counsel has been made intelligently and voluntarily and that accordingly the last of the three requirements for appearing *in propria persona* has been satisfied. However, because of the complexity of the case, the severity of the charge and the possibility, however remote, of the defendant wishing to change her mind, I'm going to appoint a qualified lawyer to act as stand-by counsel.'

Justine was on her feet, staring at the judge with open indignation, while Abrams turned away smirking.

'Your Honour, I object! My defence is to be based on *fact*, not legal technicalities. A court-appointed stand-by, or any lawyer for that matter, would only distract the jury from the essence of my defence and give the jury the wrong idea of my position.'

'But he would only be on stand-by, Miss Levy. He wouldn't even be allowed to open his mouth without your permission.'

'But his mere presence might give the impression that he's defending me.'

'The court notes, and overrules, the defendant's objection. Although the court is not *required* to appoint stand-by counsel, it has the right to do so even over the objections of the defendant. In a complex and serious case such as this, bearing in mind the danger of having to declare a mistrial in the event of the defendant changing her mind or forfeiting the right to continue *pro se*, I believe it to be a desirable precaution which need not in any way step on the defendant's toes. At any rate, the federal Supreme Court has ruled that the trial court may ignore counsel's objections in the matter of appointing stand-by counsel, in Faretta versus California, a case already cited by the defendant herself.'

Justine sat down, the seething anger showing on her face.

The judge looked around the courtroom.

'Is there anyone here from the legal aid office?'

'I am, Your Honour.' A nervous voice pierced the pregnant silence as a young African–American in a well-cut dark blue suit rose from an uncomfortable wooden seat.

'Your name?'

'Rick – I mean Richard Parker.'

The judge had adopted a serious tone, as if he were subconsciously trying to intimidate the young man. This lawyer, with his adolescent good looks and below-average height, looked like a high-school student who was too young to be there.

'Do you have any heavy commitments that might impair your ability to give this case the attention that a murder charge deserves?'

'No, Your Honour.'

Justine was looking around frantically at this nervous-looking kid whom the judge was about to appoint to be on stand-by to represent her.

'The court appoints Richard Parker to act as stand-by counsel for the defence of Justine Levy in the case of the People of the State of New York versus Justine Levy.'

Again Justine leapt to her feet, facing the judge with a brimming anger that overflowed as she spoke.

'Your Honour, this is just too ridiculous for words. He looks like he's fresh out of law school!'

'May it please the court, Your Honour, I *am* practically fresh out of law school.'

It took no more than a second for the words to register all round, and when they did the courtroom rocked with laughter. Even the normally sedate Daniel Abrams was forced to smile. Only the stoic judge and the granite-faced Justine remained impassive, like two pillars supporting an otherwise fragile structure during an earthquake. When the laughter subsided, Parker continued calmly.

'I graduated first in my class at Harvard, and I served as clerk to the Chief Justice of the United States for a year.'

He seems to be rubbing it in, thought the judge. *But why is he working as a two-bit hustler in the legal aid office where all they do is plea-bargain for the scum when he could be working for seventy-five thousand in private practice?*

But it would have been unprofessional and inappropriate

to verbalize these thoughts. In any case, by this stage he was watching Justine, wondering how she was going to handle the embarrassing situation that she had got herself into.

'Your Honour, without prejudice to my objection to a court-appointed lawyer, I apologize to Mr Parker for any aspersions I may have inadvertently cast on his professional abilities.'

Justine Levy's voice was silky smooth as she adroitly carried out the impromptu salvage operation.

As she took her seat once again, Parker complemented the performance with a brief, gracious acceptance speech. Then the judge spoke again.

'In order to give stand-by counsel for the defence a chance to study the case and confer with the defendant, I will grant a thirty-day continuance on my own motion and set the date of a further pre-trial motions hearing at the eleventh of next month. I will set the trial at that time when I see how crowded my docket is. Are there any motions on bail?'

'Yes, Your Honour,' said Justine quietly. 'I move that I be released on my own recognizance. It is a matter of public record that my impending arrest was known long before it occurred. In that time I made no attempt to evade arrest or conceal my whereabouts. I made it clear in all my pre-arrest that I welcome the opportunity to have my day in court. For these reasons I move for a release on recognizance.'

'Mr Abrams?' the judge beckoned, inviting the prosecutor's predictable response.

'Your Honour, the People oppose both bail and ROR. The accused has been indicted by a grand jury for the most serious offence in the New York penal code and the arraignment judge decided at that time that there were sound reasons to hold the accused in custody. I see no reason to regard those circumstances as having changed. There is a danger that as long as she is at liberty she will be in a position to use the press to generate publicity favourable to her case.'

'That may be, Mr Abrams,' said the judge. 'But that can hardly be grounds for denying bail or ROR. The only purpose of both bail and remand is to ensure that the accused shows up for trial. As far as media publicity is concerned, that can be handled by a joint gagging order imposed equally on both parties. But such an order cannot be linked in any way to bail or ROR.'

The judge tightened his facial muscles to resist the urge to smile at the discomfort and frustration on the ADA's face.

'In that case, Your Honour,' said Abrams, 'I ask that bail be set at an appropriately high level, taking into consideration the defendant's large inherited real-estate assets.'

'I see no need for that,' the judge responded. 'I am impressed by the accused's arguments and have no doubt that she will show up for trial. Accordingly, the accused is released on her own recognizance.'

The stampede for the exits began. Several bailiffs held back the press and spectators from one of the exits, clearing a path for Justine and Parker. As they left the room, Parker sidled up to Justine and started walking beside her.

'You know they say that anyone who tries to conduct his own defence has a fool for a client?'

'In my case they've doubled the handicap by sticking me with a fool for a lawyer.'

Ignoring Parker and brushing aside the more tenacious of the media people who had slipped under the arms of the bailiffs, Justine marched out of the courtroom. Parker stood there gaping for a second, until a reluctant smile cut across his face.

2

A wedge of sunlight cut through the layers of afternoon cloud and struck the mirrored façade of the shopping centre. Sean Murphy watched it with growing fascination as he crossed the footbridge towards it. A moment earlier the sky had been overcast with grey ruffled folds. But almost in time with his approach, the clouds had parted like a theatre curtain opening on the first act of a classical tragedy. And now the shopping centre stood there illuminated by the single ray of sunlight, as if held in the warning beacon of a spotlight. It almost seemed as if someone up there knew that the place was being singled out for special treatment.

If there is *anyone up there*, thought Murphy, bitterly, *he probably does know that it's been singled out.*

There was nothing unusual in his blue denim jeans and matching jacket. But his friends back in Derry would have found it hard to recognize him today. At the very least they would have been surprised at his change of appearance. For today he sported a beard, and his normally red hair was now almost black. Sean Murphy knew better than to take chances. These shopping centres almost invariably have security cameras, he knew. The investigators of the anti-terrorist squad of Scotland Yard, or the shadowy men of the Security Service, would sit for hours sifting through the pictures after the incident, and a man with a shoulder bag entering half an hour before and leaving a few minutes later was sure to attract attention. He couldn't stay longer because that would merely increase the danger of identification.

It would be especially dangerous if his face appeared in pictures from several of the incidents. So a change of appearance was in order, and he'd make himself look different in each attack. He smiled with wry amusement as he recalled the old Irish phrase 'to be sure'. It wasn't just the phrase which made him smile, it was the memory of a joke his wife had once told him about a Catholic woman taking the pill.

'She took *two*,' his wife had explained. '*To be sure! To be sure!*'

But the amusement gave way to bitterness as he remembered his purpose, and remembered also that his wife was no longer with him. He was here to fire another salvo in the long-running dispute between the Irish people and the British, a dispute that had claimed so many.

Sean Murphy's wife had been just one of the more recent victims, and now Murphy was all set to become one more of the victimizers. But that was not how he thought of himself. He was a fighter in a war that others had started.

'Can I play with the trains?'

'Not now. If you're a good boy, I'll buy you one *next* Christmas.'

She regretted saying it as soon as the words were out of her mouth. With another one on the way, she didn't know how she could even think of train sets, especially with Roger out of the picture, and contributing the minimum. But Tommy had a way of mellowing the heart with his lovely bright smile and big blue eyes. It was almost a pleasure to give in to him. And now with Roger shacked up with that tart from the beauty salon, Tommy was all she had. Why shouldn't she spoil him?

Of course, Tommy could be quite a handful. He'd just got over the 'terrible twos' and now here he was at three starting to assert himself. She hoped he'd get on with his brother and not be jealous when the little one came along and started getting some of the attention that he had got used to monopolizing.

Play it by ear, her mother had said, and on these things her mother was usually right, just like she'd been right all along about Roger.

'But I want to play with it *now*.' He started to cry. It wasn't loud, not the attention-seeking whining of a manipulative child. These were real tears, silently streaming down his cheeks. It wasn't the gift he wanted, it was the reassurance. After the divorce, Pauline Robson had got into the habit of using small gifts as a way of letting Tommy know that she still loved him. It was a form of over-compensating for her husband's absence. He had started blaming himself for the fact that 'Daddy isn't here', and she had responded by giving him presents as well as the usual hugs and kisses.

But it was a method of reassurance that she could ill afford. And like a drug, it produced diminishing returns. Now, for good or for ill, Tommy had come to look at presents and gifts as the measure of his mother's love for him. And to him, the refusal to buy a present was a sign not of financial hardship but that the precarious love of his only remaining parent was slipping away.

Pauline stopped and knelt down in front of Tommy and held him gently in her arms.

'I'll tell you what,' she said. 'How would you like me to make your favourite strawberry jelly sponge cake when we get back home?'

His face lit up through his tears and he smiled and nodded gently.

'OK,' he said, in that cute little voice of his that melted her heart yet again. She dried away his tears gently with the tips of her fingers, then took his little hand in hers and walked on. She knew that she'd have to let him ride the toy horse before leaving. At least, she told herself, it was the one thing the shopping centre provided that was free.

In the shopping centre Sean Murphy went to work quickly. He had two devices, and clear instructions: one in a place where it would cause maximum panic and the other near an exit, timed to catch the fleeing crowds.

The 'devices' each consisted of five hundred grams of Semtex, a detonator, a battery and a timer. He hadn't made the circuit, but he had tested it. This was how the Irish National Liberation Army worked: one soldier made the circuit and the other checked it. They were a disciplined organization, like the IRA from which they had split, even going so far as to use standard military ranks. The last thing they needed was a bomb blowing up in the hands of the delivery man. There were enough Irish jokes in circulation already! There was no requirement that the circuit had to be checked by the delivery man, but it did have to be checked by someone other than the person who made it.

When the Irish Republican Socialist Party first split from the official IRA, Sean Murphy hadn't taken them seriously. It had seemed like the formation of one more talk-shop, like Sinn Fein, the political wing of the IRA. But when they set up INLA, their own secret militia, and sent out a recruitment agent to persuade him to join, he was intrigued by their agenda. They wanted not just a united Ireland, but a united *socialist* Ireland, one in which the spoils and wealth would be shared out among the poor and not just hoarded by the rich. In their methods, they were not so different from the IRA – they believed in using a mixture of violence against British soldiers and bombings of public houses and shopping centres on the British mainland. But their broader and more future-oriented agenda appealed to the revolutionary in Murphy. So he joined the Irish National Liberation Army, coming in with the rank of lieutenant because of his experience in the IRA.

He noted, when they first introduced themselves, that they didn't use the word 'republican' in their name. The recruitment agent told him that this was because they didn't want to cause confusion in America with the Republican Party. But he suspected that another reason was subconsciously involved. It had finally dawned on them that republicanism versus monarchy wasn't really the issue: it was freedom versus tyranny. After all, Oliver Cromwell, their historical arch-enemy, had also been a republican. He was the man who had overthrown King Charles I and had him beheaded.

Yet he had crushed the fighting spirit of the proud sons and daughters of Ireland with the savagery and brutality of the most arrogant of kings.

Murphy's own baptism of fire was well in the past. But he nevertheless felt that tinge of apprehension which preceded every mission. Each mission was new and there were always things that could go wrong.

His previous bombings had all been directed against soldiers in the six counties of Northern Ireland. They entailed placing huge 200–500-pound bombs by the roadside and detonating them when British soldiers drove by in armoured trucks or troop carriers. For reasons of frugality, the British government preferred not to buy troop carriers made of the strongest armour plating available and opted instead for a compromise between price and strength that offered their soldiers very little protection against the huge roadside bombs of the IRA. These bombs were made from nitrogen-based explosives rather than Semtex, supplied in the form of animal droppings by the local farmers, who in many cases sympathized with their cause and their methods. This was the oldest explosive of all, the one that the Chinese had invented a thousand years ago.

The danger with these bombs was that, unlike the smaller Semtex bombs, they were relatively unstable. Also they were to be radio-detonated and it only took one hobbyist with a remote-controlled aeroplane to send the delivery man to an early martyrdom. The usual precaution was to sweep the frequency band with a radio receiver and survey the area visually before inserting the blasting cap and arming the device. But an undetected hobbyist could still cut into radio silence before the delivery man got clear.

With Semtex bombs it was different. The explosive was somewhat more stable than urea/nitrate-based explosive and the bombs were detonated by either a timer or a mercury switch rather than a radio-controlled pulse and blasting cap. He had activated the timer in the car and now had less than twenty-five minutes to place the devices and get clear.

Placing bombs in a shopping centre is not easy. In addition to the security cameras, there is a dearth of places to plant bombs. For security reasons, there were no garbage bins and even if he could get an attendant's uniform, he could hardly plant a bomb in one of the flowerpots in front of the hundreds of shoppers milling about. He could plant it in a toilet tank but it would cause minimal damage in both material and human terms.

It used to be possible to plant small incendiary devices in the pockets of clothes. But now the clothes retailers sewed up the pockets of their display garments, making it rather more difficult to drop such IRA or INLA gift bombs into them. An unattended package left in the open would attract attention faster than one could walk away from it. So Murphy made his way over to a large bookshop. From the entrance he proceeded to a section that sold school exam revision books. He figured that at this time of year they would be the slowest moving item in the bookshop. The section was almost empty, tending to confirm his assumption. Spreading his fingers wide, he pulled three books from a shelf with one hand and inserted the bomb with the shorter time setting at the back of the bookshelf, placing it on its side so that it occupied a minimum of space. He returned the books quickly in front of it and then made his way out of the bookshop and the shopping centre.

Although there were no garbage bins inside the shopping centre, there were several in the forecourt outside. Under the guise of disposing of an old evening newspaper, he deposited the second bomb in the bin closest to the entrance.

Srini Shankar was just coming out of the bank. He was a light-skinned man, and to look at him you couldn't tell that he had been born in Bombay. He worked at the nearby hospital and had slipped out during his lunch break to withdraw some cash. Now he remembered that he also wanted a book of crossword puzzles. He was an avid enthusiast of the famous *Times* crossword and enjoyed doing puzzles on the evening train home.

The front of the bookshop was stacked with the latest bestsellers. But he wasn't interested in them. He made his way to a quiet section at the back of the bookshop where he found the crossword puzzle books, between chess books and high school examination revision books. There was quite a wide selection. He decided to browse.

3

In the dawn light Central Park always looked tranquil. When the muggers and rapists and innocent merry-makers finally went to sleep, the natural tranquillity of this island of trees and grass in an ocean of glass and concrete finally prevailed. Not that all muggers were night owls. Some were early birds who set out to catch the worm – the worm in question being the joggers whom the muggers regarded as easy prey. Most of the joggers were now resigned to the risk and relied on police decoys to keep the threat in check. Guns were outlawed in New York and those who carried mace or pepper spray or electric shockers knew that these were virtually useless, as the muggers were always on their guard against them.

Justine adopted a different approach. She kept a metal paper cutter with a retractable blade up her sleeve and had loosened the elastic stitching there to let it slide out easily when she needed it. To keep the sleeve shut she simply held it with her fingers as she ran, taking advantage of the fact that it was a long sleeve. On the one occasion when she had needed it, she had handed over a wad of dollars *before* letting the knife slip into her hand and using it. Her passive handing over of the money had lulled the mugger into a false sense of security and the gun was no longer aimed at her when she slid the blade into its extended position and lunged at one of the eyes that only a second earlier had lit up at the sight of the money. He had fallen to the ground bleeding and writhing in agony, but still holding the gun. But his grip on the weapon loosened as the pain continued, and Justine had calmly walked around him, taken the money back and jogged on. With her mother ill at the time, the last thing she needed was to be the subject of a *cause célèbre*, even though she was confident that she could win it. Now she had no such qualms and nothing to lose.

She wondered what story the mugger told the hospital, or the police. Probably, she suspected, that *he* had been mugged. But then again he still had the gun to explain. A smile came to her lips. It was one of those unfinished episodes in her life that hadn't troubled her at the time, but aroused her curiosity now.

The asphalt swept by at a pace made relentless by the swiftness of Justine's feet. It wasn't just the calories she was burning up; it was the frustration. Being out of jail gave her a modicum of freedom, but she couldn't escape the sense of confinement wrought by those long hours. This at last was the breath of freedom that she craved.

She was dressed in the colour of the sea, her tracksuit and running shoes dark blue. She jogged energetically past the older and less tenacious health freaks who were trying to recapture their youth. She both admired and pitied them. At least they were doing something and not just sitting down passively waiting for whatever meagre share of good fortune life was ready to hand them. But for all that they were just following a fad, copying a trend instead of trying to set one. Jogging was the 'in' thing and Central Park was the 'in' place.

She sometimes used to flee to Central Park, deserting her mother when her father's erratic temper got too much for her to bear.

But it wasn't always possible to flee. Suddenly it all flooded back to her, like a wave sweeping over a lonely swimmer, pulling her under and threatening to drown her in painful memories.

The violent rage in her father's voice bellowing at her

mother in another room as Justine lay in bed waiting with desperate longing for sleep to engulf her.

The cringing helplessness of her mother, not yet the rock of refuge that she was to become.

The sound of vicious slapping as the hands of a shell-shocked victim of someone else's making lashed out at the woman he loved, beyond his own control as well as hers.

The advancing thud of bare feet along the uncarpeted passageway as the cries of anger and fear drew nearer.

The hurried opening of the door to admit a frightened woman in a torn nightdress whose tears mingled with the blood that oozed from the sides of her lips.

The rapid slamming and locking of the door before the battle-crazed stranger could enter.

The hammering of an iron fist against a solid oak door, an accompaniment of human thunder to the silent prayer that went up from inside the room.

The soft bodies of mother and daughter pressed against each other in silent fear and patient hope, helplessly clinging together as they waited for the paroxysm of rage to pass and the bitter sobbing to begin.

Justine spat on the ground and raced on, stepping up her pace as if to leave the past behind her. There was a fresh, natural look about her firm body and smooth complexion. In a word, she looked healthy. Only a single line of bitterness crept into her smile and gave away the fact that she couldn't capture the inner tranquillity that she had known as a child before her father's return from the jungles of South-East Asia.

Somewhere along her route, she passed a discarded copy of a two-day-old newspaper. 'Pretty Poison to go to trial', read the headline, borrowing a reference to a movie from before her time.

Trial by the media was part of the price one had to pay for having a free press. It would have been tempting to dismiss it as too high a price. But not for Justine. She never saw events out of context. Nevertheless the headline worried her, not because it boded ill for her trial, but because it reflected a lopsided view of justice on the part of the public. They knew about Sean Murphy and what he had done. They knew that he had blood on his hands. Yet there had been no public outcry for his extradition. Some Irish Americans had even tried to portray him as a soldier for a righteous cause.

She passed another old newspaper. But this one she didn't even bother to look at. She seldom noticed things or people when she jogged. To the runners whom she overtook, it almost looked as if her face held a thousand-yard stare, the look that haunted the faces of so many shell-shock victims, including her father. But there was no hint of recognition on their faces, no sign that they knew who she was. Not that Justine would have cared. She was too busy savouring the freedom of being out of doors.

No freedom for Richard Parker, though, as he sat at his untidy desk. A busy man's desk, he liked to call it. The shades were up, but the light of dawn that fell on the desk was too weak to read by. A desk lamp, shaded by smoked glass to the tone of the midday sky, threw a pool of light over his notes and the large volume of case law that lay open before him. The hours of immobility had taken their toll on Parker and he felt the soreness of bone and cramp of muscle that were the doubtful reward for his Herculean endeavours. At the back of his mind was a vague recollection of having started last night with the city lights as his backdrop and the headlights of cars drifting by in a display of kinetic tapestry. Sleep had descended upon him some time after midnight, but he couldn't remember when he had emerged from it. He had simply resumed working as soon as the willpower had seized him. It was a familiar pattern: first he found a ruling that appeared to offer promise, then he saw a cross-reference to another extract containing further information, and his hand reached up to another shelf, to pull down another volume for scrutiny. With his other hand, he frantically scribbled down his notes.

Suddenly he put his pen down and stretched his legs under the desk. He wished he didn't have to be there. He longed to sleep. But more than that, he longed to go out into the open, to inhale the fresh air. He would have turned green with envy if he had known that Justine was jogging in the dawn light of Central Park.

*   *   *

Sean Murphy slammed the receiver down angrily. The telephone was out of order and now he'd have to find another to deliver the warning. It was Birmingham all over again. They'd checked both phones only the day before. But the telephones had been vandalized since then by the kind of scum who damage other people's property for pleasure. In Derry and the Falls Road area of Belfast, the IRA disciplinary squads would catch the vandals, or other members of their families, and smash boards with spikes into their kneecaps. But thinking about that didn't help. He had to find another pay-phone, and quickly. The bombs were meant to kill, but part of their strategy was to give the impression that while they sometimes attacked civilian property, they tried to spare civilian life and limb. So he raced from the street, trying to get to another phone on time.

Justine was beginning to work up a slight sweat, but was still running with ease. To look at her now, Parker would have been surprised to notice how harmless she seemed. Gone was the fiery tigress who had refused his help and stepped boldly alone into the arena to face an experienced prosecutor. Gone was the rock of granite who had confronted him with a surface of cold indifference when he tried to reach out to her with friendship. Now she was alone, with no enemies in sight and no mental armour to shield her from the cut and thrust of the enemy, or from the burden of a needy friend.

But it was hard to define what was left.

As the ground rolled by beneath her feet, the eyes of men settled upon her. They licked their lips at the sight of her long legs and the curve of her tight, round buttocks as she drifted past them. But they knew that it was just a daydream. Even stripped of the cold anger that shielded her in the courtroom, Justine was too distant from the ordinary mortal to be available to them. As she sped on relentlessly, she became even more distant, leaving her admirers trailing behind her. But her face was no longer forbidding. Now and again she even flashed a benevolent smile at some random stranger. Her whole manner seemed to say: *I'm happy to be alive*.

*   *   *

Not so happy was the man who was watching her through the telescopic sight of a sports rifle.

He had a rough and rugged look about him, and although only in his late thirties, he looked old. His face was ravaged by hatred, the unadmitted hatred that he felt not only towards Justine but also towards humanity in general. As far as he was concerned, the trial was just a middle-class formality.

He pressed the butt of the rifle into his shoulder and leaned into it, his left knee bent with the foot forward, the trailing leg straight with the foot pointing outward. The index finger of his right hand moved towards the trigger. In his mind he could already see the pretty young head exploding, the juices spilling out from the brain. For a few seconds he held Justine's head in the cross-hairs of the telescopic sight, relishing the feeling of power and the knowledge that he was striking a blow for the cause.

She would die now.

His finger moved and a single shot rang out.

'OK, Tommy, you've had your turn on the horse. Now let the other children play.'

'Again,' said Tommy in that sweet little voice of his, giving his mother a flash of that angelic smile.

'All right, one more time.'

But it was not to be. For suddenly a voice boomed out of the public address system.

'Owing to a security alert, customers are requested to leave the shopping centre immediately.'

A murmur of panic moved through the crowd and in seconds people were walking, or in some cases running, to the exits. Pauline Robson scooped Tommy off the horse and strode quickly towards the nearest exit, converging on it in time with countless others.

But inside the shops, the announcement went largely unheard and many people stayed where they were, blissfully unaware of the danger that faced them. Less than ten seconds later, the bomb in the bookshop exploded, blowing a hole in the right side of Srini Shankar's torso.

At the sound of the first blast, the restrained panic in the shopping centre erupted into full-blown hysteria. People began stampeding towards the exits, pushing others to the ground and trampling all over them to get out.

Pauline had more respect for her neighbours than most, and tried to bring up her son that way, in spite of having to do it alone. But she had a responsibility to protect her child, and when she saw the panic set in among the hordes around her she knew that she had to get Tommy out of there. But to charge into the crush would only expose him to greater risk. So she held back while the more predatory of the survivalists barged their way past others and charged out into the murky daylight. Only when the crowd thinned out did she carry Tommy, who was now whining and kicking, to one of the exits. It was as she reached the exit that the powerful background murmur of the crowd was shattered by the thunderclap of the second blast.

Several joggers heard the thunderclap. Some of them, the seasoned veterans of New York City, even recognized it. It was a .22 in the hands of a savvy, street-wise sixteen-year-old. The man who had been aiming a rifle at Justine fell to the ground. The bullet from a Saturday night special had lodged in his brain. The boy with the gun had originally targeted the girl who was jogging in the white shorts and shirt as his next victim. But when he spotted the man assembling the rifle his plan changed. It was unlikely that the girl was carrying as much money as the 'piece' would fetch on the black market. He didn't know how to dispose of that kind of heat, but Ozzie would. Ozzie always knew how to find a market for that sort of thing. He wouldn't use it himself. He preferred an Uzi with a short barrel and an automatic rapid fire for drive-by work. But he had contacts on the street and he could unload it for a tidy sum or some dynamite coke to sell to the pushers on their turf.

He moved quickly, disassembling the gun and returning it to the case from which the man had produced it. He idly wondered who the gunman was. He wouldn't have touched him if he'd seemed like a professional hit-man. But the kid knew that this was no pro. Oh, he knew how to use a rifle all right, but that didn't make him a pro. No pro would stand out there in the open assembling a rifle and then aiming it, even at dawn. Aside from the joggers, he would have known about the muggers and the cops staking out their decoys. Also it was obvious he wasn't an Italian-American. Since when does an Italian-American have red hair? It was obviously someone who knew his guns better than he knew the city, in other words a foreigner.

Justine was blissfully unaware of how closely she had brushed with death. She was jogging in a secluded area of the park, hidden from public view by trees and shrubbery. Her pace was slackening now and she was sweating heavily, but still enjoying herself. It was only when she began to feel tired that she appreciated her strength and endurance. Whenever she started jogging she felt as if she were charged with energy like a fresh battery. It was this urge to unwind and break into a sprint that used to get the better of her when she first started running a few years ago. Now she could keep it in check and pace herself better. She always ran the first few hundred yards at a somewhat faster pace than a normal everyday jogger, but she had been running for some time now and the pain was beginning to make itself felt.

Finally she slowed down to a halt, dropped to her knees and then sprawled out flat on her face across the soft grass. She rolled over on to her back, stretching her arms and legs like a frisky kitten, a combination of smile and yawn spreading from one end of her lips to the other.

Murphy was walking back from the phone box towards his car. He had given the warning and used the coded message to confirm its authenticity. But it had barely got there in time to justify the propaganda claim that they had given prior warning. As he opened the car door he noticed that the clouds had blocked off the sun again, as if the curtain had closed on the first act of the drama.

4

'Are you ready for the Levy trial?'

Daniel Abrams looked up, unfazed by this sudden intrusion. Jerry Wilkins, the Manhattan DA, had just barged into his office without knocking, as he reviewed the office's case load. He was mildly annoyed. It was bad enough that he had to do the more mundane work while the DA made the public appearances. The least Jerry could do was let him do it without interruption. But Abrams knew that when Jerry got excited he couldn't control himself, and he didn't make an issue of it. That was the way they worked around here. They saved the formality for the courtroom.

'She's got that smartass black kid from the legal aid office that the judge appointed as stand-by. But she still gets to proceed *pro se*.'

Wilkins beamed a smile at him.

'You worry too much. It's just a case, like any other. And it's rock solid. Don't look so worried. She isn't going to walk away from this one!'

'Look, I don't think you realize how serious this is.'

'The hell I don't,' said the DA, still smiling. 'I've just got too many cases to worry about. And so have you.'

'Yeah, but this is political.'

'It's all political,' said the DA, pulling up a chair.

'Yeah, but this is headline news coast to coast,' said Abrams.

'Maybe,' conceded Jerry, 'but this time it's a winner. Whatever jury she gets, she's sunk. Your people don't cover for their own the way some people do. You're too busy trying to appease the Gentile establishment. If anything, they'll bend over backwards to convict, even if they have reasonable doubt.'

'But this black kid could be trouble. He's young, he's hot and he's ambitious.'

'Well, that's three strikes against him,' said the DA, smiling facetiously.

'And he's black,' added Abrams, determined to emphasize the fact. 'We've got a black lawyer defending a Jew. The press'll love it.'

The DA shook his head.

'Let me tell you something about the legal process, Danny boy.'

Daniel Abrams looked up and put his pen down.

'OK, let's hear the latest pearl of wisdom from the forensic fount of omniscience.'

The DA, who tended more towards the streetwise than the academically inclined, let the remark pass over his head without comment.

'We know that there are advantages and disadvantages to conducting one's own defence. The main disadvantage is that the average citizen doesn't know the law, and even if he does he doesn't know courtroom technique. Even when a defendant uses skilful courtroom technique it often comes over as self-serving and tends to alienate the jury. He looks like he's just plain cunning and out to beat the system. On the other hand the defendant often comes over as the victim of the system, or as the hero who's taking on the establishment, especially a cute number like the one you've got in the firing line.'

'So what's the *good* news?'

'Well, the way things stand now, it's still an amateur up against the professionals. But with a court-appointed stand-by, it *looks* like she's being properly defended. That means that her mistakes will hurt her, but she won't get the sympathy of the lone warrior swimming against the powerful tide.'

'You're mixing your metaphors,' said Abrams, shaking his head. 'Anyway, it may sound all right in theory, but you weren't in court this morning.'

'What are you saying?'

'I'm saying your assessment is wrong. Any which way she's going to look like the underdog going uphill against the odds! You know how the public roots for the underdog. Hell, with her looks and this own-defence gimmick she'd be odds-on favourite if the cops had caught her standing over the victim with a smoking Magnum!'

'Considering Murphy was poisoned, that doesn't surprise me,' replied the DA through a childish smile. 'Unless you mean a frothing Magnum. But then again it was supposedly poisoned tequila.'

Abrams made a sweeping gesture, dismissing the DA's jocular remark.

'Look, cut the wisecracks, Jerry. You know what I'm getting at.'

'So what do you suggest I do?' asked the DA.

'Let me assign it to a woman, preferably a young, attractive one.'

'It won't work. The local press has latched on to the fact that she's Jewish.'

'Well, no one can accuse us of anti-Semitism! A third of the staff are circumcised.'

'They might accuse us of bending over backwards to prove that we're not philosemitic. This whole issue is just too sensitive. If we drop it we look bad. If we fight it we look bad. But at least if we fight it we don't have to take responsibility for the outcome. And we've got a grand jury indictment to justify bringing the case in the first place.'

'All right, I'm not saying we have to drop it, but at least let's pull the rug out from under the anatomic bombshell by putting up a woman in the opposite corner.'

The DA was shaking his head. 'You're thinking of how it'll look to the jury. If you want to step into my shoes you'd better learn to start thinking about how it looks to all those millions of people watching the seven o'clock news.'

'Why should they object to a lady lawyer?'

'They won't. But as long as the press is making an issue of the fact that it's a Justine *Levy*, it has to be one of your people waving the cape.'

'We've got Jewish women on the staff. What about Hannah Segal?'

Jerry Wilkins shook his head.

'Wet behind the ears. She's not ready for this kind of heavy-duty *tsuris*.'

'Well, there's Debbie Winkler. She's got a good track record. She nailed two murderers and plea-bargained three weak cases to manslaughter in the first.'

'She's too deep into the Morton case to be pulled off now.'

'So give it to Judy Klein. It'll give her a change from sex crimes.'

The DA smiled a knowing smile, leaving Abrams puzzled.

'She's already getting a change. If you took the trouble to attend a few office conferences once in a while you'd be more up to date on the personnel situation.'

'She's quit?' asked Abrams, as if he'd just heard of the passing of an era.

'You're forgetting, Dan, we're an equal opportunity employer . . . pioneers of liberalism.'

Abrams looked blank.

'Maternity leave!' the DA exploded, exasperated by his colleague's momentary obtuseness.

'So who's taking care of the body shop?'

'Harvey Shine.'

Abrams slumped back in his chair, defeated.

'Besides,' the DA added, trying to sound comforting, but with a hint of gentle sarcasm in his voice. 'This is your chance to score a touchdown in the public eye. You could end up leapfrogging me to the state A-G's office.'

'Great!' said Abrams, the vitriol blending with the mock enthusiasm. 'The only problem is we've got the Grand Canyon where the motive should be.'

The DA brushed this aside with a deprecating gesture.

'You don't need motive to get a conviction.'

'Maybe not in law, but we're talking reality. Have you ever seen a jury convict without a motive in a *circumstantial* case?'

'Yes, as a matter of fact I have, in the MacCreedy case—'

'That's completely different,' said Abrams. 'MacCreedy was a psycho and it stood out a mile. They knew he didn't *need* a motive. This is different. If they're going to sign their names to a piece of paper that says she did it, they're going to want to know why. Otherwise the lack of motive is going to plant itself in their minds as reasonable doubt no matter *how* strong the physical evidence.'

'What did Interpol come up with?'

'Nothing. Scotland Yard has zilch. Murphy had no criminal convictions, thank God, and he was only implicated in just this one case. One of the people he supposedly killed was a radiologist. The Levy girl was studying medicine. Maybe there's some connection there.'

'You don't really buy that do you, Dan?' asked the DA.

'No. But I can't make a better connection. I hope I can sell it to the jury.'

'I think you're misreading the situation, Dan. We're talking *vigilante* killing.'

This time it was Abrams shaking his head, but he did so wearily.

'She doesn't fit the profile.'

'Maybe not. But patterns are only averages. In any case, you've got an ace in the hole on this one.'

Abrams raised his eyebrows sceptically, wondering if this was a lead-in to another of Jerry's smartass jokes.

'What ace?' he asked cautiously, realizing that he was going to have to play Costello to the DA's Abbott.

'Usually a lady defendant acts all weak and weepy-eyed, like she couldn't hurt a fly. This one's playing tough.'

'So?'

The DA sat forward. He could see that once again his former disciple wasn't with him.

'Let me give you a piece of advice, Dan. Let her play it the way she wants to. Strike that! Let her play it like it is. If she doesn't want to play the weak little pussycat, fine! Let her play tough, and make damn sure the jury sees it. Then when you point the accusing finger at her and brand her a murderess, they'll all buy it.'

'I still don't see why I have to be the fall guy,' said Abrams.

Jerry smiled the mischievous smile that alerted Abrams to an impending wisecrack.

'That's what it means to be one of the Chosen People.'

'Now how did I know that was coming?'

Chosen People indeed.

5

'How the fuck did it happen?' Declan McNutt's voice rang
out in its strong Northern Irish Catholic accent. It was neither
the hard accent of a Protestant 'Ulsterman', nor the brogue of
a Catholic from the Republic, but something in between.

'We're still trying to find out,' Padraig O'Shea replied
nervously. He knew that when Declan was this angry, he
was perfectly capable of lashing out at anyone. The man was
a psychopath. That was why the Irish National Liberation
Army recruited him. They had sent a man whom they thought
was a pro to America, but for operations in Northern Ireland
they preferred men like Declan, men who would probably be
in mental hospitals if it weren't for the British government
making huge funding cuts to the National Health Service.

When the Irish Republican Socialist Party broke from the
Official branch of Sinn Fein, the political wing of the Irish
Republican Army, in 1974, to promote a more socialist
agenda, they knew that they were taking a risk. The IRA
did not readily tolerate dissent. Five years earlier, the IRA
had faced another rift, when members of a less Marxist and
more religious persuasion had split to form the Provisional
wing. The official IRA had reluctantly accepted the *fait*

accompli of the Provisionals' breakaway, because they didn't want internal strife to detract from the *real* war against the British.

But that didn't mean that a smaller breakaway faction could count on the same leniency.

So when the dissenting radicals set up their military wing, the Irish National Liberation Army, they kept it secret even from most of their own members. And when their activities became known, they were quite open about the fact that they recruited psychopaths.

But neither their initial attempts at anonymity nor their subsequent use of psychopaths helped them when they faced the wrath of the Official IRA. In an event reminiscent of the night of the long knives, the Official IRA took action against them, wiping out eleven of their leaders. In the event, the INLA survived and resurfaced later. But by then the IRA had no real need to take action of their own. For within a short time of the INLA's re-emergence, the organization had itself split into two factions which were mercilessly setting out to destroy each other in an uncompromising civil war of their own.

'Well, what the fuck do we know so far?' Declan snarled.

Declan was clearly still angry, and Padraig knew that there was no way to appease him. He'd just have to ride out the storm and be careful not to say anything to set him off. At times like this, Declan could be difficult to deal with, even if one considered him a friend. He was a big man, six foot three and two hundred and twenty pounds, a former building labourer, with solid muscles developed by hard work on building sites rather than pumping iron in a gym. Padraig, who worked out in a gym but was of no more than average height and lean build, knew that if Declan turned violent it was not within his power to contain him, and probably not within his speed capability to make an effective escape either.

'As far as we've been able to find out he was going to make the hit in Central Park, where the girl goes jogging every morning. For some reason he was doing it with a rifle, even though he could've got close enough to do it with a handgun—'

'He doesn't use handguns,' said Declan with an acidic sneer

in his voice. 'He's an ex-mercenary and a top marksman. He only uses long-barrelled weapons. Perhaps if you read the reports they send down from Head Office once in a while you'd know what was going on.'

For a moment, Padraig considered making a wisecrack about at least being *able* to read. But seeing the implacable look on Declan's face he thought better of it.

'Well, anyway, it appears that a black teenager was seen running away afterwards with the rifle case. The gun wasn't found on the body, but it turned up later when the police raided a street gang hideout in an old derelict building. A cop was shot in the raid. But they found the gun and caught several of the gang members.'

'Did they catch the bastard who shot Seamus?'

'We don't know. None of the gang members made bail, but none of them are talking either. They have the same code of silence we have.'

'How dare you compare those bastards to us!' Declan's voice rang out in murderous rage, forcing Padraig to recoil in fear of imminent violence.

'I didn't mean it that way. I'm just saying that they haven't talked, so we don't know if they caught the scumbag or not.'

He had tried to sound chummy, as if he were agreeing with Declan and sharing his hatred of the street gang culture. In fact he understood this culture well enough, just as he understood the teenage joyriders of the Six Counties. They had no hope, nothing to live for. All they could do was mark time with acts of petty hooliganism or vandalism and try to make a bit of money peddling dope on street corners and fighting to control their territory from other gangs. But Declan was not open to reason and was past listening by this stage.

'Seamus was a good man, a man who was ready to lay down his life for our cause. Those nigger kids are worse than the joyriders the IRA knee-caps. They steal and kill for fun. They've got no cause to fight for. They believe in nothing. Their fathers had a cause in the sixties, but they don't want to fight for it any more. They've given up the struggle. They just sit on the stoop and make excuses for being the miserable little failures that they are. All they want to do now is snort cocaine and smoke crack. They have no stomach for a real fight so they spend half their time killing each other and the other half killing themselves.'

'I know. But perhaps it's all for the best. Maybe it's a sign that we shouldn't make any more attempts on the Levy girl.'

Declan reached out and grabbed Padraig by the throat, shoving him hard against the wall.

'All for the best? That one of our brothers in arms was killed by some monkey who dropped out of society? All for the best that some Jewish whore who murdered one of *our* freedom fighters is still walking around, while Sean Murphy lies in the cold ground, branded a terrorist by those who never knew him.'

Padraig was by now gasping for breath and he felt his eyes almost popping out. He had seen this look on Declan's face before when he had dealt with a woman who had suggested to him that it was no longer the time to kill, but rather a time for conciliation and peace. She had backed off and apologized after he had given her a couple of black eyes and shoved her face down a toilet and held it there for almost a minute. But Padraig was different. He didn't recognize the ceasefire any more than Declan did. All he wanted was to preserve the organization as a functional entity.

'I'm not saying that there's anything good in his dying, Declan,' he choked. 'I'm just saying that perhaps we should reconsider this whole idea of operating in America. The IRA doesn't operate there. That's where we get most of our support.'

'The IRA are a bunch of mealy-mouthed weasels,' Declan replied, slackening his grip. 'The reason they don't operate there is because that's where they get their funding from. They've sacrificed their independence to Mammon. That's why they hate us so much. Because they know we haven't compromised. They *know* that we're the ones who are in the right, but they haven't the balls to do like us. They're too scared of offending the Establishment. So while *we're* taking back the loot that the bankers have stolen from the people and using it to fund the next stage of the revolution, they're swaggering around saying' – and here he put on his high-pitched, whining voice – "'We're no threat to anyone. We're not left-wing revolutionaries. We don't want to overthrow the capitalist system. We just want to get the British out of the Six Counties. Then we'll lay down our arms and let everyone live in peace.'"

He reverted to his normal tone of voice, still heavily laden with anger.

'Well, that's bullshit. It would be bullshit if it was true and it's bullshit if it's not. Half of them are yellow-bellied hypocrites who haven't got the guts to come out of the closet and live as real revolutionaries and the other half are shameless collaborators who think all there is to the liberation of Ireland is winning back the Six Counties and handing them over to a bunch of capitalist reactionaries in the South. Well, that's not what we signed on for. We're here to change Ireland in a *meaningful* way, and if we have to trample over a few American conservative toes or even corpses in the process, we'll fuckin' well go ahead and do it!'

Even through his pain, Padraig was forced to laugh at the way Declan had presented it, while Declan, sensing that the laughter was approval, eased his grip and, after exchanging a smile with Padraig, released it altogether.

'OK, Declan, you win. We'll send someone else.'

'Someone else,' said Declan, the eyes and tone of voice still angry. 'You've gotta be out of your fuckin' head.'

'I don't understand,' said Padraig, fearing the worst.

'No, you fuckin' don't!' Declan blurted out, his anger turning into a beaming smile bordering on laughter. 'You think I want to send *you* to do it.'

Padraig was unable to keep the relief from his face. That had been *exactly* what he feared. 'Then what?' he asked, still nervous in the face of the unknown.

'I'm going to go there and do it myself, in the courtroom . . . as an act of justice.'

6

Eight months had not anaesthetized the public to the potential
drama of Justine's trial. Nor had political scandals and wars
sated their appetite for excitement. The throngs who had lined
up outside the court and filled its seats were as densely packed
as those who had crowded in to see Justine at the pre-trial
hearings.

When the court came to order, the judge went through
the token preliminary of asking each side if they had any
motions. Abrams, who had covered everything he wanted
at the pre-trial, had nothing further to add. But Parker,
although technically only on stand-by, decided to have a
desperate stab at pre-empting the outcome of the trial.

'I have,' he said quietly. He should have risen before
speaking. But he was so sure that his effort would prove
futile that he barely lifted himself off his seat and slumped
back a second later.

'You're only here on stand-by, Mr Parker,' Justice Harold
Wise responded in a guarded tone. 'However, as this is such
a preliminary stage in the proceedings and the jury have not
yet been impanelled, I'll hear what you have to say.'

The judge saw Parker struggling to hold his face neutral

in response to this early break. The temptation to smile was undermined by the solemnity of the judge's tone and the nervousness he felt in the face of this sudden and unexpected moment in the spotlight.

'Your Honour,' said Parker, as he rose with deliberate dignity from his chair, trying to project the image of a much older man. 'In view of the incessant and prejudicial reporting of the background to this case by the press, I move that the charges against my client be dismissed on the grounds that the pre-trial publicity has made it impossible to get a fair trial before an impartial jury. I also ask for the customary right to present my arguments in full.'

Abrams rose quietly to deliver his counter-punch.

'Your Honour, I oppose the motion. If counsel feels that pre-trial publicity has had such an effect then he should move for a change of venue. Furthermore he's had eight months in which to file a written motion and I would oppose any delay in the proceedings to accommodate oral arguments at this stage.'

'Yes, the point is well taken. I might have been more amenable to a motion at this stage if it had come from the defendant herself, or if she had changed her mind and asked that her stand-by counsel take over her defence. But in the absence of such a motion from the defendant or a change of mind about appearing *pro se*, the motion is denied. However, I will consider a motion for change of venue if I hear one.'

Parker was looking frustrated.

'Your Honour, as the publicity has been nationwide, it's hard to see where the trial could be held to escape the effects of the publicity. Therefore, if the court will not entertain a motion for dismissal of charges I move for a postponement, so that the trial can be held when the publicity and its effects have subsided.'

'Again, Your Honour,' Abrams responded, 'the People oppose the motion.'

'Again, I agree with the prosecution. The motion is denied.'

Usually judges put on an elaborate show of listening diligently to the long-winded arguments of learned counsel before announcing the foregone conclusion. But this was a no-nonsense judge who saw no need for such a display of hypocrisy. Aside from that, this was Justine Levy's show, and *she* hadn't moved for a dismissal of charges. The judge knew what Parker was feeling right now – as if a knife were twisting in his stomach. He now had what he thought of as an unsympathetic judge and a predatory prosecutor to contend with, in addition to an uncooperative client.

'Counsel can determine the partiality or bias of prospective jurors in the normal manner, by examination of individual veniremen.'

'Nice try,' said Justine caustically. She was angry with Parker for interfering, and she took no trouble to hide the fact.

The judge spoke again.

'The defendant may both challenge for cause and make peremptory challenges. Stand-by counsel may question the panel with the defendant's permission and may advise her, but will have no right to make challenges, not even for cause. Bring in the panel.'

The panel of prospective jurors was led in and the process of jury selection got under way. The judge recognized the woman sitting next to Abrams. She was a psychologist by training and a 'jury consultant' by profession. He didn't entirely approve of this: it gave the better-financed side the advantage. Usually that meant the defence, as the prosecution couldn't afford to use them in all cases and therefore, normally, didn't use them at all. But in this case, with Justine playing the Lone Ranger and Abrams dipping into the public coffers to use this case to advance his political career, it was the other way round. Jury consultants used anything from residential data and related public opinion surveys to clothing, body language and facial expressions to determine whether jurors were sympathetic or unsympathetic to the cause, and more importantly whether or not they would be sympathetic to the line of defence that their clients were going to offer. A woman who killed her violent husband would not want a retired military man on the jury, for example. A policeman accused of beating a black suspect would want a white middle-class jury, preferably in an area where a lot of policemen lived, to ensure an acquittal regardless of the strength of the evidence. Jury selection was not exactly an art, more an inexact science, like medicine.

Abrams rose and began asking a serious-looking man in his forties a series of routine questions about his job, number of children and whether or not he had followed the newspaper coverage. The man, James Lawson, was a businessman, had three children and had read about the case. In an important trial like this it was routine for the lawyers on both sides to look up the jurors' records of previous jury service. Daniel Abrams had records of the entire panel before him and he knew who were the 'convicting' jurors and who were the 'acquitting' ones. James Lawson was a convicting juror. He had served once before on a jury in a trial for fraud in which the defendant was found guilty. It was a different sort of case. But it showed that Lawson had no qualms or hesitation about finding a person guilty, knowing that the person was going to have to serve a custodial sentence.

'Acceptable to the prosecution,' said Abrams and sat down, confident that Justine would find no grounds to challenge for cause and knowing that she would have to use up one of her peremptory challenges to block him.

Richard Parker was staring at his own records, deep in thought. He too knew about Lawson's voting record in his past jury service, knew also that he had to find a way to get Lawson off the jury. Jurors tend to follow patterns – patterns that speak of their character in the same way as their voting patterns in an election. Some tend to give the defendant the benefit of the doubt. Others tend to put their faith in the police. But he could do nothing without Justine's consent. The judge had made it clear that she was running the show. And Justine had made it clear that she didn't want Parker's help.

Unless you're defending a client who has taken what the average American would see as legitimate revenge, you have to pick jurors who tend to acquit if you want to have any chance of getting your client off. When the DA decides to go to trial and doesn't offer or solicit a deal, you can bet your bottom dollar that the odds are overwhelmingly in his favour.

Justine rose slowly.

'Mr Lawson, would you classify yourself as a conservative?'

'I'm a libertarian,' replied Lawson matter-of-factly.

'Would you like to qualify that answer?' Justine followed up.

'No.'

Normally, questions about jurors' politics or religion are ill advised, as they might tend to alienate the prospective juror, and sometimes others on the panel as well. However such questions are permitted, and the lawyer or *pro se* defendant is free to ask them at his or her peril. In some cases they are even necessary, because of the high political or religious profile of the case. When Rabbi Meir Kahane was murdered, for example, the liberal Jewish lawyer defending the man who was caught running from the scene with the murder weapon was able to secure an acquittal by using peremptory challenges to secure an African-American jury and then repeating *ad nauseam* the false assertion that Rabbi Kahane hated blacks.

The present case also had political implications. It was the trial of a girl for the premeditated murder of a man whom many Irish-Americans and others thought of as a freedom fighter. But there was no easy answer to the question of what sort of juror she needed. A juror with little knowledge of international affairs might believe in the freedom fighter myth that the IRA had successfully propagated in much of America. An intelligent juror might see through the freedom fighter myth, yet disapprove of *any* vigilante action, seeing it as a threat to the stability of society. A liberal might see her as a girl from a privileged background with no excuse for taking to crime. A conservative might see her as a threat to law and order. An Irish-American might see her as the enemy. A Jew might feel the need to bend over backward to show that he or she was not biased in her favour.

Justine appeared to think for a moment.

'So what do you think of, say . . . Joe McCarthy?'

'He stank,' replied Lawson, flatly.

The delay in his reply had been too brief for him to have been weighing up his answer in his mind.

Abrams was staring at Justine with tense suspicion.

'I notice you don't pull your punches, Mr Lawson,' said Justine, looking him full in the face.

'I didn't get where I am today by treading softly,' he replied, meeting her eyes, unblinkingly.

'Acceptable to the defence,' said Justine, taking Abrams and the judge by surprise.

Parker's heart sank under a wave of confusion and fear. What was the stupid girl doing? Was she determined to lose the case, and her freedom along with it? Was it some twisted lemming instinct? Swimming out to sea to face certain death?

Abrams was barely able to conceal his delight. She had handed him a gift on a plate. And yet, the delight began to ebb almost immediately, leaving a creeping feeling of doubt in its wake.

The next prospective juror was a housewife. Abrams had no record of previous jury service for her, but he passed her after a few brief routine questions. Parker knew why. He was acting on the assumption that she would be envious of Justine's youthful good looks and embryonic professional career. Parker shared the assumption, and knew that a wise lawyer would work triple duty to get this woman off the jury, using a peremptory challenge if necessary.

But now it was Justine's turn, and Parker could only hope and pray.

'You say you have four children. Are any of them especially talented?'

'All of them,' replied the woman, slightly defensively.

'Did you always want to be a homemaker?'

There was a look of uncertainty on the woman's face, as if she were trying to recapture a distant recollection. But the look was tinged with regret.

'No. I studied linguistics and literature. I was going to be a professional translator. I've also done some creative writing. Short stories and articles.'

Justine nodded.

'The sort of thing you can do from home?'

'Yes,' the woman replied, this time with a hint of suspicion in her tone.

There was a ruffling motion on the other side of the courtroom as Abrams turned away, smiling.

'Did you work after you got married?'

'Yes.'

'And after you had children?'

There was another moment of hesitation, as if the woman were holding something back.

'Well, like I said, I did freelance work . . . but nothing outside of the home, if that's what you mean.'

Justine cast a glance at Abrams and then turned back to meet the woman's eyes.

'Were any of your children accidents or mistakes?' she asked.

The room had been quiet to begin with. But when Justine asked this question it fell silent. Justine was brazenly insulting a prospective juror who was not initially against her, with virtually no possibility of challenging her for cause. All she was doing was wasting a peremptory challenge.

Oh God, thought Parker. *Why don't I just give her a knife so she can slash her wrists?*

'No, young lady, they weren't!'

As before, the woman had hesitated in surprise at the question. But the response, when it came, was as vigorous as could be expected.

'Do you still do creative writing?' asked Justine, continuing as if nothing had happened.

Parker was thrown by this question. He had forgotten what the woman had said about creative writing, and in any case he couldn't see the relevance of it.

'Part of the time,' the woman replied. 'But not as much as I used to.'

'Why not?' Justine asked encouragingly.

'I don't have the time. I'm bringing up four children, don't forget.'

'But none of them are really young.'

The tone was argumentative, but mildly so.

'They still need attention. They've got talent, it needs to be nurtured.'

'You mean you didn't give up your career, you just exchanged one for another.'

For the first time since her *voir dire* began, the woman smiled appreciatively, as if learning something about herself.

'Exactly.'

'Do you think you'd have given up full-time gainful employment if your children hadn't been so talented?'

'Well, they were talented because I devoted so much attention to them. Strictly speaking I don't believe in talent. I prefer to call it ability.'

'But would you agree that being a homemaker wouldn't be so rewarding if it weren't for your children's ability?'

'Yes,' the woman conceded. 'That's certainly true.'

'Then you consider human ability to be something important.'

'I consider human ability to be the *only* thing that's important,' the woman replied with mild reproof.

'So did *my* mother,' said Justine matter-of-factly.

Then she looked over at the judge.

'Acceptable to the defence,' she concluded.

Abrams's smile had given way to a scowl that he could barely hide. In the space of a minute, Justine had turned things around, from facing an enemy to addressing an ally.

To Parker, there seemed to be a pattern in Justine's selections. It was discernible, but the underlying logic behind it remained obscure. When a truck driver came under consideration, she accepted him without even looking up. But when another venireman ogled her with undisguised lust she challenged him without batting an eyelid. She gave the go-ahead to a woman who ran a used-car business, but kept questioning a woman who served as merchandise manager for a large department store until she found grounds to challenge for cause.

Once in a while she asked a strange question, the reason for which Parker, Abrams and the judge could not figure. 'Have you heard of Lizzie Borden?' or 'What did you think of Joe McCarthy?' or 'Was Christopher Columbus crazy?' But she seemed to pass them regardless of their answers. It was as if she were planting the seeds of some thought in their minds, as the illustrious Sam Liebowitz had done when he asked jurors if they were familiar with Nietzsche, in preparation for his celebrated defence of Laura Parr. But with Liebowitz the fruit of the seeds was very clear: to suggest to the jury in advance of the prosecution's case that the 'victim' of the murder was in fact a bully and a thug who enjoyed inflicting physical suffering on women and who had used violence on the defendant immediately prior to the shooting, even though there were no signs of violence on her body or in the room. In Justine's case it wasn't clear *what* would grow from the seeds.

7

Justine stood before the bathroom mirror, holding the bottle of peroxide in her right hand. As she looked at her reflection she began to doubt that the plan made sense. She could never look convincingly platinum blonde. The sight of her deep red hair drove home to her with the most devastating force that the most she could hope for was a pale mousy shade. If anything it would only draw attention to herself without improving the chances of her plan's success.

She decided instead to concentrate on the clothes. She knew that Murphy had a preference for blondes, but he would tolerate a girl with red hair as an acceptable alternative if she looked like the kind of cheap slut that he went for. He was the kind of man who liked to tour the singles bars and pick up a different girl every time. She had watched him for several days now, at a discreet distance, following him through the trail of New York bars and discos. Following him had been the hardest part. He liked to walk through the urban combat zones where it isn't safe for a decent girl to walk alone. But she had persevered.

As the sun sank like a smouldering flame and the city dissolved into the bland, lifeless tone of the evening twilight, she had followed him like a panther stalking its quarry. She had followed him past greasy pimps and heavily painted hookers. She had followed him past the stooges of the sidewalk con artists as they enticed the mark into a rigged three-card monte. She had watched him from the shadows of the ethnic ghettos as he strolled and played the game of living footloose in New York. She had tailed him through the singles bars and pick-up joints. She knew him inside out. She had seen him change the colour of his personality like a grass snake, as he slithered through the slums and sewers of the concrete jungle.

Occasionally she glanced up at the penthouses above for a moment's relief from the cockroaches and sewer rats below. Just as there were two Americas, so there were two New Yorks, with one placed squarely on top of the other. But they were divided along the lines of personal choice. The top hadn't climbed there over the corpses of those beneath. Rather, they had aimed for the stars and leapt with all the might they could muster, while the low life rushed in to fill the vacuum.

It was down among the low life that Justine had wandered as she pursued her quarry. She hated it. But she had little choice.

As the curtain of dusk descended around her, she looked up again at the majestic towers of the skyline, drawing comfort from the squares of light hanging there in the night sky like sparkling gems against black velvet. These were the windows of the penthouses, where the curtains never needed to be drawn against the darkness, where the sense of adventure was untainted by the stench of the garbage that littered the streets.

She kept to the shade, avoiding the misty pools of light thrown by the tall, lean streetlamps on to the cold grey stone of the sidewalk. From lightless corners she had observed him as a zoologist observes his laboratory specimens. She had studied him in action while he spotted his prey and homed in for the kill. She knew every movement and physical gesture of his routine. The only thing she didn't know were the words. But these didn't matter. She would find out soon enough. The important thing was that she knew what kind of girl he liked. She knew the look . . . and she knew the type . . .

She left the bathroom and entered the mahogany-panelled bedroom. It was fitting, she thought, that she was doing it here and not in her own bedroom. It was a large room in a large apartment, and she was now the owner.

Some people would have called her lucky to be the owner of one and a half million dollars' worth of New York City real estate. But as she shivered in the emptiness of the apartment, she didn't feel lucky today. Bitter was more the word.

She went over to the full-length mirror, still wearing the bathrobe. Even modestly covered up, with only the calves and forearms to hint at the shape and form of the rest, there was no denying the beauty that would carry her plan through to midfield. From her teens onward she had never lacked dates or boyfriends, and only her mother's friendly firmness had kept the distractions at bay and the social life in reasonable proportion, to allow her to progress with her studies. Justine had the willpower to study, but having a determined mother to guard the portals made all the difference between pressing on and falling by the wayside.

Looking at her reflection in the mirror now, Justine could see the source of the potential problem. She had the smooth complexion, the gentle bone structure and the firm, voluptuous figure that appealed to the traditional tastes of adolescent boys. And she had blossomed early, making her a prime target for the high-school headhunters.

She realized now that in a way she *was* lucky – lucky to have been blessed with good looks and lucky not to have been toppled by them. And yet Justine, who seemed to have all the breaks, didn't feel lucky at all. A stupid war miles away in Asia had deprived her of her father's mind and a bullet from the past had deprived her of his physical presence. Disease had deprived her of her mother and the aloofness that she had developed while studying had deprived her of any lasting friendships.

She sat down on the bed, slipped her arms out of the bathrobe and threw it behind her. There was a brusque anger in her movements as she picked up the tight-fitting purple T-shirt, pulled it over her head and smoothed it down over her body. It was followed by a pair of frilly briefs of black lace. She didn't know how far the charade would go but she thought she had better be prepared. Just knowing that she was wearing them gave her the feeling of the part that she had chosen to play, and also gave her confidence about turning in an authentic performance.

She returned to the mirror to study the results so far. It was a pleasing picture. She certainly looked like his type. But her eyes were irresistibly drawn from the thighs and hips, which would capture his attention, to the face, which she would have to turn into a mask to conceal her real feelings. It was a sad face, which cried out for sympathy. But Justine bridled with the stirrings of an inner rebellion at the thought of sympathy. If the sorrow showed on her face it would destroy her plan. She would have to work harder to conceal it.

But she would also have to struggle to hide the anger.

The purple shorts came next. They matched the T-shirt in both colour and style . . . and carried the same suggestion. She stepped into them and pulled them up with a swift movement. They hugged her form, showing it at its best, or at least hinting at the offer. The whole scenario was repulsive and loathsome, but without the bait there was no way that she could lure that vile man to his destruction.

The combination was complemented by a pair of high leather boots in white. With every item of apparel in place, she stood before the mirror with her hands on her hips. A hard, cruel smile broke out across her face. But it was not the smile of one who had no feelings. It was the smile of one who could feel too much.

8

'Ladies and gentlemen of the jury,' Daniel Abrams's voice rang out. 'Before you sits a young lady accused of the crime of murder. This is a serious crime and it is not an accusation which a grand jury would make lightly.'

There was a stirring in the jury benches as several of the jurors sat forward. Strictly speaking a grand jury indictment is not a finding of guilt or even an accusation, but a finding of the fact that there is a case to answer. But the press and public frequently take it as a preliminary verdict of guilty, and most prosecutors are only too happy to avail themselves of this popular misconception.

'It is the contention of the prosecution that Justine Levy caused Sean Murphy to die of poisoning. It is the People's case that she did this wilfully, deliberately and with the most meticulous premeditation.'

The Assistant District Attorney stood by the wooden rail in front of the jury, addressing the twelve representatives of the people in a powerful strident tone as he blasted away at their senses with his opening volley of rhetoric. He was, by repute, a subtle prosecutor rather than a power prosecutor. But today he was changing his style in order to give a boost to his political career, and also to render him numb to his own doubts about the justice of his case.

'You will hear medical evidence as to how Sean Murphy died, how Miss Levy entrapped him into inviting her for dinner and then brought along a bottle of tequila as part of her plan to poison him. You will hear how the defendant took, from the medical school where she studied, certain equipment which she used to extract poison from canisters of insecticide, thereby avoiding having to sign for the purchase of a poisonous substance. You will hear evidence of how she purchased insecticide from which she extracted this poisonous substance. You will hear how she disguised her appearance before the crime and then went back to her old appearance *after* the crime, thereby indicating criminal intent. You will hear how she met the deceased in a bar and went off with him the night before the murder.'

There was an eerie quiet in the courtroom during the pauses between Abrams's sentences, the kind of silence one expects to hear in the fraction of a second before the verdict is announced. The judge, a seasoned observer of criminal proceedings, noticed a strange kind of unease hanging in the air, an unfamiliar kind of tension written in lines of earnest intensity across the faces of the numerous spectators. It was one of those cases that holds the public in its grip.

But there were cases and there were cases. It had always been so. There were the cases involving the rich and famous, which had drawn the public in droves, to root for their hero or to gloat over a fallen idol whom they hated or envied. There were the crimes of particular viciousness when the public had shown up to witness the undoing and punishment of the miscreant who had outraged their sense of morality. There were the serial killers, finally brought to book after tireless months of investigating by the authorities – killers who had taunted the police with their crimes and were finally hunted down and brought before the judge in chains, their days of gloating over. There were the helpless victims, the battered wives and abused children who finally and belatedly fought back with more force than the law allowed. And there were the deceitful ones who tried to portray themselves as belonging to that tragic category, their cunning lawyers taking advantage of the fact that the victim is not directly represented by the prosecution and knowing full well that the dead cannot answer back.

Each of these trials had their own peculiar character which marked them out from each other. But all of them had one thing in common: the tension came at the end, while excitement and curiosity characterized the beginning. With the case of the People of the State of New York versus Justine Levy all of this was different. The tension that was usually reserved for the build-up to the verdict pervaded the courtroom from the very beginning. There was none of the usual tendency of spectators to look at their neighbours and whisper to them. They seemed afraid even to *look* at their neighbours, as if their faces were somehow an implacable reproach to themselves.

Abrams proceeded to outline his case in more detail, describing the first meeting between Justine and Sean Murphy, the type of poison used and how it affected the nervous system, and the events at the hospital. Then he paused for dramatic effect.

'But there is another dimension to this case apart from the purely technical one, an aspect which is in fact more interesting than the dry scientific details.

'I am referring,' Abrams continued, 'to the moral aspects, and also of course to the related psychological aspects. These form the backdrop to this case.'

At the defence table, Justine showed no emotion, only a kind of quiet attentiveness, her face as closed to the outside world as that of a seasoned poker player.

'In a way this case is a tragedy, members of the jury. A tragedy written by the hand of fate on the subject of human nature, on the theme, I should say, of the *ugly* side of human nature.'

Again he paused, monitoring the jurors' reactions to his words. It was one of those carefully planned dramatic pauses that he had practised hundreds of times. Then, in time with his words, he began tapping on the rail in front of the jury with his right hand.

'A *medical* student, a girl who was learning how to *save*

human life, instead chose to use her knowledge to become a destroyer by *taking* the life of one of her fellow human beings.'

Now came the technique that Jerry had taught him when he was a greenhorn in the DA's office and Jerry was the up-and-coming whiz kid who served as his mentor. He half turned and pointed with an extended finger and outstretched forearm towards Justine. It was the perfect courtroom ploy. As long as he gave the impression of personal sincerity it couldn't fail. However Justine reacted, she would look guilty. She could smile, blush, swallow, look demurely away or burst into tears – the result would always be the same. As long as the prosecutor sounded sincere to the jury, they would believe him and dismiss the defendant's response as a ploy or an indirect confession of guilt.

'There, ladies and gentlemen, sits an evil woman who has blood on her hands, a woman who committed cold-blooded murder. She would have you believe that she's nothing more than a girl, but she is most manifestly a woman. She lost her childhood innocence the day she decided to play God!'

He lowered his hand and started pacing in front of the jury.

'Ladies and gentlemen, I know that the defendant is young and pretty. But I urge you, members of the jury, not to be swayed by her looks or her youth. Such sympathy would be wholly misplaced. Spare your sympathy instead for her victim, Sean Murphy. He paid a heavy price for liking her and trusting her: he paid with his *life*.

'You might think that because the late Sean Murphy was himself accused of murder, in a foreign country, this in some way justifies the actions of the defendant. But I need hardly remind you, members of the jury, that our sacred tradition calls for a government of laws and not of men. It was for the courts to decide what do to with Sean Murphy, not one lone vigilante. The courts decided. But she didn't agree with their decision, so she decided to take the law into her own hands.

'I do not know what connection, if any, existed between Justine Levy and her victim. It may be that in her own twisted way she thought that she was acting in revenge for her profession. Murphy was accused of murdering a doctor. Justine Levy is a medical student. Perhaps she thought that it was up to her to avenge his death. Of course, it was the revenge of a sick mind, as revenge so often is. But human life is a sacred thing . . . and that is why we have laws to protect it.'

He looked intently at the jury for a few seconds and then returned to his seat.

Some of the jurors were surprised that the prosecutor had no more than speculated on the motive, and his speculation had been pretty weak at that. What they didn't know was that motive was the prosecution's weak spot from the very beginning.

'We've got to find it,' Abrams had told the DA. 'We'll need it if we're going for murder.'

'I don't see why,' the DA had replied, unperturbed. 'We can prove what she did. We've got expert testimony. There are no chain-of-custody loopholes, and she's fully *compos mentis*. The case may be circumstantial, but it isn't weak. It comes straight from the forensic lab and it's solid. Just make sure you get a jury that trusts scientists and you've got her nailed from opening credits to sunset finale.'

'Jerry, listen to me. You said yourself when you handed me the file that it's going to be an uphill task prosecuting a pretty girl who's been through what she's been through, especially if the jury finds out about it. Now you're trying to reassure me that we have a strong case and that all I have to do is present it. Well, you were right the first time. It's not just enough to present the case. To prove murder I'm going to have to show intent to kill.'

'Oh, come on, Dan! You think all those preparations don't add up to a premeditated plan?'

'Maybe it was a plan to frighten.'

'Oh, that's ridiculous!'

'Is it? We still don't know *why!*'

But no one at the DA's office had a clue what the motive was. They had taken a straw poll and the most popular explanation was, perversely, jilted lover. That this unlikely explanation was not supported by so much as a shred of evidence did nothing to mute the speculation.

Loved-Murphy's-victim ran a strong second followed by Murphy-killed-someone-in-her-family. A straight vigilante killing had only two votes: the DA and his secretary.

Not content with the results of the poll, Abrams had put a team of three young rookies from his staff on to the task of finding a motive. They had badgered Interpol and Scotland Yard, who were uncharacteristically obstructive. They even made some enquiries with the BBC, in case they were sitting on some secret information for a documentary, to embarrass the British government. They had even investigated Justine's political past to see if she had any connection with Unionist paramilitary groups in Northern Ireland. But they had drawn a blank on all counts.

'The defence can either make its opening statement now,' said the judge in a tone of mild boredom, 'or reserve the right to do so after the People's case is concluded. Miss Levy, the choice is yours. I suggest however that you confer with your stand-by counsel before deciding. If you wish I will grant a brief recess in order to give you time to confer.'

Parker leaned over to Justine and whispered: 'I suggest you let me speak now to undermine the impact of his speech.'

'How do you propose to do that when you don't know the facts?'

He leaned back, defeated, as Justine rose.

'I'll speak now, Your Honour.'

She turned to face the jury, looking at one juror in particular: James Lawson.

'Lizzie Borden took an axe and gave her mother forty whacks. When she realized what she'd done, she gave her father forty-one. That rhyme has been known to children since the turn of the century, when the trial of Lizzie Borden took place. Not many people know, even today, that Lizzie Borden was acquitted.

'In the 1950s, a demagogue by the name of Joe McCarthy made a series of wide-ranging but factually hollow accusations to the effect that various figures in public life were communists. Although he never proved so much as one of his accusations, he was greatly admired by many people and hailed as a defender of our system against the evil of communism. Today we look back on McCarthy as a liar and a demagogue who hurt many innocent people with his false accusations. Most conservatives regard him with embarrassment rather than admiration, while radical libertarians go even further and regard him with contempt.'

Abrams exchanged a puzzled look with his second-seat colleague. The judge looked on impassively, admiring Justine's technique and fascinated by it. Strictly speaking, the only proper purpose of an opening statement is to present the outline of one's case and to state the elements of that case which one intends to prove. Abrams knew that he could object to Justine's soliloquy as not being a proper opening statement. But his instincts told him to hold back, so as not to give the impression that he was trying to suppress her case. Whatever Justine was trying to accomplish by her rambling monologue, he was confident that there could be nothing in it that would harm his case. All she could do would be to confuse the jury and give them the clear impression that she was mentally unstable, perhaps even unstable enough to commit murder.

'When Christopher Columbus set sail to the west in search of a new trade route to the riches of the eastern world, he was warned by uneducated people around him that the world was flat and that he'd fall off the edge. This was in spite of the fact that educated people had known since the time of the ancient Greeks that the world was round.'

A ripple of laughter wafted through the courtroom and broke into embarrassed silence in the face of the judge's reproving look. It relieved the spectators to hear such a snippet of humour from the hard-faced Justine, however brief. But it was over almost as soon as it started, without even a fleeting smile crossing her face.

Abrams shifted awkwardly. He was recognizing the common factor in all of Justine's anecdotes, finally realizing what she was up to. But he had left it too late to make a valid objection. The judge would not look kindly on it if he tried to block her now. All he could do was ride out the storm and try to put his case back on track when he called his first witness.

'The point I'm getting at, members of the jury, is that it's all too easy for a lot of people to believe something and for all of them to be wrong. It's easy even for *intelligent* people to get caught in the grip of mass hysteria. We see it in the lingering assumption that Lizzie Borden was guilty. We remember it happening during the McCarthy era. And we can even read about it in the time of Christopher Columbus.'

She paused for a moment to let her point sink in.

'All I'm asking you to do is keep your minds open until you've heard all the facts. You've read about this case in the papers and heard about it on TV and some of you have come here with your minds already made up. You've seen the case in close-up. Now stand back and take another look.'

She sat down to a silence that was as deafening as any thunder, a silence that weighed in so heavily it allowed the jurors to hear not only the beating of their hearts, but even the creaking of their souls.

9

'Were you always this stubborn?' asked Rick Parker.

He was edging his way along between the chairs towards a table in the corner, his tray held high in the air as it passed precariously over the heads of the lunchtime crowd. Justine gave him a quick backward glance, catching sight of him briefly as he struggled to keep up with her while she deftly manoeuvred towards the table she had chosen.

'I'll let you figure that out for yourself,' she replied, dismissing the question coolly as she led the way through the throng of customers with a degree of self-confidence that bordered on bravado.

'I reckoned that if you wouldn't let me defend you in court, at least you'd let me buy you lunch. I'd like to feel that I'm earning my keep in some way.'

They slid easily if without grace on to the olive-green Formica seats. The act of sitting down offered Parker a sense of relief, a feeling of taking shelter from the lunchtime rush even if they were still in the thick of it. In the comfort and safety of the corner, it was as if nothing in the world could harm them.

'I'm a good lawyer, you know. If only you'd give me a chance.'

She took a bite out of her pastrami sandwich as if consciously relegating his question to second place.

'I don't doubt you,' she replied. 'I want you to know that. I'm sure you're a damn good lawyer.'

He smiled in gratitude at the few crumbs of flattery she was ready to throw his way. But she killed his reviving confidence with her follow-on.

'It's just that what you have to offer me really has no bearing on my defence.'

He looked at her, not exactly hurt, but openly vulnerable.

'Why don't you tell me what you're planning?' he asked. 'I mean your defence. Maybe I could help you.'

'I'll tell you when I tell everyone else, in court.'

'You mean you're going to testify?'

The fear in his voice was genuine. But it came over as sarcasm.

'I believe I have that right,' she replied, struggling to inject a note of coolness into her tone.

In the silence that followed she took another bite out of her sandwich while Parker studied her face.

'You're a tough cookie,' he said, to break the silence.

She said nothing.

'Does that mean I'm going to have to work blind?'

'You're only a stand-by counsel. You don't have to work at all.'

'I could help you on points of law. I could raise objections to Abrams's tactics and block evidence that may be harmful to you. But if I do it blind I could make things worse. Can't we work together on this one?'

'My defence is going to be very simple: the truth. I don't need your help with that. I have nothing to hide and no reason to erect a barrier of technicalities. Your field is the law. My concern is the truth. That's what I'm going to give them.'

She continued eating while he watched her, his puzzlement increasing. Her face remained as inscrutable as her words. He couldn't penetrate the enigma. Finally he too started eating, realizing that he was going to make no headway.

For a couple of minutes they ate in silence, the tension

still lingering. All the while a thought was eating away at Parker, a thought he was afraid to verbalize. But he knew that he had nothing to lose.

'The way you're carrying on before the jury, they'll think you're tough enough to commit murder.'

It was so unexpected that she was forced to stop eating and look up at him.

'I am.'

With a valiant effort, he stopped himself from choking. She seemed to be holding back a smile, as if secretly amused by the effect her words had had upon him. She was about to attack her food again. But he couldn't leave her remark hanging in the air like that, a cloud hovering over them.

'Do you want to spell that out?' he asked.

'What I'm trying to say is . . .' Justine seemed to hesitate for the first time. '*Whatever* I do . . . it's what I *want* to do . . . and it's what I think is right.'

'That sounds ominous,' he replied.

'All right, let me make it a little clearer, Rick. You don't know a damn thing about me. You don't know if I'm guilty or not. If I am you don't know why I did it. For all you know I could be a murderess. Yet you're ready to fight for me as hard as if you were sure that I *was* innocent . . . *but no harder*. In other words, Rick, you don't care about whether or not justice is done. The only thing you care about is *winning*.'

'That's not true!' But the denial was too emphatic to be sincere. There was no pain in his cry, just vehemence. 'OK, you're right, I *do* care about winning. But I also care about the rights of the defendant. The defendant has the right to the best defence possible. It's for the jury to decide on the facts.'

'Spare me the platitudes, Rick!' she spat out contemptuously. 'You let the cat out of the bag when you said "defendant". You didn't say "you". You used that anonymous impersonal word "defendant". Admit it, Rick, you were reciting the standard formula you learned at law school.'

But he sensed that there was more than contempt in her reply. There was anger, as if something he had said had caused it. It was not him, he realized. It was what he said – what it represented. His remark had set off something within her, or touched a raw nerve, and he felt that if he could find out what, he would find himself holding the last piece of the puzzle, the key that could unlock the mystery.

Half a minute ticked by while they attacked their food in earnest. Only briefly, and imperceptibly, did Justine glance up to notice Rick's boyish curly hair. By the time Rick summoned the courage to look up again there was no sign that she had ever looked away from her food.

'I liked your speech. It really knocked Abrams off course.'

'It was nothing. I just had to open their minds. But you won't be hearing much from me for a while. I plan to let Abrams run the circus from now, at least for the time being.'

'There was something I wanted to ask about . . . your strategy when it came to jury selection.'

'What did you make of it?'

'Well, one minute you seemed to be antagonizing the panel by the kind of questions that a rookie like me would know not to ask, almost as if you were hell-bent on challenging them or else really wanted to impanel a hostile jury. Then the next minute you said something to win them over to your side. Very often it was just a single word or sentence. And there were some cases where you almost assaulted them with impertinent questions and then won them over by looking them in the eye without smiling and saying "Acceptable to the defence," as if you were exchanging some sort of coded signal.'

'Did I challenge any of them?'

'You used up all of your peremptories.'

'So I wasn't capable of winning them all over to my side.'

'Well, no, it wasn't that. Some of them seemed like they were incapable of getting angry about anything.'

'What's that got to do with it?'

'Those were the ones you challenged.'

'And what sort of jury did I get for my trouble?'

'I'd say a jury of hard-heads. Tough, unemotional people. People like you in fa . . .'

As he trailed off into the silence of realization, she nodded her head slowly as if to underscore the lesson he had just learned.

'It's true,' she said. 'I did win them over as friends before the trial started. But that wasn't what I was trying to do. They liked me because they recognize me as one of them. But I wanted *them* because I recognize them as being like me, at least partly. Let Abrams rant and rave about "that unfortunate man" or "that wicked lady" and I'll come right back and spell out the facts, including the ones he's trying so hard to sweep under the rug. By the time this trial is over there are going to be no secrets left between me and the jury.'

'There was another thing I noticed, though. When you made your opening speech, you kept looking at just one juror, James Lawson, I think. Don't you understand that by singling out one juror like that you're antagonizing the others? That's something I learned in a course on jury psychology. Also it might make Lawson nervous.'

'He's not the type to get nervous. He's a self-made millionaire who worked his way up from the gutter. You saw what he was like: tough as nails.'

'But I still don't see why you did it,' Parker persisted.

'OK, well, first of all I picked Lawson because of all the members of the jury he seemed like the most self-confident, one of the most intelligent and certainly the one with the most commanding presence. Incidentally, you may have noticed that I also went out of my way to impanel an intelligent jury. I challenged some veniremen with paper degrees because they looked like they weren't capable of independent thought. You know the type, the kind that can only bite into a mouthful of knowledge too big to swallow and then spit it out in the examination room. At the same time I gave the green light to the kind of people who learned on the job and haven't surrendered their minds to stale conformity. They're not the kind who think the world is all roses and candies and they aren't the kind who can't think at all.'

'But still, why did you address everything to one juror?'

Her face softened, flattered by the earnest sincerity of his question.

'Rick, imagine that at the end of the trial, when the jury retires to consider their verdict, you're allowed to go into the jury room to argue the case all over again and answer any questions or doubts they may have. Imagine further that the judge allows you to stay in the jury room throughout their deliberations and remind them of all the facts and points that are favourable to your case and to challenge any point that may be unfavourable. Imagine that after the prosecutor has finished his closing argument and thinks he's had the last word, you can come along and undermine everything he's said. Imagine further that you can meet with and speak to each and every juror separately and customize your arguments to their peculiarities, to allay their doubts with individual arguments directed at each one in turn. Would that give you an advantage?'

'I'll say!'

'Now let's consider a variation on the theme. Suppose that you aren't allowed to go in there yourself, but you're allowed to send in a friend to do all these things on your behalf.'

'I guess that would still be an advantage, maybe even a better one, because with a friend to do it for you it wouldn't look like it's self-serving. That's why it's always better to be represented by a lawyer.'

He couldn't resist that last dig.

'All right.' She sailed on, brushing aside his final comment. 'Now imagine that this ambassador of yours is intelligent and persuasive, as well as being a shrewd judge of human character.'

'I guess it would give me an *overwhelming* advantage.'

'Well, Rick, James Lawson is going to be my ambassador in the jury room.'

He swallowed the cola in his mouth and almost launched into a coughing spasm.

'Do you mean to say that you cooked up a deal with a juror?'

In the space of a fraction of a second the look of satisfaction was swept away from Justine's face. What stood in its place was regret. There was no hint of any fear of being revealed or anger at being insulted, just an immense disappointment.

'Rick, if I'd cooked up a deal with Lawson, either before or after he was impanelled, do you think I'd make it so obvious by staring straight at him in public all the time?'

'I guess not.'

'Then doesn't it occur to you that the rapport I've built up with him has taken place exclusively in the courtroom?'

Parker said nothing. He sat watching her in helpless fascination, still trying desperately to unravel the mystery. She made no effort to fill the silence. But when it was clear that her words had penetrated the surface of his understanding, she continued.

'Rick, I've never seen that man before the day he was selected for the jury and I haven't spoken to him for so much as a second outside the courtroom. What I'm doing is communicating with him *inside* the courtroom. I'm addressing my arguments to him, reaching out to him in the courtroom and turning him into my ally. There's nothing devious or underhanded about it. I'm just showing him how much we have in common.'

'Are you sure you *have* anything in common? I mean, like you said, you've never met him before.'

'Rick, if you can't see it then it's just as well that I'm conducting my own defence.'

He carried on eating, not understanding why Justine's words hurt him.

It was Justine who reconnected the lines of communication between them.

'We've talked enough about me. Tell me about yourself, Rick.'

'Do you want the full story or the condensed version?'

She looked at her watch.

'We're due back in court at two thirty. You'd better strip it down to the basics.'

'I grew up in New York City and graduated from high school at seventeen. I did well on my SATs and got into Columbia where I majored in psychology. I graduated *summa cum laude* and got into Harvard Law School where I graduated first in my class. I did my legal internship with the Chief Justice of the United States and then took a job at the legal aid office.'

Parker's brief summary of his personal paper chase had made light of the extraordinary difficulties he had faced every step of the way. His relentless march towards the bar had been a succession of tough but carefully planned stages.

The young Rick Parker had passed up basketball games and parties in order to study, encouraged and urged on by his wise old uncle whose lavish praise convinced him of his own worth. He took little part in high-school sports but was a keen member of the debating society.

It was a difficult struggle, although the academic aspect was the least of his difficulties. He sailed through what was supposed to be hard work with a minimum of effort. The only problems were his brother's fists and the old man's belt during his brief spells out of prison. He discovered that there was a fundamental difference between his approach to learning and that of his peers. They tried to memorize first and understand later. His method of learning was more economical. He sought to integrate any new fact or principle into his existing knowledge. Once he *understood* something new it was automatically committed to memory with no need for further effort on his part. All this to achieve an ambition that he had settled upon at the age of ten: to become a lawyer.

'You know, we haven't really talked about you at all,' he said cautiously. 'I don't mean the case, I mean you personally. Who you are and where do you come from?'

'You mean with all your lawyer's emphasis on preparation and reading you didn't have me checked out by a private dick or go snooping around my friends?'

'That's not the way we do things in legal aid. Besides, I didn't have the money to hire a private investigator or the time to do it myself.'

'So you come right out with it,' she said approvingly. 'Well, I like your style. At least you're straight.'

'So what about it?' he asked, sensing that 'being straight' was very much part of her creed. 'Will the real Justine Levy please stand up.'

In the space of a few seconds, two emotions vied for control in Justine's mind: regret and joy. She frowned, threw back her head, smiled and then looked at the space on the table between their plates.

'I was born in 1973 when my father was in the Reserve Officer Training Corps programme and my mother was working as a secretary to a real estate broker. When I was two my father was sent to Vietnam as an adviser. It was 1975 and he was one of the last people to be sent there before the war ended. I mean before it *really* ended. He saw the fall of Saigon and the mad scramble of the people to get out before the barbarians took over. Then they brought him out, or at least what was left of him.'

'In a coffin?'

'Yes and no.'

'Paralysed? Injured?'

'He was blinded by a shell.'

'Shrapnel?'

'Rick, for God's sake will you stop trying to guess and let me tell it like it was!'

He swallowed nervously and mouthed a brief apology.

'It was concussion blindness. Physically he made a complete recovery before he was even brought back. He got his sight back within a few days. But when you're stuck out there on a battlefield with shells falling all around you, and you can't even see what's going on, it does something to your mind. That's what happened to my father. He was never the same.'

She broke off, as if fighting some inner conflict. But she wouldn't share it with Rick. There was a part of her that still had to remain private.

'He came back suffering from what they now call "post-traumatic stress disorder". He went through seven years of alternating passivity and violent spells. Finally he splattered his brains all over the wall with his service revolver.'

Rick winced. For all his legal work with street punks and the scum of the earth he was still squeamish.

'Seven years? That would have made you nine at the time.'

'That's right. I walked into the room just in time to see him do it.'

'Oh God . . .'

It was an unfamiliar feeling, the lump in his throat. He stopped speaking, unwilling to trust his voice.

The enigma of Justine Levy was beginning, just beginning, to unravel.

'Wait. It gets worse later. Anyway, that was the day I

decided to study medicine. Well, it was a noble enough ambition, and I figured it was a good way to help people, and there was money in it which didn't hurt either. My mother gave me all the encouragement in the world. She studied and took her real-estate exams and became a real-estate broker herself. Now I'm living in a duplex penthouse that we got for seven fifty grand, and it's probably worth one and a half million now. Then my mother got ill and it all started to fall apart.'

'What did she have?'

'Infiltrating lobular carcinoma. It had already metastasized by the time it was detected.'

'What happened then?'

'I wanted to quit my studies and just stay home and take care of her, but she wouldn't hear of it. We had medical insurance and some money put aside, but to cover the costs of a day nurse and my medical studies we had to sell off some of her jewellery. Only she refused to sell the apartment. She wanted to keep it for me. She didn't know it, but I took a job as a waitress to supplement the income. It was just as well because I wanted to make sure that she got a private room when it reached the point where she required hospitalization.'

'And *then* what happened?' asked Rick, now wary of trying to anticipate the twists and turns of Justine's life history.

'I should think that's obvious. She died. And now, at the ripe old age of twenty-three, here I am all set to end my days of freedom on a murder rap.'

'How did you feel about not spending much time with your mother?'

He was looking for signs of guilt.

'I wanted to. But she insisted that my studies must come first. She knew that she wouldn't be around much longer and she wanted to be sure that I had a secure future. She didn't want me to spend my whole life regretting the lost opportunities that had passed me by. On her deathbed she told me that whatever I decided to do, I should do it well. She told me that my good looks could be both a blessing and a curse. I could use them to give me the pick of the men, but I could also lapse into a safe marriage for security and never get to make the most of my mind, because the alternative was all too easy. She knew what it was like being married to the wrong man – I mean he *became* the wrong man – and she didn't want me falling into that trap.'

'Did it come as a shock to you?'

'What?'

'Your mother's death.'

'No, of course not. I knew it was coming – even without my medical studies I knew it. At first, when it wasn't clear how advanced the malignancy was, she tried to play it down and dismiss it from my mind. But once she knew that it was terminal she made sure that I confronted reality and didn't try to hide from it. She made sure that I was prepared for the inevitable. But it was still painful. It was harder on me than for her. She could take it, I couldn't. She forced me to accept it and prepare for what was to follow. Even in her illness she was still the pillar that I had to lean on.'

'Did you resent it?'

'The fact that she gave me strength? The fact that she showed me how to face up to tragedy? The fact that she taught me how to stand on my own two feet so that I could give her the strength when the time came? Would you have resented it?'

'I'm sorry. It was a stupid question.'

He took a deep breath and let a moment of silence pass.

'Did anything happen to hasten her death?'

'No. But nothing happened to stop it either.'

There was a trace of sharpness in the tone, a cutting edge of anger. It seemed to strike at odd intervals, defying any pattern of expectation.

'When you objected to me defending you, was it because I'm a man?'

'You're asking me if I hate men?' she asked incredulously.

'I'm trying to figure you out,' he admitted, too desperate to hide behind the stalking-horse of small talk.

'You're barking up the wrong tree.'

'I just thought that if your mother never remarried after your father's death, maybe she was man-shy . . . and maybe it was contagious.'

'My mother was one of a kind.'

'Were you close to her?'

'Most of the time.'

He leaned forward again, but this time only slightly, almost imperceptibly.

'You mean you were estranged before she died?'

'No, nothing like that. It's just that there were times when we couldn't talk to each other, at least about certain things.'

'Did you patch it up before she died?'

'Long before. This was when I was in my early teens.'

'Can you talk about it now?'

She flicked her hair back girlishly and looked up at him.

'What do you want to know?'

'What was the problem?'

'It wasn't *one* problem, it was lots of things. I guess that was part of the problem. I had too many things on my mind all at once. I was going through a bad patch at school and I swore I wasn't going back there. I don't mean academically, it was what they call interpersonal relationships. I was fourteen at the time and just starting to get interested in boys.'

Justine's mind drifted back a decade in time.

'She could've just pulled rank, but she knew that wouldn't solve the problem. So she took me off to Florida for a vacation right in the middle of the semester. She didn't try to make me talk about it. She just let me wander off on my own and swim. I could tell that she wanted me to open up, and I really *did* want to. But I just couldn't.'

A tear appeared in the corner of Justine's left eye. Rick squirmed with embarrassment at this uncharacteristic sign of weakness. He tried not to stare, fearful that she would close up again. After a momentary pause, Justine continued.

'Then . . . just a couple of days before we were due to leave, we saw a young couple strolling on the beach in the late afternoon with their baby. The baby's father was tossing the baby into the air and catching it. Then he started swinging it towards the sea as if he was going to throw it in. The baby was chortling away quite happily at its father's antics.

'We were watching from a fair distance and it was such a pleasure to watch. Then my mother said to me: "Such trust it has in its father. Why can't you have that kind of trust in me?"

'Well, that just did it. I mean I just broke down and cried on her shoulder. I explained my problems, at least as well as I could. I didn't really understand them myself. But she seemed to understand. Anyway, it wasn't plain sailing after that, but between us we managed to get things straightened out.'

The tears were streaming down Justine's cheeks.

'It sounds like she was very special to you.'

She wiped away the tears with an angry gesture.

'Let's get going,' she said, rising. 'It's almost two thirty.'

He watched her walk away, a question mark hanging over him, his mind racing to find the key to the mystery, the formula to unravel the Gordian knot.

She was soft then, he thought to himself. *Her family tragedies had hardened her. But what had finally set her off?*

10

She was fifty-six years old. But neither her white hair nor her gaunt body could give her a look of frailty. She held an inner strength which in some indefinable way projected itself to those around her. Watching her as she walked towards the witness stand without so much as a sideways glance, Justine could see, in the self-confidence of her gait, an efficient, competent professional who knew her job.

'Please state your name and occupation,' said Abrams, as he approached her.

'My name is Miriam Liebowitz and I am a forensic pathologist with the Manhattan coroner's office.'

The spectators, for whom science was little more than an esoteric activity of élite fraternities, were looking at her in awe. But the jury, which Justine had impanelled with painstaking precision watched her only with a kind of respectful appreciation.

'Would you please tell the jury your qualifications.'

'I studied at Princeton and Stanford. I practised medicine at City General for five years and at St Matthew's for three. I worked as a medical examiner in the Atlantic City coroner's office for seven years where I rose to the rank of deputy

chief medical examiner. Then I moved to New York with
my husband, where I've been working as a medical examiner
for the last eleven years.'

Abrams continued to establish Liebowitz's qualifications
by eliciting testimony about her previous cases and then
moved to the nuts and bolts of the case.

'Were you called upon to perform an autopsy on the night
of September the seventh of last year?'

'I was.'

'And what identification did the body carry?'

'A tag on the big toe of the left foot bearing the letter M
and the number 3-8-7-5-9-4.'

'What does the M stand for?'

'Male.'

'Your Honour,' Abrams's voice intoned heavily, 'the People
had intended to call the deceased's mother who resides in
Northern Ireland to testify as to the identity of the body.
However, she is seriously ill and it would be potentially
damaging to her health to come here for a second time.
I have a sworn affidavit containing her identification with
explicit reference to the toe tag as well as the two agreed
documents: Sean Murphy's passport and driver's licence. I ask
the court to admit the affidavit as People's exhibit one.'

The game was clear to everyone present, at least all of
those conversant with courtroom procedure. It was one of
the classic courtroom ploys: bring in the victim's sick mother
and have her deliver her faltering testimony to identify the
body of the deceased as that of her poor son whom she
always hoped she'd see again in happier circumstances.
That was why he hadn't raised the issue of the affidavit
at the pre-trial motions hearing. He'd obtained it already
as a precaution against the mother's premature demise and
the need to obtain other identification, but he hadn't wanted
to use it. Parker knew this, and he was whispering to Justine
that as the affidavit had been obtained before the pre-trial and
not mentioned there she could object to its introduction now.
However, they both knew that Abrams was already doing the
next best thing after parading the old woman before the jury
and that was describing her and putting her there in spirit.
Given that Abrams couldn't bring her over because of her

health, any delay would merely force him to seek and the judge to grant an adjournment or continuance while other formal identification was obtained. This would leave the jury with the memory and mental image of the sick old woman robbed of her son by a heartless young woman, who showed herself to be devoid of compassion in the courtroom.

It was with these thoughts in mind that Justine rose with a mellow look on her face.

'Your Honour, may it please the court, in order to spare the prosecution any further problems and to spare the deceased's mother, I am ready to stipulate that the body identified by toe tag M 3-8-7-5-9-4 was that of Sean Murphy as identified in Mrs Murphy's affidavit.'

'The stipulation is accepted,' said the judge as Justine sat down.

Abrams then proceeded to ask a series of questions to establish the details of the autopsy, keeping the language as simple as possible. He had given all his expert witnesses a stern lecture before the trial. 'Don't get over-technical. Talking a lot of scientific jargon won't make the issue any clearer to the jury. You may give the jury the impression that you're a master of your field and that you know what you're talking about, but the other side can call other experts who can do exactly the same thing. When that happens, the jury doesn't know who to believe and they give the defendant the benefit of the doubt.'

They had all nodded vigorously; some were already familiar with courtroom technique, were old hands at this game and needed no pep talk. But their presence in the room provided group reinforcement to hammer home the message to the others.

'So what I want you to do,' he continued, 'is keep your testimony as simple as possible. If you have to go into a complicated concept, use a commonplace analogy to clarify it. For example, a blocked artery could be compared to a clogged-up drainpipe.'

He always used the clogged-up drainpipe analogy because it was easy to understand and effective in illustrating the principle.

After a few concise questions to Miriam Liebowitz and some

lucid answers, Abrams was ready to bring his deceptively brief direct examination to a conclusion.

'So could you tell us, then, what was the cause of Sean Murphy's death?'

'Atropine poisoning.'

'Your witness,' said Abrams with a wave of his hand in Justine's direction.

A tense cloud of silence descended on the courtroom as everyone waited to get their first taste of Justine's cross-examination. Parker was leaning towards her, talking in a frantic whisper.

'Did you hear what she said?'

'Atropine poisoning. Now keep your voice down.'

'But you were supposed to have given him—'

'I said keep your voice down!' hissed Justine.

'Does the defence have any questions?' asked the judge forcefully.

'No, Your Honour,' said Justine.

The tension broke in an explosion of chatter as the judge adjourned the hearing.

11

'I don't know why the British keep calling the IRA terrorists,' said Veronica McGlaughlin, sweeping back a wisp of hair from her face to emphasize her well-groomed looks. 'There are always casualties in war. The IRA are fighting against an occupying army. Most of their actions are directed against British soldiers. And as freedom fighters with a just cause they have the right to use all means to secure their just aims.'

Veronica McGlaughlin was the spokeswoman for Iraid, a shadowy organization that officially collected money for the families of imprisoned IRA terrorists, but unofficially financed IRA terrorism itself.

'And what gave you the right to drag my little boy into your war?' screamed Pauline Robson.

The tears were streaming down her cheeks like a river. 'Your precious IRA and INLA are a bunch of terrorist scumbags! And so are you!'

Pauline Robson was by now hysterical with the grief of the pain and suffering which she had relived, and would go on reliving in recurring nightmares for the rest of her life. She broke down in a sobbing fit, her hands clasped over her eyes, her fingers tearing at her hair. The camera captured her anguish and held the moment in frame for a few seconds longer before returning to Veronica McGlaughlin, challenging her to reply to the onslaught, as the nation held its breath and morbidly looked on, wondering how she would respond.

Carefully, Veronica told herself. *With dignity. Always with dignity.*

She picked up the red light of the active camera with the skill of the trained PR professional that she was, and looked millions of Americans in the eye. She remembered well her course in media manipulation from the PR firm. Don't be indignant, be hurt. That was what this woman was doing, straight from the heart without any formal training, and that was what Veronica knew she also had to do. It had worked against Joe McCarthy in the Army-McCarthy hearings, and it was working for this woman. Veronica had to turn it around and make it work for herself now.

'What that woman won't tell you,' Veronica said, with a delicate balance of sympathy and gentle criticism, 'is that she feels guilty about her son's death because her boyfriend sexually abused the boy.'

'That's a vicious lie!' Pauline screamed with the last of her breath before the strength of her vocal cords gave out. But by then it was too late. The entire audience was in uproar and the studio camera showed that there was only a minute on the clock. People on all sides were shouting, some for the woman and some against her. Others wanted to return to the subject of the original discussion. But there was no going back to it. Pauline Robson was frantically trying to get to Veronica McGlaughlin, but she was being restrained by several members of the audience. There would be no more discussion of Northern Ireland that evening. And the last thing people remembered was Veronica's accusation of child abuse and the woman's angry reaction when confronted by it.

The television set clicked off, and the sound and picture abruptly vanished.

'And that's the way to do it,' said Veronica.

'So what does that prove?' asked Padraig.

She was seated in the living room of Iraid's Derry safe house with Padraig seated and two IRA minders standing over him. The meeting had been arranged at the behest of Veronica, after the killing of the assassin in Central Park had made it clear that the INLA was planning to kill Justine Levy, in breach of the well-established Republican code of not operating in the United States. Papers found on the assassin revealed that he was close to Declan McNutt and Declan McNutt was in turn close to Padraig O'Shea who now sat before Veronica and her two IRA gorillas. They had brought him with minimal force, bundling him into a car without brandishing their firearms and sitting him down without tying him up or gagging him. But there was a hint of violence in the air, as if the mood could turn nasty in the blink of an eye if they didn't get their way.

'It proves that in America there's a right way and a wrong way to do things.'

'What do you mean?' Padraig persisted.

Veronica sighed. At times, Padraig could be very stupid.

'It means that in America, public opinion is everything. Wars aren't fought and won on battlefields any more: they're fought and won on the pages of the press and in TV studios. A few close-up shots of Richard Nixon with five o'clock shadow, together with a little bit of vote-tampering, handed a narrow election victory to Kennedy in 1960. A single image on TV of a South Vietnamese soldier pointing a gun at the head of an unarmed Vietcong and blowing his brains out decided the outcome of the Vietnam War. The sight of a young Kuwaiti woman crying on TV about babies ripped out of incubators by Iraqi soldiers persuaded people to support sending a huge international but mostly American military force to the Persian Gulf to restore the Kuwaiti royal family, after the Iraqi invasion. You've heard the saying "betwixt the cup and the lip"? Well, in America, a few small factors can determine the course of history, and nine times out of ten those are factors that swing public opinion one way or the other. That's why we have to be careful to avoid mistakes.'

'You're a fine one to talk,' said Padraig sarcastically. 'Where were you when our boys were being killed in the fight against the British? You weren't always active in the struggle.'

'No, but I always sympathized with the cause.'

'Sure,' Padraig sneered, 'and you were recruited not because of your skills or courage as a fighter and not even because you're such a great speaker. It was because of your good looks. Because you look pretty and photogenic in front of a TV camera.'

'If that's intended as an insult it isn't going to work, because it confirms the point I'm trying to make. In a country where the ability to win an election is governed by sound bites and appearance rather than solid ideas it was deemed expedient to have the public persona of our cause represented by a well-groomed, photogenic young woman like me. You can't expect the average American to understand our cause, and nor do we want him to. He might end up thinking that we're living in the past instead of adapting to the present and building towards the future. That's the way the Americans think, with their total lack of any sense of history.'

'Well, if they're that shallow, then why should we care what they think?'

'Because we still need the financial support of the Irish-American movement and the support of their judges against extradition. We've eliminated most of the competition in drug smuggling with the punishment squads, but that isn't enough to cover the costs of weapons, even with cheap imports from the former Soviet bloc. We need the deep pockets of the Irish-American community to keep us in business. And we needed their demographic support for judges who won't extradite us when we use America as a place of refuge. We have that support at the moment because state judges are elected and some areas have large Irish-American communities. But if the Irish-American community itself turns against us, we lose our power base.

'That's why I trained and studied my ass off learning how to "do press", as they say there. I learned how to present brief, snappy sound bites, how to heckle at potentially dangerous arguments and steer the discussion away and how to break the flow of the other person's arguments by well-timed interruption. Why do you think I accused her of condoning child-molesting? It brings out the disgust and revulsion of Middle America, the political mainstream that controls the floating vote. Child-molesting is always a good one because it doesn't have to be proved. It's enough to make the accusation to swing the tide of public opinion against your opponent. Accusations of child-molestation come cheap, but they can be a deadly weapon when they're used right.'

'Now it sounds like you're boasting about character assassination,' said Padraig in a sardonic tone.

'I'll let you into a little secret, Padraig. I have nothing against that woman. I even feel rather sorry for her. But her reputation was a casualty of war, just like the toddler and the doctor were casualties of war. Sean Murphy killed two people in the cause of the liberation of Ireland. I assassinated that woman's character in the pursuit of that same cause. I didn't like it, but I had to do it. But the one thing I didn't do is create *sympathy* for her. I didn't say that her son deserved to die, or that his death didn't matter. I attacked her and suggested that she had wronged her son too. I put her on the defensive. There's no point killing a few British soldiers and civilians if we end up losing the battle for public sympathy in the country where we get our major financing.'

'And what's that got to do with us?' asked Padraig defiantly.

'What I'm trying to tell you, is that if you kill the Levy bitch now, we'll look like cold-blooded murderers. Maybe you can kill her after the trial is over when she's in prison. You can make it look like a drug-related prison killing. We may even be able to help you with that. We have contact with black liberation groups in America and we might be able to cut a deal with them.'

'And what if she's acquitted?' asked Padraig.

'That shows how little you understand of the American scene. She's not going to be acquitted. We already know the case against her from the grand jury hearings. She left her prints all over the bottle containing the poison and she has no valid defence. The one thing she might have been counting on was the sympathy of the jury. But in this case she's lost their sympathy by being too hard. She's made it clear that she isn't the poor little orphan girl, but the tough and vicious bitch who lured a man to his death with her body and then poisoned him with cold-blooded premeditation.'

'Juries in America often go against the evidence. Remember those four police storm troopers who beat up that black man?'

'That was different. In that case the judge helped the storm troopers beat the rap by transferring the case away from the place where the crime was committed to an area where a lot of cops and ex-cops lived. He did it on the pretext that the storm troopers couldn't get a fair trial in the area where they beat up the motorist. To secure the acquittal of a guilty person in the face of conclusive evidence to the contrary all you need is the right jury. But you have to know how to get it. Justine Levy doesn't. That's why she's going to lose. You'll note that she challenged all the soft-headed, faint-hearted people off the jury. What she's got there is a convicting jury. Only like you, she's naïve when it comes to playing politics in America. She doesn't know the rules of the game. That's why she's painted herself into a corner. That's why she's going to be convicted. And when she is, then she'll be at our mercy. It's very easy to kill a person in prison, you know. It's just a case of slipping the word to the right person, and maybe also some money.'

'Well, assuming you're right, what's this to do with me?' asked Padraig, nervously.

'Let's not play games, Padraig,' said Veronica. 'We know that you and Declan were behind the assassination attempt on the Levy girl.'

'What if we were? The assassin is dead and the Levy girl is still alive, so there's no more to be said.'

He tried to rise from the armchair, but the 'heavy' behind him pushed him back down again. The man was almost as strong as Declan and Padraig knew that he had no chance of leaving against this man's will, which in turn meant without Veronica's permission, as she was calling the shots.

'I'm afraid there is, Padraig, because we know how you people operate. The assassin was killed a few days ago. That means you're probably already planning to send another. We can't afford to let that happen. So we need to know who you're planning to send.'

'I don't know,' said Padraig, the fear welling up inside him.

The gorilla behind him silently clamped his arms round the

back of the chair, while the other started tying him up. Now the fear was twisting inside him like a knife.

'It's the truth I'm telling you. You know what Declan is like! He plays his cards so close to his chest you're lucky if you can get a glimpse of them! Why don't you ask him?'

'We would,' Veronica replied. 'But we don't know where he is. Now perhaps if you'd like to tell us that we can bring *him* here and ask *him* these questions.'

The heavy was now tying his legs to the castors of the armchair.

'I don't *know* where he is. *He* finds *me* when he needs me. I never know where he is. You know how paranoid he gets.'

'Yes,' said Veronica. 'And we also know how you're scared shitless of him and wouldn't want him to know that you betrayed him. That's why you wouldn't tell us where he was even if you knew it. But that's also why we have to ask *you* these questions.'

'But how can I answer them, when I don't know the answer meself?'

'We think you do, Padraig,' said Veronica, 'and we have to find out. We mean you no harm, but we have to find out who, when and where.'

The larger of the two IRA men was now rolling up his left trouser leg while the other was opening a case. As the bigger man stepped aside, the other took out an object shaped vaguely like a gun. But it wasn't a gun; it was an electric drill.

Padraig's eyes filled with tears and his stomach was convulsed with terror as he realized what was about to happen.

'I'm telling you the truth! I don't know what he's planning.'

'We can do this the easy way or we can do it the hard way,' said Veronica. 'But one way or another you'll give us the truth.'

The heavy was plugging in the drill and switching it on . . .

'I'm telling you the truth!' Padraig screamed. 'Declan told me he was going to send someone else, but he didn't say who! He only said he wasn't sending me 'cause I wasn't up to the job. He said something about getting a real man!'

The IRA man with the electric drill was now advancing towards him, a murderous gleam in his eyes.

'You know Declan never had much respect for me! He treated me as his lap dog but he never confided in me!'

'Last chance before the pain begins,' said Veronica.

'Please! God help me, I know nothing!'

The heavy behind him clamped a sock in his mouth and taped it over.

'You know the drill,' said Veronica, before adding 'Excuse the pun' with a pang of guilt. 'When you want to talk just nod your head and we'll give you a chance. But if you don't talk you get it worse the next time.'

He was frantically nodding his head already.

'It's late now,' said Veronica. 'I gave you your last chance before the gag was put in place. The rule is once the gag is in place you get one dose of the pain and then you get the chance to talk again.'

His head was shaking frantically from side to side and the tears were streaming down his face in anticipation of the searing agony. The drill advanced towards his left knee-cap. He tried to free his leg but it was secured firmly by the ropes. The drill made contact with his knee, cutting into the bone and sending a spasm of unbearable agony up his body to his brain.

Even through the gag he emitted a heart-rending cry of pain. But to his interrogators, heart-rending was a concept devoid of meaning. The smaller IRA man pulled off the tape. Padraig spat out the sock and coughed as he gasped for air. He was choking on his tears of torment, knowing that the pain was beyond endurance, knowing that he may well have suffered permanent damage already, and knowing that after this he would have to go into hiding lest the INLA kill him in the most painful fashion for the act of treachery he was about to commit.

'It's Declan himself!' he cried in desperation. 'It's Declan himself!'

'What do you mean?' asked Veronica.

'I mean it's Declan himself. He said he was going there to do the job himself because he couldn't trust anyone to get it right.'

'I don't believe you,' said Veronica, unsure of whether to believe him or not, but determined to test him.

'It's the truth I'm telling you!' he screamed, terrified at the prospect of another rendezvous with the drill. 'That's why you haven't been able to find him. He's gone there already.'

'How can you contact him?' asked Veronica.

'I can't. He made sure not to leave a trail.'

By this stage, Veronica believed him. She knew that he had hit the fear barrier as well as the pain barrier, the point beyond which those under interrogation can no longer hold out. She had seen it before in the other interrogations she had witnessed or supervised. This was a man who wanted nothing more than to avoid further suffering and get out of the room with his life intact.

'OK,' said Veronica to the others. 'He doesn't know anything more.'

'Are you sure?' asked the bigger one.

'Positive,' said Veronica. 'We'll have to track Declan down directly, using our airport contacts. If he was stupid enough to use his own name. But in any case, if you've got pictures then we should be able to find him.'

'So what do we do with him?' asked the big one, shoving Padraig on the shoulder blade.

'He says he doesn't know how to contact Declan and he's probably telling the truth. But Declan might contact him and he might talk. Deal with him. I need some fresh air.'

With that, Veronica McGlaughlin left the room.

'Pleeeease! I swear on my mother's grave I won't tell him a blessed thing!'

The smaller IRA man was fitting a silencer to a .38, while the bigger man was refitting the gag, choking Padraig's final pathetic plea for his life. Strictly speaking only a .22 can be effectively silenced, but with a .22 the danger was that the bullet would lodge in the brain without actually killing the man, leaving him a vegetable. With a .45 there was a danger of a high-velocity exit, as well as a noise that might attract attention. For indoor executions, the .38 represented the ideal compromise. The smaller man picked up a cushion from the sofa and held it to Padraig's head. Then, pushing the gun right into the cushion and aiming it at the temple, he squeezed the trigger and fired off a single shot. Padraig's head recoiled and then lolled limp against his shoulder as his body drooped sideways as far as the ropes that bound him to the chair allowed.

12

'When I first saw Murphy he was in an extremely agitated state.'

Abrams's after-lunch witness was Bernard Stern, the doctor who had treated Murphy at the hospital.

The courtroom was even more crowded now than at the start of the trial. The press coverage of the early sessions, the fact that Justine was conducting her own defence, the drama of a young woman on trial for murder, and a medical student at that, all made for the kind of living drama that drew the crowds, and the public interest was growing, in tune with the media publicity.

'Could you elaborate?' asked Abrams.

'Well, when I arrived he was ranting and raving hysterically. He had a low temperature, ninety-three point seven, and was shivering and trembling. His breathing was heavy although he wasn't hyperventilating. He had chest pains and watering eyes. Most significant, from a diagnostic point of view, he claimed that he'd been poisoned.'

'You could object,' whispered Parker to Justine. 'It's blatant hearsay.'

At the back of his mind, Parker knew that the objection

would probably be overruled. This evidence was clearly part of the *res gestae*, the sequence of events that forms an integral part of the crime, and was therefore an exception to the rule barring hearsay evidence.

'Drop it,' Justine replied.

'What about the symptoms which Murphy described?'

'Well, it's hard to say really. He didn't actually describe anything coherently. As I said, he was ranting and raving a lot.'

'Did he give you anything?'

'He gave me a bottle of tequila which he said he believed contained poison. He claimed that he had imbibed some of the contents of the bottle without realizing what it contained.'

'At this stage, Your Honour,' Abrams continued, 'I would like to introduce the bottle and its preserved contents as People's exhibit two and ask the witness to identify it.'

'If the witness marked the bottle for identification with some non-removable, non-repeatable mark before it left his possession then I'll accept this witness's identification of the item. Otherwise I'll have to rule against it at this stage on the grounds that insufficient foundation has been laid.'

The judge already knew where things stood on this matter. But the facts had to be entered into the record. He turned to the witness.

'Dr Stern, did you mark the bottle for identification?'

'No, Your Honour.'

'In that case I'm going to have to rule against its admission at this stage. If the People can establish chain of custody between this witness and one who did so mark it, then the court will admit it in evidence.'

Abrams appeared unperturbed by this. The bottle had been handed to someone else and could be linked to the crime by chain-of-custody evidence. He'd just have to call a couple of extra witnesses from his witness list. In the meantime, he resumed his cross-examination.

'What did you do when he gave it to you?'

'I handed it to a hospital orderly called Brian Colt and told him to take it to Professor Ostrovsky in the toxicology lab and have him analyse it. I also phoned through to Professor Ostrovsky to tell him that it was on the way.'

Abrams looked up at the judge, satisfied.

'Your Honour, I have no further questions of this witness at this time.'

'Any cross-examination?' asked the judge, looking down at Justine.

'No, Your Honour,' said Justine calmly.

The judge and jury eyed her, puzzled. She had gone to great trouble to get a particular type of jury. But now she was offering them nothing by way of evidence, and not even a hint of her defence. For now at least the tension and waiting had to continue.

13

The clouds were overshadowed by Justine's face and by the occasional human figure that drifted by in the background. She was standing in front of a drug-store, her face almost pressed up against the glass. But it was not what lay behind the window that held her attention. It was her own reflection. The face that had always looked so familiar when she had seen it as her mother now looked like a stranger when she saw it as herself.

The face was dominated by a pair of eyes that seemed frightened to look at her, as if there were something all too forbidding in what they saw. It was as if she were afraid to see what she had become. It was a face that could never remain indifferent, even when it was ignored by others as they went about their daily business. Neither the bitterness nor the hopeless yearning could mar the ivory complexion, the sky-blue eyes that blazed with the heat of an inner anger, the delicate curve of the proud lips in a pained frown that yet refused to acknowledge defeat. No amount of suffering could camouflage the beauty of the woman . . . the girl . . . the woman.

She walked on a few steps and turned, barging the glass

doors aside with the cool intensity of the cowboy hero entering a saloon in a classic western movie.

The drug-store offered a comprehensive array of products. But she had no thought of browsing. She was here to implement a plan. She knew that she couldn't just go into a shop and ask for poison, except perhaps rat poison. If she *did* buy a pure poison product she would have to sign for it. But there are other forms in which poison is sold besides the pure form. Many household cleaning products contain poison. If one knows what one is doing one can acquire poison without any difficulty.

Her hand wandered along the shelf until it came to rest on a large spray can of insecticide for non-flying insects. She checked the list of contents and only when she saw that it contained pyrethrum did she deposit three identical cans of it in her basket. The cosmetics counter of a nearby Five and Ten supplied her with the sleazy-looking purple lipstick and eye shadow to go with the clothes that she had already bought.

For a while she thought that it might actually be fun, playing the role of the bimbo while she lured her enemy on to the rocks. But to get in so close, to have to listen to his self-righteous platitudes, and to feign sexual interest, it was all too revolting. *Besides, how can one have fun when one is grieving?*

At her last station on the track, a liquor store, she bought a bottle of tequila.

She wasted no time when she got the items home. Using the Rotavapour that she had borrowed from the laboratory, she set to work extracting the pyrethrum from the insecticide.

The moment of truth was drawing near. The preparations were almost complete. But the ritual dressing was only the first stage of the bullfight. Still to come was the cape work, the banderilleros and the *coup de grâce*.

14

'Passengers for flight BA103 please make their way to Gate Eleven!'

Airports always held a thrill for Declan, although he had been accustomed to air travel from the start of his career. Whenever he passed through one he knew that he was either entering or leaving a danger spot. Sometimes both. For airports were always under scrutiny by police and security forces.

But the United States was safer than most. They were on the lookout for Islamic terrorists, not Irish Republicans. They still regarded the Irish Republican movement as freedom fighters, in spite of the efforts of the Levy bitch to discredit them. They had maintained that view even in the face of the unfortunate events of the Murphy episode, clearly accepting that the child and the doctor were simply casualties of war and not victims of murder. So Declan's arrival here should not pose any security problems for himself or for the American authorities. There were no warrants out for his arrest and he had not been declared *persona non grata*. As far as the authorities were concerned he didn't exist at all.

Outside Ireland and Britain he was not even known, and

even within those countries he was not a public figure, just a name on a couple of lists from a handful of law enforcement agencies. He had been arrested for throwing petrol bombs at the British Army, and was known to the Royal Ulster Constabulary for intimidation offences. But he had not yet attained the stature of international terrorist.

He couldn't be sure, though. He had taken advantage of the IRA's revolutionary contacts network to train in Libya. It was possible that the Israelis knew of him. Their legendary Mossad was said to be so good they sometimes knew the names of a group of aeroplane hijackers within hours of the plane being seized, even if the organization hadn't yet revealed its name. When the American embassy in Teheran was seized by Khomeini'ite students, Mossad gave a list of names of the student leaders to the CIA. If the Israelis knew of Declan McNutt, they would certainly have told the Americans.

For this reason, Declan was not travelling under his own name. Whether or not the Americans considered an INLA freedom fighter likely to enter their country, they may have put his name on a watch list. He knew that as a member of a breakaway group he couldn't count on the same sympathy as the IRA had in the United States. He looked around furtively as he stood in the queue at immigration control.

When his turn came at passport control, he handed over his red European Union passport, the document that somehow blurred the distinction between Ireland and Britain and threatened to make the dispute irrelevant. The girl at the desk flipped it open with a practised gesture and scanned its machine-readable information with her hand-held laser scanner. She watched on the screen while the name and details appeared, checking perfunctorily for that warning check mark that would appear in the top right corner if he was listed in the 'black book', that roll of undesirables and people with outstanding arrest warrants long since transferred to a few minuscule bits of iron oxide in a computer. If he had been so listed, she would not have heard any noisy alarm. Nor would she have pressed a secret foot pedal or challenged him herself. Rather an alarm would automatically have gone off in the immigration control room and the controller would have called up the desk on his video monitor panel and dispatched half a dozen heavily armed men to approach the desk from all sides to take the man into custody. However, no match for the name was found, no check mark appeared in the corner of the screen and no warning alarm sounded in the control room. Instead the details simply went into the computer, recording the arrival of one more visitor to the United States via New York's Kennedy Airport.

The girl handed him back his passport with a pleasant smile.

'Enjoy your stay in the United States, Dr O'Brian.'

15

'And what did you do with this bottle that Dr Stern gave you?'

Brian Colt was a boy, no more than seventeen. He had been working as an orderly at the hospital on the night Murphy arrived. But he wasn't being paid for it.

'I took it to the toxicology lab and gave it to Professor Ostrovsky.'

'And you gave it to Professor Ostrovsky personally?'

'Yes, sir.'

'Just let me tear this guy apart,' Parker whispered, leaning over to Justine. Even without the courtroom experience of a Daniel Abrams, he could smell blood now, having checked out the witness's background. And he homed in with the killer instinct of a shark.

'Leave him alone,' she said firmly, realizing that Abrams was drawing near to the end of his direct examination.

'Are you crazy? If we can break their chain of custody over the bottle we've broken their case. Without the bottle they can't prove a damn thing.'

This was spoken in a loud whisper. Abrams's 'second seat'

heard it. But not Abrams himself. He was too busy rounding off his direct examination of the witness.

'Has he given you any reason to believe that he's lying?' asked Justine.

Parker sighed. At times this girl could be incredibly naïve.

'No, but it's possible that I can shake him. I can destroy his credibility in the eyes of the jury.'

'But unless you can get him to recant, the prosecution will still have the chain of custody that they need to make the bottle admissible. Anything you do to that poor kid will only affect questions of fact which would still have to go to the jury. Aside from that you'll be hurting the kid for no good reason.'

'We have to take the breaks that the case gives us. And that "poor kid", as you call him, happens to be . . . well, you'll soon find out.'

'Rick, whatever else that boy may be he isn't a liar; at least, he isn't lying in this case. Whatever you do to hurt that boy, it won't help me. It'll just add one more problem to the problems he's already got.'

'You know what he is, don't you?' said Parker, finally realizing.

'Yes,' she said quietly, 'I know what he is. I know all about it: armed robbery; he was the lookout, and he lied at the trial. They gave him three hundred hours' community service. But that's all past history. Now he's serving out his sentence as a hospital orderly. You want to ruin him for life? At his trial, his identity was protected as he was a juvenile. You want to splash his name all over the front pages? Have people point him out in the street? Make him feel as if people are talking about him behind his back?'

'Justine, I can't force you to let me cross-examine him, but I can tell you one thing: if you don't impeach his character and break their chain of custody then you may as well look forward to spending the next fifty years behind bars.'

'Does the defence have any questions?' asked the judge irritably.

A flush of crimson swept across Colt's cheeks and sweat broke out all over his body as a swelling heat twisted his stomach and rose up through his chest, past his pounding heart to his dry throat.

'Rick, it's funny how you can be so ready to hurt someone you don't even know when it suits your case and yet still play the great liberal humanitarian the rest of the time.'

Parker nodded slowly in reluctant admission of defeat. Justine looked up at the judge. 'No questions, Your Honour.'

16

He felt bitter. Bitter about the fickle press that ignored his
cause because it was no longer politically chic. Bitter about
a world that tolerated imperialism when it was practised by
so-called 'Western democracies'. Bitter about a pope who
criticized communism but objected to liberation theology
which was aimed at the overthrow of Fascism.

We can't count on anyone else, he told himself. That's how
it's always been.

Ourselves alone.

He downed the remainder of his pint in one huge gulp and
ordered another.

With his back to the mirrored doors, he didn't see the
well-stacked girl in purple walk in. But in the other mirror,
the one behind the barman, he noticed the heads of lonely
men turning to take note of the new arrival, alerting him to
her presence.

The stunning redhead tossed her head back, shaking the
spirit of life back into her hair. Moments later she cast her
gaze around with an air of proprietorial contempt, as if she
were looking for someone in particular. The gesture kept the
men at bay, at least for the time being.

The double doors that opened on to the Green Light were more or less central, with the strobe-lit dance floor to the left of the rectangular room and the well-stocked bar to the right. But the symmetry was broken by the ceiling which was higher over the dance floor than over the bar on account of the balcony restaurant which overlooked the gyrating revellers below. Justine turned right, her eyes settling on her prey. She headed for the dimly lit bar. It was an L-shaped arrangement with about ten seats on both sides. Although six or seven seats were free on the side near the dance floor, Justine chose the other side, the quieter side, sitting down on the only vacant seat.

She looked around discreetly. The area around the bar was illuminated by subdued lights set into several long rectangular flowerpots in the corners. But even in the dim light she felt the eyes of dozens of men on her body, their thoughts doing what their hands dared not. This was a place where men went to make a quick score and where women went to get picked up without all the stalling and small talk. She forced herself to ignore it, and focused her attention on the disco area.

The brown-haired man in olive-green needlecords and blue shirt who sat to her right didn't seem to notice her, although the man to her left could have sworn that she pulled her high stool a few inches to the right before she sat down. She was fumbling around in her purse looking for something, pulling out a cigarette and inserting it clumsily between her lips.

Should I light it? wondered the loser to her left. Am I her type? Am I a bit old for her? Will she care about my pot belly and receding hairline? Is she under-age? Too late! Dammit!

The man to her right was lighting the cigarette. Not a word had passed between them. He had just stretched out his hand in a manner as proprietorial as that of the girl when she had entered the room, and lit the cigarette, the skin of their hands barely brushing in that first moment of innocent physical contact that would either erect a barrier between them or break the ice. Their eyes had met so far only in the mirror. But they looked like they were kindred spirits who both thought they owned the world. The man, confident of his superior strength as the final arbiter of claims, relished the thought of taming her.

'Does a pretty girl come to a place like this to drink alone?' he asked.

'Is the Pope Jewish?' she replied.

There was a second of silence for station identification, and then he burst out laughing. She smiled in response.

'What can I get you?' he asked.

'A tequila sunrise.'

He snapped his fingers aggressively at the barman: the standard macho gesture for impressing girls. She didn't look impressed.

'A tequila sunrise for the lady.'

He wondered about her. Her clothes made her look cheap but her face held too much concentration and purpose. It wasn't the vapid look of a dumb thrill-seeker.

'You're Irish,' she said after the moment of silence he had let pass in order not to show that he was too eager.

'No prizes for guessing that.'

'Would there be any prizes for guessing that you're *Northern* Irish?'

'Now how would you be knowin' that?' he asked.

'There are a lot of Irishmen in New York. I recognize the differences between the mellower Eire accent and the harder Northern Irish accent.'

'And what do you prefer?' he asked, looking straight at her, 'hard or mellow?'

'Hard,' she replied, meeting his eyes without flinching.

'I suppose you're a student, then?'

'Now how would you be knowin' that?' she asked, imitating his accent.

'Your age. Most girls your age are students in this country, most white girls that is. Even if they're studying something as useless as liberal arts with its paper degrees that aren't worth wiping your arse on. Colleges are as common in America as pubs are in Ireland.'

She flinched at his crudeness, but let him continue.

'Anyway, it's not unusual to meet college girls in places like this. College girls are after the same things as most other girls, and most boys for that matter.'

'Am I that obvious?' she asked good-humouredly.

'Let's just say I know how coy you college girls are about admitting what you want, especially in New York.'

'You've been reading too much Dorothy Parker.'

There was no anger in her tone, and she held his eyes with a cheeky smile on her face. He knew that he was riding on the right track.

The barman arrived with her drink. Murphy paid him, handing over a hundred-dollar bill even though he had several tens and fives. Justine pretended not to notice the fives and tens and looked on, feigning the appropriate degree of awe as the face of Ben Franklin slid across the bar. The barman dawdled off to bring the change.

'What are you studying, then?'

'Pest control.'

'Are you serious?' he asked incredulously.

'Well, actually, medicine.'

Murphy's right hand rose into the air, holding his glass between them in a respectful salute.

'I'll drink to a girl who's studying for a noble profession, Miss . . .?'

'Levy. Justine Levy.'

'To your health, good fortune and success.'

He swallowed a man-sized gulp and slammed the glass down. Justine sipped her drink delicately. She regretted not having practised drinking beforehand. She was supposed to look like a hard-drinking woman of the world with morals as loose as her clothes were tight. But it wasn't working out. The performance just wasn't coming off right.

She took another sip, keeping her eyes on Murphy. His eyes held hers, suggesting that he was getting the right signals and knew it.

'You're a strange one you are,' he said casually.

'Why?' she asked nervously.

'You haven't asked me *my* name.'

'Like you said, I'm the coy type,' she responded, gathering her wits together as quickly as the pressure between her temples allowed. 'I like to let the man set the pace.'

Oh, very good, Justine. Appeal to that streak of macho in him – the one that forms a cross with that streak of cowardice.

'Sean Murphy.'

'A pleasure to meet you.'

They chinked their glasses together and drank.

'Your parents must be very proud to have a daughter studying medicine.'

'I haven't had a father since I was nine. He shot himself.'

'Shot himself? Why?'

'Is suicide a rational act? Does it need a logical reason?'

'Just asking,' said Murphy, backing off.

'A battle-scarred Vietnam veteran. He lived with it for seven years and then blew his brains out.'

'You must've been shaken by it. I guess it left a few scars on you.'

She could have accepted pity from a close friend or even from a sympathetic stranger, but the realization that she was being offered consolation by a man whose hands were soaked in innocent blood turned her stomach. She prayed to God that the anger hadn't crept on to her face.

'I guess it did.'

'How about your mother?'

'She didn't take it as hard as I did. Seven years of living with a manic depressive toughened her.'

'No, I mean how does she feel about her daughter studying medicine?'

'She was proud of me.'

'She's got a right to be. What made you decide to study medicine? Was it anything to do with what happened to your father?'

'I never really thought about that . . . I guess it was.'

She knew that it was. It had everything to do with her father.

'Did you say your mother *was* proud of you?'

'Yes.'

She blinked back a tear.

'An accident?'

'In a way. A slow, lingering death in a hospital bed.'

'I know how you felt. My mother's dying now. I wish I could get back to see her.'

'What's stopping you?'

'The same people who wanted to hang George Washington.'

'The British?'

'The British.'

'In what way?'

'I'm a wanted man.'

'What for?'

'I'd rather not talk about it.'

'Something you're ashamed of?'

'No, I just get tired talking about it. Maybe some other time.'

You're so sure there'll be *another time, you arrogant bastard.*

'Do you feel like dancing?' he asked after a brief silence.

Justine was about to refuse, but she was in the act of drinking and Murphy had grabbed her wrist and dragged her off her stool before she had time to speak. The drink spilled over the bar as Justine slammed it down angrily. Her first inclination was to turn her anger on Murphy. Normally she would never have stood for that sort of behaviour from a man. But she remembered that she was playing a role and she stopped herself from showing anger just in time.

She wasn't used to disco dancing and she felt a bit awkward, as if the eyes of others on the dance floor were focused on her, scrutinizing her every move. She dismissed the thought as paranoia. If they were looking at her, they were interested in her body, not her dancing. In any case, she soon found that Murphy was as awkward as she, possibly more so. They had been dancing for only a few minutes when the music turned quiet and slow.

Murphy had timed it perfectly – suspiciously perfectly.

The lights stopped flashing and were replaced by a slow, undulating change of colour from blue to green to orange to yellow to red to pink to purple. The young couples – some lovers, others almost strangers – slid their arms around each other and moved in slow, gentle steps across the floor. Some of them were put at ease by the drink or by drugs. Justine was fully alert, and intended to remain so.

It was some two hours later when he drove her home. The car screeched to a halt outside the apartment building.

'Thanks, Murph,' said Justine, taking off the seat belt. 'It's been a great evening.'

He slid an arm round her shoulder.

'Hey, wait a minute. Aren't you going to invite me in for coffee?'

She half turned and smiled uneasily.

'I've got an exam tomorrow. I'll take a raincheck.'

She realized, too late, that an intelligent man would wonder why she went to a nightclub on the eve of an exam. Fortunately for her, Murphy was not an intelligent man.

'How about dinner tomorrow? We can make a celebration of it.'

'That's assuming I pass.'

'Sure you will . . . a smart girl like you.'

'Anyway, I hate restaurants. It's like being in a goldfish bowl . . . no privacy.'

'Who's talking about a restaurant? I was thinking about my house. If the weather stays like this we could eat by the pool.'

'Can you cook?'

'Do you like Chinese?'

She opened her eyes wide and ran her tongue along her lips.

'I love it.'

'Great! I'll send out to the Chinese takeaway.'

'Fine.'

She opened the door.

'I'll pick you up at seven. What number?'

'I'll meet you down here. The doorman suffers from an acute case of paranoia.'

She stepped out with one foot.

'Good night, then,' said Murphy.

She leaned over, kissed him chastely on the cheek and stepped out, slamming the door with moderate force behind her. Murphy licked his lips with anticipation as he watched her shapely derrière disappear into the building. With the tantalizing pangs of lust still stirring in his loins, he gunned the engine and drove off. Ten seconds later Justine emerged from the building and walked to another some eighty yards down the road.

17

The rapping of the gavel and the staccato intonation of the bailiff announced to the interested and the curious that the third day of the trial of the People of the State of New York versus Justine Levy was about to begin.

That same delicate quiet, that same hushed aura of expectation, again settled over the courtroom, as it had on the first days of the trial. Things were moving along remarkably swiftly, far more swiftly than the prosecutor had expected from a trial of this sort. Abrams knew that this was because of Justine's non-adversarial approach. If she had been represented by a lawyer, like Rick Parker, or if she had chosen to act like a typical *pro se* lawyer, these past two days could easily have turned into two weeks.

When everyone was seated, the judge went through the usual litany of enquiries as to whether the principals were present, before turning the floor over to a confident-looking Daniel Abrams.

'My first witness today,' the prosecutor began in a subdued tone that seemed to be holding something back, 'is Professor Samuel Ostrovsky.'

Samuel Ostrovsky, or Sam as he was known to his friends,

was a man of contrasts. His head carried a mane of brown hair, but the beard at the tip of his chin was almost black. He was a relatively short man, but his presence was so commanding that he exuded a look of effortless professional competence accented by a pair of rimless spectacles that had 'ivory tower academia' written all over them. When he spoke it was with a pronounced Slavic accent, but he punctuated his speech with American idiom in a way that was too natural and random to be an affectation.

'State your name for the record,' Abrams began.

'Samuel Levitch Ostrovsky,' he replied.

'And what is your occupation?'

'I am a professor of toxicology at St Joseph's Hospital.'

The next fifty minutes were taken up with a series of questions and answers designed to establish Ostrovsky's credentials as an expert witness. It was clear that he was to be a vitally important witness to the prosecution's case. His testimony was characterized by an economy of words which lacked the pompous affectations that intrude into the testimony of many professional witnesses. For example, he didn't say 'Yes, sir, that is correct' where a simple 'yes' would do. When asked to explain something he gave a brief, straightforward explanation.

He was, in fact, experienced in courtroom testimony, although by no means a 'professional witness' in the dishonourable sense of the word. This meant that he was resilient to the standard lines of attack used by defence lawyers. He was too self-confident and court-wise to be shaken by a probing cross-examination and he was too well paid for his non-legal work for defence lawyers to be able to get away with the suggestion that he needed the legal work and might therefore be tempted to make sure that his conclusions were favourable to the side that called him.

'Professor, could you tell us please where you were on the night of September the seventh of last year?'

'In St Joseph's Hospital.'

'Could you be more specific, Professor?'

'I was in the toxicology lab during most of the night in question.'

'Could you tell us about the events of the evening?'

'Could *you* be more specific?' asked Ostrovsky mockingly.

'Did you, on that evening, receive anything from Brian Colt?' asked Abrams, trying to conceal his irritation as he struggled to pry the facts out of Ostrovsky. He fought to keep his voice flat. But it was hard. Ostrovsky made a point of being uncooperative with the side that called him in order to give more weight to his testimony. But Abrams was getting excited about the prospect of using his best witness yet to tighten the noose around Justine's neck, at least in the figurative sense.

'Yes.'

Ostrovsky wasn't fazed by the smoke that seemed to emanate from the prosecutor's nostrils.

'Could you point him out?' asked Abrams.

'Yes. That young man sitting over there,' he said, pointing to Colt.

'Let the record show that Professor Ostrovsky identified Brian Colt, who has already testified as a witness in this trial.'

'So ordered,' said the judge.

This apparently trivial little exercise was to establish something called 'chain of custody' over the bottle. This was one of the requirements that the United States Supreme Court laid down for the admissibility of physical evidence. For example, in this case, in order to link the bottle to the crime, Abrams had to show an unbroken chain of control of the bottle from the moment Murphy brought it to the hospital claiming he had been poisoned at least until its contents were tested by Professor Ostrovsky, if not until it was brought into the courtroom. He also had to show that the defence was given access to the bottle and its contents and given the chance to conduct their own tests. He also had to be able to refute the claim that the bottle or its contents were somehow contaminated in transit before the defence were given the chance to examine it.

'Professor Ostrovsky, could you describe what you received from Brian Colt?'

'It was a bottle of tequila; that is, a tequila bottle with a few drops left.'

Abrams now walked slowly up to Ostrovsky, giving emphasis to his forthcoming words by the heavy, deliberate pace. The

judge had been prepared to restrict the lawyers to standing at
their respective tables. But there had been no objection from
Justine when Abrams had started walking about during his
opening argument, and the judge had warned Justine that he
would not take over routine defence for her. Even now there
was no objection. So he allowed Abrams to proceed with his
histrionics unimpeded.

'Is this the bottle he gave you?'

The professor gave it a cursory examination.

'Yes,' he confirmed, with the staccato click of a precision-
made machine.

'Did you mark it for identification before handing it over
to the police?'

'Yes.'

Again the tone was perfunctory.

'In what manner?'

'I signed a label and stuck it on it.'

'Does it still bear that label?'

'Yes.'

'May it please the court, Your Honour, I move that the
bottle now be received in evidence as People's exhibit two.'

Parker leaned over to Justine.

'You know you can still object,' he whispered.

At the second pre-trial hearing, Parker had tried to persuade
Justine to object to the admission of the bottle on the grounds
that Ostrovsky's label could have been removed or copied
and put on another bottle. It was a trivial motion which had
little chance of success. But, in any event, Justine wouldn't
hear of it.

'The bottle and its contents are admitted as evidence
without objection from the defence,' said the judge.

'Professor Ostrovsky, what did you do when Brian Colt
gave you the bottle?'

'I subjected a small quantity of the liquid inside the bottle
to various tests to determine its identity.'

He spent the next half-hour describing the tests. Several
times Abrams tried to lead him. But Ostrovsky resisted all
such efforts and delivered his testimony in his own words.

'And did you reach any definite conclusion on the basis
of these tests?'

'Yes,' replied Ostrovsky, like clockwork.

'What did you determine the contents of the bottle to be?' asked Abrams.

'A mixture of tequila and pyrethrum.'

'What *is* pyrethrum?'

'It's a nerve poison, commonly used in insecticides.'

A gasp went through the courtroom. In a rural community, no explanation of pyrethrum would have been necessary. But in an urban area such as New York City, it took Ostrovsky's explanation to alert the spectators to the fact that they had just heard something significant.

'Is it harmful to human beings if imbibed orally?'

In the spectators' section a man sat forward keenly. It was the man who had entered the country as 'Dr Paul O'Brian', but who was known in Northern Ireland as Declan McNutt.

'If imbibed in sufficient quantity,' Ostrovsky answered, with cold, professional neutrality.

'Can it be *fatal* to human beings?' Abrams pressed on relentlessly.

'If imbibed in sufficient quantity,' replied Ostrovsky with that same non-committal indifference.

'Were you able to determine the relative concentration of pyrethrum in the tequila?'

'Yes.'

'Professor, in terms of the tequila and pyrethrum together, what would have constituted a fatal dose of the mixture to an average-sized man?'

'A double,' Ostrovsky blurted out, apparently without thinking.

A burst of laughter rang out from the spectators' section. It was the first crack in the professor's façade of scientific professionalism. Or at least so it seemed to the spectators. Rick Parker was not so sure.

'Two measures,' Ostrovsky corrected, hiding his embarrassment behind a smile, although he saw very little humour in the matter.

'Professor, in your opinion, would the strong taste of the tequila disguise the taste of the pyrethrum?'

'It *might*,' said Ostrovsky, piling on the cautiousness, to avoid leaving those hard but brittle spots that cross-examiners love to exploit.

'Now, Professor, what did you do when you reached your conclusion about the contents of the bottle?'

Parker noticed that Abrams was prefacing every question with the word 'Professor' as if to imprint the title on the jurors' minds and emphasize the professional expertise of his witness. He would have objected to this manipulative practice. But he knew that Justine had no intention of doing so, and he didn't even bother to suggest it.

'I called Dr Stern,' replied Ostrovsky, 'and asked him to find out how much of the mixture had been imbibed. He told me five measures.'

Even if Parker had been representing Justine he would not have been able to object: Ostrovsky's evidence, though hearsay, was part of the *res gestae*. As such the evidence was admissible, however damaging it may have been to Justine.

'And that would be what, Professor? Two and a half times the fatal dose?'

'Yes.'

'And what did you do then?'

'I asked for a description of the patient's symptoms and was told of his low temperature and bodily trembling. I found this to be fully consistent with pyrethrum poisoning.'

'And what action did you take?'

'I advised Dr Stern to administer a dose of atropine, that's the antidote to pyrethrum. I advised him as to the quantity. He concurred with that advice to the best of my knowledge.'

Parker noticed a sense of unease in Ostrovsky as he said these words, and noted also that the words themselves had a qualifying effect more typical of a lawyer or a politician than a doctor. He sensed that this was Ostrovsky's way of avoiding moral responsibility for the consequences of his actions.

'And what did you do with the bottle?'

'I marked it for identification and put it into a plastic bag. I then locked the bag in a drawer in my desk. A few hours later I handed it over to a uniformed police officer who showed me identification revealing him to be Detective Reilly. I got him to sign a receipt for it when he took it.'

'And is this the receipt?' asked Abrams, producing a small slip of paper.

The clerk of the court brought it over to the professor, who perused it briefly.

'Yes, that's it.'

'Your Honour, the receipt has been marked as People's exhibit three, but I will be withholding it until I've established further grounds for its admission with Detective Reilly's testimony. I have no further questions of this witness.'

Abrams sat down smugly. Parker leaned over to Justine and was about to say something to her when she rose abruptly. He straightened up sheepishly as she began her cross-examination.

'Professor Ostrovsky, you said something in your original statement to the police about analysing a blood sample from Murphy. Is that correct?'

Abrams knew that the blood sample was the Achilles' heel of Ostrovsky's evidence. The professor had assured him that it was irrelevant, but the question was not about science but about the jury's subjective thoughts on the subject.

'Objection,' said Abrams, rising swiftly. 'The matter wasn't raised in direct.'

This was Abrams's first opportunity to do battle with Justine directly, and his first opportunity to 'crowd' her and show her the difference between an amateur and a professional in the context of a courtroom joust. But he was not dealing with such an amateur.

'Goes to impeach the witness, Your Honour,' said Justine. 'It shows that he overlooked pertinent scientific evidence that conflicted with his thesis, and may also have grounds for covering up his own mistakes now.'

'Overruled,' said the judge.

The jury were now wide awake and alert to the unfolding drama which had just shifted into a higher gear. This was the first witness that Justine had chosen to cross-examine, and the first sign of a genuine crossing of legal swords between the combatants, as distinct from the feinting and posturing that had gone before. The crack of blade against blade hinted at the drama yet to come.

'That's correct,' said Ostrovsky, shifting uneasily in

response to the sudden elevation in the level of the jury's alertness.

Now it was Parker's turn to sit forward abruptly, as he smelled blood of a different kind. The professor's answer was padded with surplus verbiage for the first time since he took the stand. Justine was taking him out of his regular stride.

'Could you tell us the result of that examination?'

'I found no trace of pyrethrum in the blood sample that was taken at that particular time,' he replied, placing particular emphasis on the last four words.

'How did this result factor into your diagnosis of Murphy's condition?' asked Justine.

'It . . . it didn't.'

'No further questions,' Justine concluded.

She sat down without gesture or flourish.

'Redirect?' the judge asked Abrams.

Abrams rose awkwardly and with a trace of apprehension, knowing that he had to mount a quick salvage operation.

'Does the absence of pyrethrum in the bloodstream *necessarily* mean that he hadn't orally imbibed a fatal dose of pyrethrum, Professor?'

'No, it doesn't,' replied Ostrovsky, clutching at the straw the prosecutor was offering him. 'It only means that if he *had* imbibed such a dose, it had not yet been *absorbed* into the bloodstream.'

'Thank you, Professor. That's all.'

Ostrovsky visibly sighed with relief, convinced that his ordeal was over as Abrams sat down without troubling to hide his smug satisfaction. But the relief disappeared when Justine rose confidently, without waiting for the judge to invite her to conduct her recross.

'I have just a couple of questions, Professor,' she said, emulating Abrams's emphasis of Ostrovsky's title with a hint of mockery. 'If the pyrethrum had *not* been absorbed into the bloodstream, then what could have caused the patient to display *symptoms* of such poisoning?'

The professor shifted uncomfortably. There is a German expression in the game of chess, *Zugzwang*, meaning compulsion to move. It refers to a situation in which it is a player's turn to move and he is not in any immediate danger, but whatever move he makes will put him in grave danger and cause him to lose the game. If chess players could simply pass their turn, then *Zugzwang* would not exist. But chess players, like witnesses in a courtroom trial, cannot pass their turn. And so Professor Ostrovsky now found himself in *Zugzwang*.

'Well, first of all I didn't say that the symptoms *were* caused by pyrethrum poisoning, only that they were fully consistent with it. Secondly, the symptoms might have been *psychosomatically* induced.'

Ostrovsky looked over at Abrams for reassurance. Abrams avoided his eyes, sensing what was coming, and wanting no part in it.

'But, Professor,' said Justine, adding a further note of irony to the proceedings by repeating her gentle stress on his title, 'if the symptoms were *psychosomatically* induced, then surely they would have occurred independently of whether or not he *had* imbibed pyrethrum?'

Abrams was looking at the ground, desperate to cut himself off from the collapse of one of his most important witnesses.

'That would be a fair comment,' said Ostrovsky, reluctantly.

Once again there were stirrings of excitement in the courtroom.

'Thank you, Professor,' said Justine, returning to her seat calmly.

'That was brilliant!' said Parker, a beaming smile spreading across his face as the courtroom erupted into excited chatter.

In the spectators' section, Declan scowled at the sound of Justine achieving a minor victory, even though it had no bearing on the outcome of events as he conceived it. On the other side of the spectators' section a man watched him. He was called 'Tom' or 'Thomas', and there were a great many stories circulating about his name. Some said it was short for 'Peeping Tom' because of the way in which he kept his victims under scrutiny before rubbing them out. Others said it was short for 'Doubting Thomas' because he worked alone, being too sceptical to trust anyone else. Yet others said that it stood for 'Tom Thumb' because he was quite small, too small in fact to seem like a threat to anyone. But then again a small handgun made of a composite polymer that wouldn't show up in an X-ray scan or metal detector was enough of an equalizer to make him a threat, especially to those foolish enough to underestimate him.

The IRA knew from the beginning that it was a waste of time trying to track Declan through the Irish-American network in New York, because he would have sufficient cunning to avoid them. But the one place he couldn't stay away from was the court. If he planned the hit there then he would have to case the joint. If he planned it elsewhere then, lacking an intelligence network, he would probably go there to follow Justine and find out where she lived. By the same token, the IRA man knew that he could follow Declan and find out where *he* was staying. Then they could decide what to do.

18

She remained seated in the car as Murphy went round to the other side. Her instinct was to open the door and get out herself. She had meticulously cultivated and fiercely guarded her independent spirit and had no time for the pleasantries of gentlemanly chivalry, especially from a man whom she hated. But with a great deal of hidden effort and willpower she forced herself to stay put. She had to remind herself consciously that she was here to put on an act, to play a role.

The door was opened by the same casually clad figure who had so confidently jumped at the bait that Justine had offered the night before. She stood there facing him in a polo-necked sweater and form-hugging jeans. For a moment he stood too, admiring her, wondering how he could have such luck as to have attracted this girl without even having to tell her about his adventurous past.

'You look ravishing,' he said for the second time that evening.

Justine tried not to wince. She should have known that he was the type to recite that hackneyed compliment at every opportunity. He led her through the mirrored vestibule into the mahogany-panelled living room. Justine looked around, stricken momentarily by awe and the nauseating feeling that she had underestimated her man, until she brought things into focus. A man who had employed a ghost writer to draft the semi-fictionalized bestseller about his terrorist past didn't need aesthetic standards of his own. He could hire others to do his thinking for him.

It was others, she knew, who had advised him about the halogen lamps in the corners which now flooded the room with light, but which could at the turn of a dial be dimmed to provide a gentle romantic ambiance for the grand seduction scene that Murphy had, no doubt, scheduled for later that evening.

The white plush-pile carpet felt soft to the touch as she slipped off her shoe and ran her toes along it.

'So what d'you think of the place?' he asked, reading her eyes rather than her mind.

'I'm impressed,' she replied, balancing tact with honesty.

In one cosy corner of the room, near the wall of glass that looked out on to the swimming pool, a small round dining table was set for two, with a white lace cloth, a crystal vase overflowing with bright summer flowers and, the ultimate cliché, a silver candelabra out of which rose long candles tapering off at the flames which danced in the breeze from the open kitchen.

'What's that?' asked Murphy, as Justine produced the bottle from behind her back.

'Tequila,' she replied. Then she smiled with embarrassment. 'I forgot that you said we'd be eating Chinese. Maybe we could have it after the meal.'

There was something girlish about the way she spoke which stirred Murphy's gentler instincts. He gave her a chaste kiss on the cheek.

'I'll go and get the food,' he said, depositing the bottle on the table.

Justine smiled as he left the room. She was feeling her way into the role by instinct now, like a method actress, engulfed in her assigned character.

It was later when they were eating large portions of sweet and sour rice and Szechwan chicken that Justine raised the subject that had been on her mind.

'So what was that about being wanted in England?'

'Wanted *by* England. There's a difference.'

'How d'you mean?'

'I'm wanted in the so-called United Kingdom of Great Britain and Northern Ireland, or more precisely, in the six British-occupied counties of my country.'

'Why are you wanted there?'

'I committed a political crime in England in the struggle for the liberation of the Six Counties. But I can't go back to Northern Ireland either because at the moment they're under British occupation.'

'What exactly was your political crime?'

'I planted a bomb in a shopping centre.'

'You mean like . . . one of those incendiary devices that goes off at night and burns out the shop?' she asked hesitantly.

Murphy shook his head. She watched his eyes, curious to see his reaction. There was a faint trace of guilt. But it was only a trace.

'No, it was a couple of fully fledged Semtex surprises, and the warning arrived late.'

His manner was mildly apologetic, as if he knew at some level of his consciousness that what he had done was wrong and was pleading mitigation. He knew that his intention had been to kill. But she sensed that the pictures of that three-year-old child had been too much even for this would-be man of steel.

'How come it arrived late?'

'The telephone booth that I was going to send the warning from had been vandalized.'

'Was anyone killed?'

Murphy nodded.

'Who?'

'A kid and a man called Shankar . . . Srini Shankar.'

She noticed that he had said 'a kid' in such an offhand way, that you couldn't tell that he was talking about a three-year-old child. *But then again, how do you tell a girl you're trying to get into the sack that you blew up a three-year-old?*

'Srini Shankar? Sounds like an Indian.'

'What, like Sitting Bull?' he asked, grinning broadly.

'I said an *Indian*, not a native American.'

Good, she told herself, pleased with the act she was putting on. *A typical white middle-class college girl, more concerned about political correctness than the sanctity of human life.*

'Oh, that sort of Indian. Yes, he was . . . Let's eat, before it gets cold.'

He started eating.

'What was he?'

Murphy's chopsticks stopped in mid-air.

'How do you mean?'

'What did he do?'

'Nothing. He was just in the wrong place at the wrong time.'

'That isn't what I meant. I mean what was his job?'

'Well how the bejesus should *I* know?' he lashed out more aggressively than he intended, the anger of his tone camouflaging the helpless desperation of his guilt, a display of anger being so much more manly than adopting a cringing posture in a plea for absolution.

He started eating again, and this time so did she. For a while they ate in silence. At least a minute ticked by before Justine looked up from her plate. Murphy attacked his food like a famine victim at an unexpected feast, glancing up occasionally to study Justine, who made a point of avoiding his eyes. An inner conflict was raging behind that face, and it showed.

'A penny for your thoughts,' he said gently.

Her hands and mouth stopped moving for a moment, as if a battery inside her had been disconnected.

'I was thinking about that man you said you killed,' she replied.

'I guess I shouldn't have told you about it. Now you probably think I'm a murderer.'

'Do you think of yourself as one?' she asked gently.

'Hardly a day goes by when I don't ask myself that question. I don't think I'm any different from an American pilot who drops bombs on Baghdad. The only difference is they showed the faces of the people I killed in papers. I had to look at them and remember them. And I'll go on remembering them till the day I die.

If I *am* a murderer, at least I'm a murderer with a conscience.'

'How do you cope with the guilt?'

'The same way any soldier does. I remind myself that the real guilt belongs to the enemy.'

'And who is the enemy?'

'The British government and their occupying army in Northern Ireland.'

'Then why target civilians?' asked Justine.

'Why does any army target civilians? Why did the American Air Force bomb Hiroshima or blow up bridges in Baghdad? Civilian areas are part of the economic infrastructure that keeps the government in power.'

'But what about the civilians themselves? Don't they also have a cause?'

'You really want to know?' he answered bitterly. 'Most people don't give a damn about anything until it starts affecting them. Then they go off and act all self-righteous, wagging their fingers and preaching morality at people who don't have the comforts that they take for granted. What makes people think they have a right to be indifferent to the suffering of others?'

'Maybe they just haven't got the time to fight against all the world's injustice.'

'That's what I mean,' Murphy snapped. 'They haven't got time. Perhaps if they weren't so indifferent to the suffering of others they'd *find* the time.'

'Hasn't it occurred to you that there's so much suffering in the world they couldn't find the time for *all* the world's problems. It's not that people don't care. It's just that there are too many problems to cope with.'

'That's touchingly naïve. Just go ask some sanctimonious politician who speaks out against kiddie porn. Ask him if it troubles his conscience that his clothes were made by child labour in a sweat shop in some fascist dictatorship!'

'And you'd rather kill the good for the crimes of the bad than spare the bad for the sake of the good?'

'I'd rather change the world than leave it in the pitiful state it's in – oh, I've just remembered about that

Indian. He was a professor of something . . . radiology, I think.'

He couldn't understand the flicker of emotion on Justine's face.

19

With the demolition of Ostrovsky's evidence, the game was beginning to look more like a two-sided contest.

When the court reconvened after lunch Abrams called one Detective Albert Cruz to the stand.

Albert Cruz was a tall, lanky man. He stood six feet two, but seemed taller because of his recalcitrant brown hair which Abrams inferred must surely have impeded the advancement of his career as a plain-clothes policeman because of its eye-catching conspicuousness. His face held an amiable smile. The prosecutor couldn't understand how a man with such a friendly nature could survive in the rough-and-tumble world of urban policing. Parker, who had crossed swords with Cruz before in a legal aid case, knew that Cruz's amiable manner was a façade to win over juries. He could be a bastard towards his suspects.

The early questions elicited his name and rank as well as some of the more basic information from his service record. He had won a number of citations for bravery as well as the precinct 'conservation award' for low gasoline consumption. He had played it down at the time. His off-the-cuff quip had been 'how much gas can you burn up on a stakeout?' It had made the rounds of the precinct and become a candidate for 'sound bite of the year'. But the conservation award still sounded impressive to the jury. All in all, Cruz's record read like the résumé of the golden boy of the Police Department who could do no wrong.

With these formalities of character and professional qualifications out of the way, Abrams got down to business.

'Could you tell the jury, please, where you were on the night of September the seventh at about nine p.m.?'

'My partner and I were on routine patrol on Broadway. We got a call to go to the emergency room at St Joseph's Hospital. We went there and were directed to a room where a Dr Stern was giving treatment to a man called Sean Murphy.'

'Your Honour,' said Abrams, 'this witness's identification of Dr Stern was accepted by the defendant through stipulation at the preliminary hearing and I ask that it be entered into the record at this time.'

The judge looked over at Justine.

'Miss Levy?'

'No objection.'

'So ordered.'

The identification was written into the record and Abrams proceeded.

'Could you tell the jury, please, what happened in that room?'

'Sean Murphy made a verbal statement to me which I took down in writing.'

'Did he sign the statement?'

'No, he was too weak to sign it.'

'Did Murphy say anything apart from what you wrote down?'

'Not to me.'

'Well, did he say anything to Dr Stern in your presence?'

'He said—'

'Just a moment, Officer,' the judge interrupted. 'Mr Abrams, this is hearsay and clearly not part of the *res gestae*.'

'Your Honour, this question is aimed at establishing foundation for the admission of Murphy's statement to Detective Cruz as a dying declaration.'

A dying declaration, Parker knew, carried the same weight

in law as testimony given under oath, and had one distinct advantage over such testimony: it was not subject to cross-examination. It had to be stopped. And for this purpose, he was prepared to overstep his watching brief and try to assume the status of defence counsel even without Justine's permission, if the judge would let him.

'Your Honour,' he said, rising, 'this whole question was already settled at the pre-trial motions hearing. If the prosecution wants to reopen the issue then I ask that the jury be sequestered for the duration of the arguments.'

In effect Abrams had already succeeded in his objective: he had drawn the jury's attention to the fact that there was an incriminating deathbed statement by Murphy which the defence wanted to suppress. But he would have to come up with a good reason for trying to reopen the matter, otherwise the judge would slap him with a citation for contempt of court.

'You're not empowered to act for the accused without her consent. However, on my own motion I'll hear arguments in the absence of the jury.'

On the judge's instructions the jury was led out by a bailiff. When the doors were closed behind them, Abrams was given the go-ahead to begin.

'Your Honour, in order to receive a statement in evidence as a dying declaration, the court must be shown that the deceased was dying and that he knew this to be the case. The court has heard evidence that Murphy was dying and that he did die. Regardless of the final cause of death, one of the elements of a dying declaration was clearly present. The other essential element is that the deceased *knew* that he was dying. Normally this requirement is satisfied by an inclusion of a statement to the effect that the deceased knew that he was dying in the dying declaration itself. In this case, concededly, Murphy's statement to Detective Cruz contains no such statement. However, we are in a position to show that Murphy made such a statement to Dr Stern in the presence of Detective Cruz, in the form of the words "She's a cold-blooded murderess". I submit that the use of the word "murderess" clearly indicated a belief that he was dying and thus qualifies his subsequent statement to Detective Cruz as a dying declaration.'

Parker had by now openly assumed the mantle of defence counsel with no apparent opposition from Justine. He wondered if she would let him continue as such for the remainder of the trial.

'Your Honour, I must disagree with my learned colleague on a number of points. First of all Murphy's statement to Detective Cruz was given *after* he had been administered with a dose of atropine. The doctors believed that the atropine would save Murphy. If Murphy shared this belief then at the time he made his statement to Cruz he didn't believe himself to be dying.'

'There is no proof on record that he *did* share that belief,' the judge pointed out.

'But there is no proof that he didn't, and the *onus probandi* is on the prosecution to establish the admissibility of the statement. Moreover there is clear evidence on record that Murphy knew that he had been given the normal antidote to the pyrethrum.'

'In that case it hinges on when Murphy used the word "murderess",' said the judge. 'Before or after the atropine was administered?'

He looked over at Abrams.

'Your Honour, the remark was made to Dr Stern *before* the atropine was administered,' Abrams replied, feeling the ground slipping away from under him. 'However, the court should take note of the fact that the deceased made a statement similar to the contents of his dying declaration *before* the antidote to the pyrethrum was administered, even though it wasn't written down at the time.'

'My learned friend forgets that *before* the antidote was administered there's no proof that Murphy was dying. The People's own evidence suggests that he died of atropine poisoning.'

Abrams was being put on the defensive, and he didn't like it. He hit back with what little ammunition he had.

'Nevertheless he *did* die and at the time when he arrived at the hospital he truly *believed* himself to be dying, as evinced by his statement to Dr Stern. This is admittedly an ironic situation. When Sean Murphy *believed* himself to be dying he *might not* have been dying and when he *was* dying he *might not* have *believed* he was dying. But I would argue that coincidence of the belief and the fact is not necessary.'

'On the contrary,' Parker countered. 'The belief and the fact must coincide, or at least they must both be present at the same time as the statement was made. This is a vital test before a dying declaration is recognized. The question is what did he believe when he made his statement and what was the case *in fact*. He may have believed himself to be dying when he *arrived* at the hospital. However, the legal import of his words "She's a cold-blooded murderess" was swept into oblivion by the administration of the atropine. Once that took place he may well have believed that he would live, even if it was the atropine that sealed his fate. Furthermore, the court should note that even before that, Murphy went of his own volition to a hospital where he was surrounded by some of the best doctors in the country. Presumably he went there to get medical treatment in the belief that he had a chance of survival, otherwise he'd have gone straight to an undertaker.'

Laughter swept through the courtroom.

'Mr Parker,' said the judge, scowling, 'I don't take kindly to such displays of levity in my court.'

'I'm sorry, Your Honour. The point I'm trying to make is that Murphy's actions show that even when he said "She's a cold-blooded murderess" he believed that all was not yet lost.'

The judge nodded patiently and turned to the prosecutor.

'Mr Abrams, do you have anything to add to the argument?'

'No, Your Honour.'

'Mr Parker?'

'No, Your Honour.'

'Miss Levy?'

'No, Your Honour.'

'Thank you.' The judge looked Abrams straight in the eye. 'It is clear that insufficient grounds have been established for admitting Murphy's statement to Officer Cruz as a dying declaration. Accordingly I see no reason to amend my ruling at the pre-trial against such admission. I must also observe that I don't even see any adequate grounds for the prosecution having reopened the issue of Murphy's statement, and I warn you, Mr Abrams, that if there are any more attempts to poison the minds of the jurors, by raising issues already decided, you will be held in contempt.'

Abrams looked away fearfully, realizing that while his gamble might have scored a few points with the jury in the few seconds during which they had heard it, the exercise carried a dangerously high price tag with the judge.

A few yards away, Parker was leaning over towards Justine.

'You might show a little bit of an interest,' he whispered as the jurors were led back. 'If that statement had been admitted as a dying declaration, you'd've been sunk.'

Justine showed no reaction.

20

The setting sun was dazzling to the eyes as Thomas stepped out of the brownstone. His hand slipped into his breast pocket to retrieve his sunglasses and he put them on as he turned to start walking down the street. He had followed Declan back to the apartment where he was staying and then paid it a visit while Declan was out doing his weekend grocery shopping. Declan knew the gun laws in the State of New York very well and he made sure to leave the Colt 45 automatic in the apartment. He would only take it out when he needed it. Even having the gun was against New York's strict gun registration and licensing laws, but that was a risk he had to take.

Thomas had no qualms about killing another of the INLA troublemakers, to add to the four he had notched up already. But he was operating under the same rules of engagement as other members of the Official IRA, and that meant no military operations in the United States. It was in order to enforce this doctrine that he was here in the first place. It wouldn't do if he were to enforce the rule against operating in the United States while at the same time breaking it. Of course, the rule was a pragmatic one. The purpose was to avoid *appearing* to be operating in the United States. He could conceivably make the hit look like a mugging or a hit-and-run driver. But there was always an element of risk involved in any sort of hit, and his brief had been very clear. Stop him with minimal force and only kill him if absolutely necessary and unavoidable.

In any case, there was more than one way to skin a cat. His approach was simple and involved the old principle of never doing your own dirty work when you can get someone else to do it for you. In this case, the servants of his will would be New York's finest, and Thomas needed only one tool of the trade, and it was the telephone.

He had to time it so as to make sure that Declan would be there when they arrived. He also had to make sure that they would conduct the search. They had funny laws in the United States about 'probable cause' and 'illegal search and seizure'. Evidence had been thrown out of court because the police didn't have a search warrant when they got it. Apparently American police officers were not allowed to use their initiative as their British counterparts were, a restriction that in this case did not work to Thomas's advantage.

On the other hand, they were allowed to follow their noses. A police officer's sense of smell could serve as probable cause. Incriminating evidence discovered during searches of cars had been admitted because the officer conducting the search had sworn that he could smell marijuana. The joint that Thomas had left smouldering for half an hour would certainly leave a lingering aroma that any experienced member of New York's finest couldn't fail to detect.

He made his way to the pay-phone at the end of the street. The room had no phone and he didn't want to risk being overheard by anyone else from the building by using the phone in the lobby. Now all he had to do was wait. No more than ten minutes elapsed before he saw Declan returning from the Korean supermarket with two brown bags packed with food.

He dialled the local police.

'Listen carefully, 'cause I'm only going to say this once.' He gave Declan's address and added, 'You'll find a drug dealer who's just made a score. He has a gun, but he probably hasn't got the balls to use it.'

He put the phone down and waited. It was a long wait. This was a working-class area of the city, where the crime rate was high and police response times were slow, except when it was an 'officer down'.

The police detectives arrived in an unmarked car using a silent approach. They parked a safe distance away and entered the building quickly. They had no warrant and a forced entry would have been questionable. This was one of those many cases that they'd have to play by ear. They checked for rear exits and found that the fire escape was accessible from inside the room via the window. One of them covered it while the other proceeded to the front door. He knocked and waited.

'Who's there?' came the cautious voice from inside.

'Police,' said the detective. 'Open up.'

He heard the sound of wood scraping against wood as the window was raised and the sound of someone inside clambering on to the window ledge. He knew that his partner was there, ready to cover any escape by the window. He waited a moment in case there was someone else in there who might try to make an escape through the door. Then he walked casually round to the back of the building where his partner was already reeling off the litany of Miranda rights from memory as the subdued suspect 'assumed the position' and submitted to the personal search. Later, with the suspect safely in custody, the police were able to get a search warrant and check out the house, revealing no drugs but an unlicensed firearm.

Like all suspects, Declan had been given the right to make a phone call. But he had no one to call. He asked the arresting officer if they could recommend a lawyer. The arresting officer told him that he couldn't recommend, for fear of being accused of taking kickbacks, but then added with a vague ring of sympathy, 'There are plenty of shysters hanging around the courtroom where we'll take you for the arraignment.'

Meanwhile, in an IRA safe house in the Bronx, Thomas smiled. With Declan out of the way for a while, the heat was off. But if Declan got out of custody, he might have to take further action.

21

'It makes me feel small,' said Nancy.

'It makes me feel big,' replied Parker. 'It makes me feel as if I could just reach out and grab it.'

They were standing in the torch of the Statue of Liberty, looking out at the New York skyline and the spreading bay before them.

'You know, Rick, I'm surprised you don't get on with her better than you do.'

She was a big girl, a buxom blonde. Only she wasn't Justine. She had the same full figure, but whereas Justine had the unyielding face of an Amazon warrior and the firm body of an athlete, Nancy had the fresh face of a cheerleader and the soft body of a beauty queen. While Justine's back was flawlessly straight, Nancy's was more rounded.

Several men were ogling her and eyeing Parker jealously, some with open, racially motivated hostility. It was hard to ignore Nancy. Her ample breasts strained at her white summer dress with its plunging neckline that showed plenty of cleavage.

'Why do you say that?' asked Parker. 'About being surprised that I don't get on better with her?'

'Because of what you just said . . . about being able to reach out and grab it. It's the sort of thing *she* would have said.'

'How do *you* get on with her?'

'Do we have to talk about her?'

'We made a deal,' said Parker. 'A free lunch for a financially pressed student in exchange for some routine information about Justine.'

'If it's in exchange for something then it isn't free,' replied Nancy with a cheeky smile.

'Well, you know what Heinlein said: "There ain't no such thing as a free lunch."'

Secretly, Parker was impressed by the shrewdness of Nancy's argument.

'All right,' said Nancy, sweeping her hair back in subconscious imitation of a gesture so frequently made by Justine, 'what do you want to know?'

'First of all I want to know one thing up front: do you really not have a clue why Abrams is calling you for the prosecution?'

'I swear to God I don't. Look, I don't *want* to testify against Justine and I can't for the life of me think what I said to that smooth-talking assistant of his to suggest I had anything relevant to their case. But I got this subpoena and I have to go. I haven't got the slightest idea what he's going to ask me.'

Parker was relieved by her lack of hostility. At least she wouldn't be accusing Justine of jealousy, an emotion that juries often associate with women accused of murder. But he wasn't reassured by the gap in his knowledge. He would prefer to know what Nancy was likely to say, even if it was something negative about his client. Ignorance left Justine more vulnerable. If there was a hole in Justine's case, they could prepare to plug it now rather than when it appeared in court.

'OK, let's try another line. What can you tell me about Justine?'

'That she hasn't told you already?'

'She hasn't told me very much.'

'Well, I don't know if I can add much. I mean, you've seen her yourself. She was as closed in and private with me as she probably was with you. If you have a specific question I'll try to answer it, but I don't know what you want.'

Parker thought to himself for a moment.

'What I really want is a woman's perspective.'

'To tell the truth, I tended to stay out of her way at med school. And don't even think of asking her out on a date.'

'What about a night out with the girls?'

'Not that either. I mean it was impossible to *relate* to her . . . as a human being.'

'In what way?'

'She's too hard, too tough. There's no softness to her, not even a soft centre.'

Parker felt a stab of fear. Was this the evidence that Abrams was going to present through Nancy? Negative character evidence. Could Abrams somehow get it across under the guise of presenting some relevant substantive evidence? The quiet insinuation that Justine was a hard woman who would think nothing of murder? It couldn't be. Justine's hard character had been apparent from the beginning. For good or for ill she had done nothing to disguise it, and it was hard to see what Nancy could add to it, even if she had been friendly to the prosecution, which she clearly wasn't. But Parker knew that he had to explore further. Abrams was evidently calling her for *some* reason.

'Are you sure about that?'

'Maybe there was a soft centre. Maybe that's what she was trying to protect.'

'She had a rough life,' said Parker. 'It's hardly surprising.'

'She's a born survivor, like her mother.'

'What do you know about her mother?'

'Well, I don't know if you know anything about her background – I mean her father and all that.'

'I know the basic facts,' Parker prompted, 'nothing more.'

'After her father shot himself, her mother just picked up the pieces and carried on living. She passed her real-estate exams and was all set on a new career. It gave them financial security, even a fair degree of luxury.'

'How often did you get to talk to Justine?'

'Not very often. Before she was arrested, her life consisted of two straight lines: to med school in the morning and back home again in the evening. We sometimes sat together in the cafeteria.'

'But she wasn't very talkative.'

'Oh, she talked all right, about her last class. She couldn't imagine why anyone would want to talk about anything else.'

'Didn't she ever talk about her childhood?'

'Now I *know* you're a closet Freudian. You think that's the key to it all.'

'I'm clutching at straws. Do you know anything about Srini Shankar?' asked Parker.

'Not really. I mean, the first I heard of him was after the case blew open. He was a British professor. Or an East Indian. I don't think any of his work formed part of our courses. Justine used to read everything, not just what she had to learn for the course.'

'And that could have included Shankar's work?' said Parker.

'I guess.'

'Any possibility that he was in America ever? That they had a brief affair?'

Nancy looked at Parker somewhat irritated.

'That's a load of bullshit, Rick! And if there *had* been an affair, you can rest assured the prosecution would have given it to the press before the trial even started.'

'Well, they might not have wanted to create an excuse for a mistrial with prejudice.'

'I don't know what that means, Rick. All I know is that no one on the course had even *heard* about this Srini Shankar until Justine was arrested for killing that Murphy guy and the press started running stories about his background. I've read a lot about this case in the press, and no one's even suggested that Shankar was ever in America.'

'I'm just afraid that Abrams might be holding something back. He's not obliged to tell me his case. The only thing I have to go on is his witness list. That's a list of all the people that he might be calling, although he isn't obliged to call them. That's why I was wondering if you might know something that I don't. Because if you do and you want to help Justine, now's your chance.'

'I don't know anything about any affair. I'm pretty sure that if there had been one I would have known. I never heard about Srini Shankar from Justine. I read about him in the papers. I thought that if anything, Justine was more likely to be motivated by that three-year-old child. That was a pretty gruesome thing for Murphy to do. I could see Justine taking revenge over something like that.'

'Did she ever say anything to suggest that?'

'No, but she always sided with the underdog. She felt empathy for the weak.'

'You seem to know a lot about her,' said Parker.

For the first time there was a hesitation before Nancy's reply, as if this question had taken her out of her stride, had forced her to consider a possibility she hadn't thought of before.

'We were close. But there was a part of her that always had to remain private. There may be a secret lurking there, but I don't think you'll find it until she chooses to let it out.'

A heavy silence fell between them. Nancy saw pain on Parker's face.

'Do you think you can save her?'

'I'm pitching for all it's worth. But I'm not sure if I have his measure. Abrams is a good lawyer . . . and I have a very uncooperative client. Hell, she's not even my client. I'm on stand-by. Strictly speaking I'm not even supposed to open my mouth without her permission, although I've done so a couple of times and got away with it.'

'Couldn't you work out one of those deals?'

'No way. I wanted her to cop a plea but she refused. And even if she did, Abe and his boss are using this case as a springboard into politics.'

'How do you mean?'

'The DA's got his sights set on state attorney-general and Abrams is all keyed up to step into his shoes in Manhattan.'

'Surely there are other cases they could exploit?'

'Not with this much ready-made publicity.' He shook his head wearily. 'They're going to milk this one for all it's worth and then they'll throw her dried-out carcass to the wolves.'

'Tell me something, Rick, what exactly are *you* after?'

'I told you. I'm trying to build up a picture of my enigmatic and uncommunicative client.'

'That's what I'm getting at. Is it only Justine Levy the *client* that you're interested in, or Justine Levy the *person*?'

Parker's arms slid off the parapet slowly as he turned to look at her.

'Is *that* what you think?'

She stepped back from the parapet and turned to meet his eyes.

'You said before that you wanted a *woman's* perspective. Well, I'm giving it to you.'

He turned back to look at the city, resting his arms on the parapet once more.

'Did she tell you anything else that might help me?'

She edged closer to him.

'Rick Parker,' she blurted into his ear, 'are you changing the subject?'

She smiled, expecting Parker to do the same. Instead he frowned and clenched his fists.

'Let's just say I prefer not to want what I can't have.'

'I wouldn't write her off as a lost cause just yet.'

'I can't have her unless I can save her, and even if I save her she'll see me as just another schmuck like the kind she brushes off as if they were fleas.'

'Well, now we're making progress,' said Nancy mockingly. 'At least you're ready to admit to *your* feelings.'

He spun round.

'OK, you're right, I like her a lot. But I'm fighting a losing battle.'

'Now you're selling yourself short,' she said gently.

He forced a brave smile and met her eyes.

'Are you talking about Rick Parker the lawyer or Rick Parker the person?'

22

The proceedings of the last two days had been fairly routine, taken up with police testimony and formality. Parker would have loved to have put the police witnesses under the pressure of a barrage of technical questions, but all he could do was sit and watch while Abrams led his witnesses through their laborious testimony, with not the slightest trace of resistance from Justine.

It seemed to Parker that Abrams himself was drawing out their testimony to unnecessary lengths, although he couldn't think why. Justine appeared to be suppressing a smile as she watched the proceedings, almost as if she knew what the prosecutor was up to. It wasn't until the afternoon, however, that the speculation came to an end.

The first sign came when the press began filing into the courtroom for the afternoon session, filling up their rows of seats. There seemed to be more of them than usual. This was not in itself surprising: the press contingent had been growing steadily since the start of the trial, as the networks started picking it up. But it had dwindled briefly during the more mundane parts of the testimony. Now it had risen abruptly.

But what, Richard Parker wondered, *was the DA doing in court?*

'Your Honour, in deference to my learned colleague the District Attorney for Manhattan, I am stepping aside for the examination of the People's next witness.'

So that was it, thought Parker. That was the name of the game. The whole cornball production was to enable the DA to cash in on a high-profile case with minimum risk to himself, by conducting the examination of one minor witness who could hardly put a foot wrong. The arresting officer was a fairly routine witness, and even though Parker knew that routine witnesses could be shaken by a smart lawyer like himself, there was little likelihood that Justine would take advantage of the situation.

The strategy was that the DA would lead the witness through a series of routine questions to reveal his excellent service record and then get on to the nuts and bolts of the arrest to establish its legality for the record. That would fill about an hour. If Justine declined to cross-examine, as she almost certainly would, they could all go home early to enjoy a relaxing Friday evening and a pleasant weekend.

True to form, the opening questions elicited the patrolman's name and number, the number of years he had served in the force and his citations for bravery and initiative. It was just when the DA was beginning to get confident that Justine rose.

'Your Honour, may we enquire what this witness is being called upon to show? The defence is interested in saving time and I am quite willing to stipulate as to the legality of my arrest, that my Miranda rights were read to me and that I indicated that I understood them. If there are any problems about the fingerprints, I'm ready to stipulate to them if and when the file with the prints is introduced.'

The judge looked over at the DA quizzically. The DA looked round at Abrams and whispered a word in his ear. For a few seconds they appeared to be engaged in frantic conversation. Finally Abrams rose.

'Your Honour, those are precisely the things this witness was called upon to show and we are grateful to the defendant for her cooperation.'

'In that case the witness is excused.'

Abrams remained standing.

'Your Honour, we had expected the direct and cross-examination of this witness to take all afternoon. In consequence we have no other witnesses available to testify this afternoon.'

'That would appear to be a very serious oversight,' said the judge gravely.

'I apologize to the court, Your Honour. This is really quite unexpected. We were given no indication at the pre-trial that these stipulations would be forthcoming. I'd like therefore to move for an adjournment.'

'The court does not look kindly on such unnecessary delays in the proceedings, especially when the court has such a crowded docket and the defendant is being so cooperative in expediting matters. However, in view of the incompetence of the DA's office in coordinating its business, I have no alternative but to grant the motion, albeit with the gravest of reluctance. And I feel duty bound to censure the Assistant District Attorney for his handling of the matter and I hope that in the future he will take greater care in the preparation of his case. This court is adjourned until ten o'clock Monday morning.'

23

The police had dragged their heels over bringing Declan McNutt before a judge for arraignment because of the trivial nature of his offence. The approach of the IRA and the INLA in England had always been to give away as little information as possible. In spite of his refusal to cooperate, the police made no trouble about granting his right to make a phone call, not wanting to jeopardize their case against him. He had tried to call a contact whose name he had been given back in Belfast, making sure that the police officer didn't see the number. He knew that if they were really determined, they probably had other ways of checking. But he suspected that they weren't going to try. To them this was another minor case of illegal possession of a firearm, and possible possession of marijuana for personal use. There was no answer from the number.

They had told him that they were looking for drugs. At first he thought that this was just a ploy, certain that they were on to him, even though they were of Irish origin themselves. But after they checked him out with the FBI for previous convictions, they actually became quite friendly, asking him the obligatory 'What part of Ireland do you come from?'

and going on to enquire what life was like under British occupation.

The sleazy building where he had been staying was obviously a den of low lifes. Declan had seen the type hanging around the corridors. It was perfectly natural that the police should periodically raid apartments in a place like that. This was probably just a case of mistaken identity. In all likelihood they were tipped off about another apartment and simply got the apartment number wrong. Declan assumed that he had simply got caught in the tangled web. This would explain why they didn't even know his name. They didn't know *who* they were looking for. All they had was the number of an apartment. It was just his bad luck that they caught him with a firearm.

He had originally thought of keeping the gun stashed in a baggage locker ready for use when he needed it. But he liked to be ready for action at all times, ready to make a run for it if necessary. In Northern Ireland the purpose of army raids was not always to arrest but to execute a fighter. And the INLA was also in a state of constant alertness against another IRA crackdown like the one that had almost liquidated them. It may have been different with police raids here, given the high level of sympathy and public support that they enjoyed with a sizeable section of the American public. But old habits die hard.

The question was, had his cover been blown?

'Paul O'Brian,' the young man from the DA's office said perfunctorily as Declan was brought forward. 'Possession of a concealed weapon without a permit. No priors but a foreign citizen.'

The arraignment judge leaned forward.

'Is the defendant represented by counsel?'

'Not yet, Your Honour,' said Declan. 'I've been trying to get in touch with a friend who can get me a lawyer but I haven't been able to contact him yet.'

'Are you aware that if you desire an attorney but cannot afford one the court can appoint one free of charge?'

'Yes, they told me that. But I'd like to keep my options open. If I can get in touch with this friend he should be able to get me one. If not there's an organization I'd like to contact.'

'Very well. Does the DA have any objection to bail?'

'We do, Your Honour. The suspect was very uncooperative with the police at first about—'

'The suspect does have the right to remain silent,' the judge pointed out forcefully.

'Yes, but at first he wouldn't even give his name. Aside from that he is a citizen of a foreign country and as such he might not be inclined to show up for trial.'

'Mr O'Brian?'

'Well, Your Honour, I was staying at an inexpensive hotel where people can easily get into other people's rooms through the window and someone must have put the gun—'

'Mr O'Brian, I'm not trying the merits of the case,' the judge cut in. 'This is simply an arraignment appearance to determine whether or not bail should be granted.'

'I haven't got a lawyer so I don't know how you decide whether I get bail or not. But if the DA is worried that I won't show up for the trial I could always give you my passport.'

'A good point. As there are no priors and the charge is only possession of a firearm rather than actually using it, I'm inclined to release the defendant pending trial. However, as he is a foreign citizen I won't release on recognizance. Bail is set at ten thousand dollars. And the defendant's passport is to be surrendered to the court.'

Declan suppressed the urge to mouth an obscenity. In fact it would have cost him nothing. The judge was too hardened a veteran of the bench to take notice of such things.

There was a bitter taste in Declan's mouth. *Where am I going to get ten thousand dollars?* He didn't know about such creatures as bail bondsmen. But he soon would, because several of the legal vultures were already circling in the air around him.

24

'You really screwed Abrams yesterday.'

Central Park was sweeping by as Rick Parker, tired beyond belief, struggled to keep pace with Justine. Her fitness astounded him. Admittedly, long and tiresome law studies and professional practice had turned him into something of a couch potato. But still it was humiliating to have to struggle to keep up with a girl.

'How do you mean?' asked Justine.

Even her breathing was shallower and easier than his heavy panting. From her voice you couldn't tell that she was running at all.

'The DA wanted to cash in on the publicity from your trial. That was the whole idea behind his guest appearance. He picked a safe witness whose testimony couldn't easily be shaken in order to make sure that it didn't blow up in his face. Then you pulled the rug out from under him and ruined his golden moment.'

'I know,' said Justine.

'It's all dirty politics with them, of course.'

'I guess the DA was unlucky that Abrams didn't have another witness lined up.'

'The idea was that the DA would draw it out till the end of the afternoon. I don't know how he hoped to accomplish that, but that's sure as hell what he had in mind. It may be that he *did* have another witness outside, but didn't want to chance handing him over to the DA. The idea was that the DA would question a witness whose testimony was solid. The last thing Jerry wants is egg on his face in an election year.'

A few yards away Declan was poised behind a tree, waiting for the right moment with a mixture of excitement and apprehension. One of the shysters at the Hall of Justice had introduced himself and explained about 'bail bondsmen' making a living out of putting up bail. From that point on, it had been absurdly simple getting out of jail. He had no intention of going back after making the hit. That would merely expose him to further danger. It was bad enough that he had to talk his way into a back room of a Harlem pub (or 'bar' as they called it here) and hand over a wad of cash for an unreliable 'Saturday night special' that he had stripped and oiled to make sure it was still in working order. He would hardly be using his brain if he went back to answer to some stupid firearms charge, even if he could be sure that all he would get was a fine or probation. If some idiot who didn't know him wanted to throw good money after bad getting him out of jail in the hope of seeing some return on the investment, that was his mistake. Declan had already put up ten per cent, which he would forfeit by not showing up. But that would be all he forfeited. And the bail bondsman would lose a whole lot more.

Declan had decided that it would be best to kill Justine with a silenced handgun at close range. Instead of having to dismantle a rifle and drive away with it, as that so-called 'professional' would have had to have done, he would just slip the gun back into the shoulder holster beneath his loose-fitting sweatshirt, and carry on running like any other early-morning jogger.

He hadn't brought the field glasses this time. They would have aroused suspicion. Joggers don't usually carry binoculars. Aside from that, they would have been an added burden, and he needed mobility. Besides, he knew her routine well enough from his past observations, and he knew therefore that she was getting near. He knew her schedule like the back of his hand. Any second now she would come into view. He would jog behind her, make sure that there was no one else around and execute the bitch.

She was in view now. He started jogging a few yards behind. There was a man running along just behind her, black. However, he appeared to be out of breath and she would soon open a distance between them. Declan knew that all he had to do was keep up with Justine, while the black dropped back behind them.

'I'm glad you're finally beginning to appreciate my style,' said Justine.

My God! She's on to me.

A feeling of dread swept over him.

'Well, after what you did to Ostrovsky it was obvious that if you weren't a medical student you'd probably make a very good lawyer.'

Not me, Declan realized. *She's talking to the black guy.*

It took Declan a few seconds more to recall where he had seen the black before.

So her lawyer's jogging with her?

Now the whole task of execution became problematic. Sure he could kill them both. The Irish nationalist movement had killed innocent people before, with bombs as well as guns. *In war*, he told himself, *there are no innocent bystanders, only the indifferent and the wilfully ignorant*. But deliberately shooting a bystander so that he couldn't testify was upping the ante. It would seem like a cowardly act, not like the act of a soldier. A soldier is ready to sacrifice himself as well as other people, like the hunger strikers who had starved themselves to death when they were denied the status of political prisoner in British prisons. To kill to protect his identity would not arouse much sympathy in the United States. The fact that the lawyer was a black would also count against them in the eyes of American liberals. It wouldn't be politically correct.

Declan despised American liberals and the concept of political correctness. But sometimes they were both useful. Like horse manure. He put the gun back in its shoulder holster, inside his jogging suit.

*   *   *

Rick was working up a heavy sweat now. It was an unfamiliar feeling, using muscles in his calves and thighs that he had almost forgotten existed. He had never been one for exercise, or even late-night dancing. His right arm was the only part of his anatomy that really knew what hard work was, and even then, a pen or telephone receiver was the heaviest object it got to work out with. So now he found himself stretching his endurance to the limit just to keep up with Justine, while she ran ahead of him effortlessly. He regretted having allowed himself to degenerate into so much of a couch potato. It was not as if exercise would have taken that much time out of his studies. *She* managed well enough.

There was a cramp in his stomach and a burning sensation in his chest. If he were running away from some life-threatening danger he would probably have found the strength to keep going. But there was no such danger. If anything it was pleasure rather than pain that kept him going. And the sight of Justine was at the centre of that pleasure.

His eyes, which had been focused initially on Justine's straight, broad back, had now dropped to the curve of her buttocks. He felt the first sensation of a hardening between his legs and looked away. In his loose sweat pants it might not show, but he didn't want such thoughts to undermine his ability to do his job. Getting involved with a client was the biggest no-no in the book.

Keep it strictly professional, he told himself. *Easier said than done*, his libido answered.

'Justine,' he gasped.

'What?' she asked, flicking her head round to see how far behind he had fallen.

'Can we stop now . . . I'm kind of . . . exhausted . . .'

'All right, Woody Allen,' she said with comforting sarcasm as she slowed to a halt. 'Mama's gonna take you home.'

'Your place or mine?' he asked, as he covered the distance between them in five fatigue-laden steps.

He noticed the hard, angry glance given her by the tough-looking man who jogged past her, but didn't understand it. As Rick caught up with her she held out her hands to him, helping him steady himself. He fell against her breasts all the same.

It was ten minutes later when they arrived back at Justine's duplex.

'This is some place you've got here,' said Rick as he looked around the spacious lounge in awe. He had just stepped across the threshold and was now turning around slowly, taking it all in. The room had bronzed mirror panelling on the walls, creating the illusion of even greater space, and floor-to-ceiling windows giving a breathtaking view of the city.

It had been Rick's idea that they jog together. He had erroneously assumed that the stamina that sustained him during his research all-nighters would give him what he needed to burn shoe rubber. It had taken him less than two minutes of moderately paced running to discover that he was wrong.

But jogging had not been his objective in any case, not as an end in itself. It was Justine he was after. He wanted to unravel the Gordian knot and solve the enigma. Most importantly he wanted to win her trust and get her to let him help her. He knew that he could help her, if only she would give him that chance.

'Look, why don't you take a shower while I rustle up some breakfast?' asked Justine, walking towards the kitchen.

'I've got a better idea,' said Rick, following her. 'Why don't *you* take a shower while *I* prepare breakfast.'

She turned to face him at the entrance to the kitchen.

'What's this? A man who thinks he can cook?'

'I'm something of a gourmet,' he said in a crude imitation of a French accent.

'You think you can find your way around my kitchen?' she asked, blocking his entry with her arm, the hand resting on the door post.

'I grew up in Harlem,' he said, slipping under her arm into the kitchen. 'I'm very self-reliant.'

'Quoth Shirley Temple.'

'*She* never grew up in Harlem,' he said mockingly.

Minutes later Justine was in the shower, the stinging jets of warm water cascading down on to her body, producing a kind of pleasant tingling sensation in the aftermath of the outdoor cold as the perspiration that had been trapped beneath the track suit was finally washed away.

It was a strange feeling, having someone else in the apartment again. Since her mother's death it had been a place of solitary confinement, a place in which to dwell on the past, to meditate on unjust suffering and misery. She never liked to think of the world as a place of suffering. Her sense of life railed against it. But in the year since her mother's death, this apartment had become a place of bitter memories.

Now for the first time she was with someone whom she could at least like if not love. Someone intelligent and kind to whom she could talk . . . and listen. A *friend* was the word that summed it up, a friend like the one she had lost when her mother died.

She let the water run on long after it had done its work, welcoming the feeling of being engulfed in warmth. She could quite happily have stayed under the warm torrent of water for ever. Only there was Rick, the human figure in the kitchen who held the other thing that she most wanted: human companionship.

She emerged from the bathroom in a medium-length yellow towelling bathrobe with a matching towel around her head. The smell that hit her was of frying and grilling. When she entered the kitchen she was rubbing the towel against her head, energetically drying her hair. But Parker barely looked up from his unconsummated culinary efforts. When she stood close he noticed only the ivory calves of her legs.

'So let's see if Escoffier lives up to the test,' she said, pulling a chair up to the kitchen table.

He brought the last of the food to the table and they started eating a hearty breakfast of poached eggs on golden brown toast, potato pancakes and grilled kippers. There were pots of tea and coffee on the table as well as fresh orange juice.

'Where did you learn all this?' asked Justine.

'While I was studying I used to work in restaurants: busboy, waiter, short-order cook. Your name it, I did it.'

'Well, you certainly do it well,' Justine said, as she took a bite of one of the hot potato pancakes.

'When you're number two you try harder,' replied Parker, smiling.

'With food like this you shouldn't be number two.'

'Thanks. I'm just waiting for you to compliment me on my legal skills.'

He said it with a smile, but it killed the conversation. Somehow the trial and the histrionics of the courtroom seemed so far removed from this quiet Saturday morning that the mere mention of the proceedings brought them back to an unpleasant reality and shattered their idyllic calm.

After breakfast Justine cleared away the dishes and put them in the dishwasher while Rick took his turn in the shower. While the machine went into action she wandered into the library. She hadn't entered the room since her mother died. It held too many memories, far more than her mother's bedroom. It was the room where she and her mother sat in silence, each studying, both secure in each other's presence.

It was panelled in rosewood and lined from floor to ceiling with books, many of them leather-bound. Justine remembered that she had been struck by that feeling of comforting warmth in the judge's chambers. Now she understood why. The chambers were in some ways a replica of this library. It was a feeling of homecoming, of returning to the security of the womb, of rediscovering the lost innocence of childhood.

Her life since childhood had been like a slow descent from the summit of a great mountain, periodically resting on the ledges on the way down. The ledges were stable, but had always felt precarious, and each one was lower than the one before. Her earliest memory had been of her father coming home from the hospital. Her mother had told her to be nice to him because he was very unhappy. She had tried to be nice to him, but he always got angry whenever she made a noise. Noises, it seemed, were the thing that made him most unhappy. But for all the fear she had felt in the face of his raging temper, when he died she had felt it as a great loss. She gained a feeling of stability for a while, in adolescence, as she and her mother leaned on each other for support. But then came the final blow when her mother was struck by cancer.

A long, tortuous descent from the summit of a mountain. Cut and grazed by the jaggedly protruding rocks, finding brief respite on the ledges of transient stability before the next stage

of the descent. She had never really wanted to reach the foot
of the mountain. She had always hoped that she could climb
back up to the top. No one ever told her that once you leave
the summit you can never go back up. And if they had told
her she wouldn't have believed them.

Through the open door of the library she could hear Rick
leaving the bathroom. He had used the same bathroom
she had, the one in the master bedroom. Now he was in
the bedroom . . . her mother's bedroom. She couldn't just
throw him out. But she felt too possessive about the room
to leave him there alone. She eased the door ajar and spoke
quickly.

'Are you decent?'

'Define decent,' he chuckled.

'Typical lawyer,' she said, marching in with mock defiance.

He was wearing nothing but a towel around his waist.

'So what shall we do today?' he asked, teasingly.

'Nothing.'

'Nothing?' he asked quizzically.

'It's Saturday,' she said coolly. 'My day of rest.'

'You don't look Jewish,' he mocked.

'You don't look black,' she replied.

'Touché.'

She walked up to him slowly.

'So, like . . . what did you have in mind?'

She had slid her arms around his neck and interlocked her
fingers. Her forearms rested on his shoulders. She was still
wearing the bathrobe, but in his mind's eye he could see
beneath it.

'I thought maybe we could . . . go over your . . . defence.'

He was trying to hold back. The whole thing was just so
unexpected. So unprofessional. But he could feel his arms
sliding round her waist, as if pulled there by a force that
existed outside of his own volition.

'Maybe I'll just . . .'

Her lips were moving towards his.

'. . . throw myself on the mercy of the court.'

Their lips met in a violent kiss. Their tongues touched and
their embrace tightened.

Rick's hands rose up under her robe, exploring her silky

thighs, caressing her buttocks. She freed a hand to loosen the knot of his towel. He heaved a deep breath and the towel fell to the ground. He tugged on the cord of the robe and untied the knot. As Justine's hands encircled him once again he pushed back the folds of towelling and reached out to cup one of her breasts in his hand, caressing it gently. Again their lips and tongues met and their heavy breathing intensified.

Rick's hands now encircled her waist and gripped behind her back, this time inside the robe. As he smothered her face and breasts with kisses she disengaged her hands and wriggled and writhed to ease the robe off her arms. When it reached her wrists she slipped her hands out of the sleeves and the robe slid to the floor.

He released her for a moment and they stood there facing each other, smiling, she tauntingly, he eagerly.

Whenever you're ready, her arrogant face seemed to challenge him.

He pushed her gently back on to the bed and climbed on top of her, their hands meeting palm against palm, their fingers interlocking as he pinioned her to the bed like a helpless yet willing prisoner. He entered her with a gentle thrust and she bit her lip as she suppressed a gasp at the back of her throat. He worked slowly at first, building up the pace in tune with the encouragement of Justine's gasping breath.

They disengaged their fingers, and Justine's nails bit hard into Rick's back. He raised himself on his hands, entering her more deeply now as her breathing grew ever more frantic. She arched her back and seemed to emit a wild cry as she crossed another frontier. He raised himself again with another thrust, deeper and harder than the last. She slid her legs out from under him to encompass his torso with her firm thighs. Her feet crossed over and interlocked behind his back, trapping him in a scissor lock as tight as that of any wrestler.

They were now almost gasping for breath as the pace of their efforts accelerated from the intense to the frantic. When it reached fever pitch their bodies shook with a violent explosion in simultaneous rapture.

25

'Why did you join the Irish National Liberation Army?'

A shimmering glow emanated from the swimming pool. It was lit from below the waterline by shielded lights at the side, and every time the water stirred in the evening breeze a glimmer of light rose from the rippling surface.

'Do you know anything about the history of Ireland?'

'A bit. Not much.'

She had been reluctant to give away how much she knew about the subject, from many hours of reading and research, because she didn't want their meeting to appear to have been anything other than a result of chance. A middle-brow college co-ed out on the make, looking for an easy pick-up, not an intelligent young woman with an interest in Murphy's past or the political history of Ireland.

'Well, I won't bore you with a long history lesson. I'll tell you about my personal tragedy. The Unionists were going to hold one of their Orange Order marches through a nationalist area. The British government decided to stop them for once, because of the sensitivity of the times. They ordered the Royal Ulster Constabulary to halt the march. That led to a stand-off for a few days between the marchers and the RUC.'

'And what happened?'

'The RUC were ordered to disperse the Orangemen. But they refused. That's because they supported them. So the British government just gave in and allowed the march to go ahead.'

'And she was killed by the Orangemen?'

'No, what happened was the RUC ordered a curfew of the Catholics who lived in the street in order to let the Unionists march there. My wife was returning home from doing the shopping. She tried to get into the street. The RUC blocked her way. She tried to force her way through, insisting that she lived there and they couldn't stop her walking to her own home in her own street. At the same time some of the other residents of the street tried to come out of their homes. The RUC turned violent and started lashing out and hitting people blindly, just like the B-Specials did a generation before. Then the nationalists started throwing petrol bombs and the next thing you know the RUC were using their guns. And my wife . . .' There was a break in his voice '. . . was killed in the crossfire.'

She was afraid that he was going to cry. This was the one aspect of what she was doing that filled her with dread. She couldn't stand the thought of seeing a man cry. She had seen it before, with her own father. And it had been the harbinger of so much misery to come. It had been the warning sign that preceded his suicide and the subsequent years of toil and struggle for her mother.

She could stand the thought of a *woman* crying. She had seen her mother cry many times when her father was alive. One of the things that she regretted most, after the death of her father, was that her mother had *lost* the ability to cry. But she couldn't stand tears in a man. She knew that men were weak. But their weakness was supposed to manifest itself in anger, not in tears. A man's anger was the storm that she could ride out with the iron will that her mother had instilled in her. But a man's tears were pathetic, like a rock crumbling to dust in one's hands, instead of erupting with fire like a volcano.

The thought of seeing a man cry made her sick.

But Murphy held out. There were no tears. He probably

thought it unmanly to cry. But there *was* anger. It was his anger that had driven him to terrorism, the anger that had smothered his sense of morality and rendered him numb to the pain of others. It was the anger that enabled him to restrain his tears. It was that restraint which cost him his life. In that instant, he remained a man whom Justine could hate, and not a miserable specimen from whom she would have felt the urge to turn away in disgust.

'I'm sorry,' she said quietly, as Murphy lowered his head. 'That's what happens when the killing starts. It doesn't stop.'

'What are you talking about?' he asked, looking up.

'In your efforts to drive the British out by force, aren't you just killing more innocent people?'

'You can hardly call the British innocent.'

'They didn't *all* kill your wife.'

'My wife's death was just the symptom,' he snarled angrily. 'It made me realize what I should have realized before. It's the British presence that's the disease. Think of our actions like radical surgery, to get rid of a cancerous growth.'

He didn't realize why, of all the things he had said, this was the first to make her wince. She reached over to the bottle and filled their glasses with tequila.

'But they could say exactly the same thing. The relatives of an IRA bombing victim could claim that all the Roman Catholics are in some way to blame for the crime and kill a Catholic in revenge.'

He was drinking tequila as she spoke, fascinated and somewhat puzzled by the sudden display of intellectual confidence from someone who only a few minutes earlier had been a spoilt middle-class, middle-brow college girl whose knowledge of current affairs appeared to go no deeper than the 'we must stop oppressing the Third World and plundering the environment' variety. And more than puzzled by it, he was a little afraid of it, as if her knowledge of the matters of which he spoke was in some way a threat to him, as if he were deprived of the advantage of superior knowledge. She continued speaking.

'Then your side can say that all Protestants are to blame,' she continued, 'and kill one of theirs. And there you have it, sectarian killings.'

'You *do* know something about Ireland,' he said, surprised.
'Like I said, I know a bit.'

'Then you must know that the British aren't innocent. They've been occupying my country for the last four hundred years. Over the years the people of Ireland have been forced to pay a tithe to the Church of England and forbidden to teach the Roman Catholic faith to our children. Our lands were confiscated, and Scots Presbyterians were settled in our midst. We were effectively disenfranchised by gerrymandered constituencies in Stormont until it was belatedly closed down by the British. We were discriminated against in housing, education and employment and then assaulted by militant Unionists when we tried to demonstrate peacefully against that oppression in the 1960s.'

'I'm not saying that you haven't been the victims of injustice. The blacks of America have also been the victims of injustice. They were kidnapped in Africa and brought over as slaves. They were flogged and chained. When the constitution gave them the vote, they were disenfranchised by literacy tests. Even in the 1960s they were forcibly segregated in the south. We had state-imposed apartheid *in the United States*. And if the legacy of British oppression of the Irish survives, so do the lingering after-effects of white oppression of the blacks! But does that mean that the remedy is to give them a separate black state? Does that mean that it's all right for a black to kill a policeman? Or plant a bomb in Nieman Marcus or Bloomingdales?'

'Perhaps they'd get some justice if they did.'

'You think you can correct every injustice of the past by turning the clock back to a halcyon age that never really existed? Sometimes you have to turn the clock forward to a new solution.'

'That's just another way of saying we should give up the struggle.'

'Well, someone has to make the first gesture.'

'But why should it be *us*? Why don't *they* make the first sacrifice?'

'Because *you're* the ones who are crying out for justice. Doesn't it occur to you that peace is sometimes of higher value than where the government sits? At least you have access to the democratic system. And don't say you haven't used it when it suited you.'

Murphy recoiled physically at her outburst. But he leaned forward aggressively when he replied.

'You say that we're fighting the battles of the past. But they're still killing Nationalists. Maybe not on the scale that they did in the days of the Black and Tans, but they're still doing it. They're still beating up Catholic teenagers and harassing us, and brushing off our legitimate complaints with a wall of silence or a conspiracy of lies. Have you ever wondered why so many moderate Catholics become extremists? It's because of the way they're treated by the British. It's impossible to remain a moderate in Northern Ireland.'

'And what about the way you treat your own? Punishment beatings with sticks and spikes for alleged petty crimes. No trial, no right of appeal. Gangs of masked men acting as judge, jury and executioner?'

'If we can't rely on the occupation government to maintain justice, then we have to do it for ourselves. That's the way it's always been: *Sinn Fein*, ourselves alone.'

She flicked back a wisp of hair, mockingly, and looked straight at him.

'Doesn't it occur to you that the dispute renews itself with each new person it touches? You proved that by your own example.'

'I know,' he said bitterly, with another break in his voice. 'But don't you see it's too late for me. I've already been touched by it. And the scars will never go away.'

His head dropped, and again he appeared to be damming up a floodtide of tears.

'And what about those people you killed, the child and that Indian doctor. Will the scars of *their* loved ones ever go away?'

'We weren't *trying* to kill them. They were just casualties of war. It's tragic, and I regret it, but it happens all the time.'

'And you expect their families and friends to be more forgiving than you were?'

Murphy was drinking again, trying to find his courage at the bottom of a glass.

'I can't ask them for forgiveness. I can only hope that they see that the cause of their pain came long before me. And that cause won't go away until the old wrongs are righted.'

'And then we end up back where we started,' said Justine. 'Trying to right the wrongs of the past.'

'Not all the wrongs,' replied Murphy, almost pleading for understanding. 'Just the major ones.'

'You mean just the ones that bother *you*.'

'*No!* I mean the ones that have left a lasting impact.'

'They've *all* left a lasting impact . . . on someone . . . somewhere. Only that's the part you never see.'

'I mean the kind of injustices that we *can* put right,' said Murphy, the whining tone persisting as the drink took hold. 'At least let's put those wrongs to right. Then we can start to rebuild and restore.'

'And if in the process you commit a few wrongs that *can't* be righted?' asked Justine. 'If, in the pursuit of your justice, you inflict a few scars that *never* heal, like the ones you bear from the death of your wife? What do you say to the victims of *those* injustices? What do you say to their families and friends?'

'I can't comfort them in their grief, any more than I was comforted. I can only say that those who died were casualties of war.'

Justine picked up her glass and started walking towards the pool.

'Does that include your wife?'

Murphy swivelled round to face her.

'Yes, it includes her. She was a casualty of war just like the others before and since. But it was her death that made me realize there *was* a war, and that I couldn't escape from it. I didn't take up arms to avenge my wife. I took up arms to end the war that claimed her.'

Justine turned and met his eyes coldly.

'You could end the war with surrender just as easily as with victory.'

'But why should we? You say peace is of value in its own right. But when I lost my wife I lost the one woman who represented all that peace has to offer: the peace of a happy home.'

'And you think that because you lost that gift, you had the right to take it from others?'

'What right do *you* have to condemn me? By your own admission you know very little about Irish history. So what right do you have to pass judgment?'

Justine turned and flung her glass away. It shattered on the ceramic tiles by the pool.

'Do you know about the life histories of your victims?' she asked coldly. 'Do you know anything about *their* causes before you blast them off the face of the earth? You say that I have no right to condemn you unless I know about the history of *your* country and *your* cause. Yet you feel free to terminate human lives without knowing anything about *their* personal histories!'

Murphy recoiled. He had expected a retreat, not a counter-attack.

'Do you think I'm proud of what I did?' he whined, begging for her understanding. 'Do you think I'm happy that two innocent people were killed because of me? Do you think I don't go to sleep every night regretting that I took the life of an innocent child and a man who helped others?'

They stood there facing each other in anger and bitterness. She feared that she had let it go too far too soon. Without the poison it wouldn't work. She spread her hands in a gesture of helplessness and sighed, as if surrendering to the force of his self-righteous indignation. Murphy's heavy breathing grew lighter, as the anger of the moment passed.

26

'And how long have you been an evidence technician at the 46th Precinct?'

'For seven years.'

There were empty seats in the spectators' section for the first time since the trial began, as if public interest were waning. The proceedings were degenerating into their technical phase and could no longer compete with the glamour soaps to hold the public's attention. Also, the trial didn't seem to have a sex angle as some of the tabloids had promised. The public felt cheated and were voting with their feet for a more interesting form of entertainment. If the DA couldn't satisfy them with a saga of lust and greed, then they'd go elsewhere for their titillation.

'Now could you tell us about the events of the night of September the seventh.'

'Detective Reilly gave me a plastic bag containing a bottle which from the label appeared to be a bottle of tequila. It was closed by a cork but the bottle was not full.'

The witness was Lieutenant Hogarth. Unlike many other evidence technicians he was college-educated and but for

departmental politics would have headed the police laboratory in his precinct.

'Do you see Detective Reilly in this courtroom?'

He looked around quickly.

'Yes, sir, I do.'

'Could you point him out, please.'

'That man over there,' he said, pointing to Reilly.

'Let the record show that the witness pointed to Detective
Reilly.'

'So ordered,' said the judge.

All of this was to establish chain of custody over the bottle
until the point when fingerprints were identified.

Hogarth was twenty-eight years old, and presented a very
conservative image with the judge and jury alike. He wore
a dark suit like a man accustomed to such attire and with
his neatly trimmed hair he looked the perfect picture of the
upcoming young corporate executive, a yuppie who played
by the establishment's rules.

'What did you do with the bottle when you received it?'

'I removed it from the bag on to a clean Formica surface and
spray-dusted it with fine black powder for fingerprints. I then
photographed the fingerprints with a fingerprint camera.'

'Who developed the pictures?'

'I developed them myself in the darkroom adjacent to the
fingerprint lab.'

'Is this the usual procedure?'

'No, it's more usual to delegate. But on the graveyard shift
we have only a skeleton staff, if you'll excuse the pun, so I
did it myself.'

Rick Parker made a note and thrust it in front of Justine.
It read: 'Staff shortages, most violent crimes committed at
night, work pressure, could have caused mistake, let me
cross-examine.' Justine shoved it away contemptuously.

'Did you compare the fingerprints in question with the
defendant's fingerprints?'

'I did.'

'With what result?'

'I found four total and seven partial prints belonging to
the defendant.'

'Did you compare the fingerprints on the bottle with

those taken from the body of the deceased Sean Murphy as contained in the autopsy file?'

'I did.'

'With what result?'

'I found seven total and nine partial prints belonging to him.'

'Were there any other prints?'

'Yes, I identified others belonging to Dr Stern and Professor Ostrovsky.'

'Could you tell *when* the defendant's prints were made in relation to the others?'

'There is no direct procedure for determining this but some of the partial prints of the defendant were partly covered by those of Sean Murphy and Dr Stern and some of those of Sean Murphy were partly covered by those of Dr Stern and Professor Ostrovsky.'

He then used an overhead projector with enlarged slides and pointer to show this in more detail.

'Did any of the prints of the defendant cover any of the others?'

'No.'

'And is it possible to draw any heuristical conclusions from these facts?'

'It is highly probable that the defendant touched the bottle before Sean Murphy, the deceased, and that Dr Stern and Professor Ostrovsky handled the bottle after Murphy.'

'Thank you, Lieutenant Hogarth.' He turned to Justine. 'Your witness.'

'No questions.'

27

He had taken the dishes into the kitchen. For Justine the chance had finally come. She pulled the vial out of her pocket, snapped off the lid and poured the contents into the bottle. The 'contents' was enough pyrethrum to kill a horse, pyrethrum that she had so painstakingly extracted from the cans of insecticide. She could hear the clattering of dishes in the kitchen and knew that he was still there, but she quickly returned the vial to her pocket. She then threw away the contents of her new glass in a flowerpot, refilled the glass from the bottle and positioned both the bottle and her glass next to her place, well out of Murphy's immediate reach.

Murphy emerged from the kitchen carrying a tray on which stood a steaming china pot and two small cups. A minute later, they were facing each other across the table, drinking coffee.

'So how did the British get on to you, then?' asked Justine.

'They caught the man who sold me the explosives, and the bastard snitched. They almost arrested me. But I gave them the slip and signed up on a US-bound freighter in Liverpool.'

'But how did you manage to stay here?'

'I married an American girl.'

Justine looked around, as if expecting to see his wife there.

'Oh, don't worry, it didn't last. But it gave me a residence permit. I think she was more attracted to my money than to me, after I sold my book.'

The book in question was *To Fight for Freedom*, written by Sean Murphy 'with Martin Resnick'. It was a quintessentially American product, the outgrowth of a collaboration between a ghost writer and a 'celebrity'. And Murphy was as much a celebrity as any anorexic model strutting down the catwalk, or any hooker caught giving a blowjob to an actor.

Some British politicians called his book 'The memoirs of a terrorist'. Murphy had supplied the raw material, along with rambling political polemics which meant little to the American reader. The 'co-writer' had toned it down and turned it into a fast-paced piece of popular journalism.

'But if the British know you're here,' asked Justine, 'can't they apply for your extradition?'

'They tried,' Murphy replied with a smile. 'The judge threw the case out.'

'On what grounds?'

Murphy smiled again.

'Well, you can't be extradited from America to stand trial for a political crime, just like you can't be tried for one *here*. I had one hell of a smart lawyer: Robert Hershkowitz. He's one of those high-profile lawyers who specialize in representing celebrities. He argued that my crime was political and the judge accepted his argument.'

She had heard it all before and it didn't impress her. But by now the game of cat-and-mouse had run its course. The ballet had completed its set-piece choreography and now nothing remained of this verbal *pas de deux* but the grand finale. She sat forward, smelling blood, her heart racing and her nerves tingling. It had been so easy to plan and prepare, driven as she was by anger. But it was not so easy now. Not so easy to take a human life, however miserable and unworthy that life may be. This was the time for the final confrontation, and if she didn't do it now, she wouldn't do it at all.

'Blowing up a radiologist and a three-year-old child?'

He went white and the hairs on the back of his neck stood up.

'You know about the child?'

He remembered that he hadn't mentioned the child's age.

'I know about the whole thing. Why do you think I let you pick me up in that nightclub?'

'Let me . . . pick you up?' he stuttered, a tinge of confusion creeping into his tone.

She nodded silently, her implacable eyes confirming her power and her silence underscoring her victory.

'It was a set-up?' he asked, grasping the beginnings of her plan, but uncertain of where it was leading.

'Right from the word go.'

'But why?' he asked, the confusion ceding ground to a faint trace of fear.

'You forfeited the right to ask that question when you murdered two people whom you didn't even know.'

Her eyes remained unyielding, holding him a prisoner on the spot where he sat.

'Knowing them has nothing to do with it. It wasn't a *personal* matter. Can't you understand that? It was *political*.'

'Murdering a child is political?' she asked incredulously, the resurgence of anger sweeping over her like a tidal wave, even though she had heard this kind of nonsense a hundred times before.

'Well, it was politically motivated.'

'On that basis,' she said, 'I could kill an American soldier to protest American policy in Central America and claim immunity from prosecution.'

'Sounds like you're preaching again,' he said sneeringly, trying to play down his confusion.

She reached out towards the bottle and fingered it delicately, almost lovingly.

'It's funny how something so small can stop something so big.'

'What are you talking about?' asked Murphy, confused, and sensing a growing hint of menace in her voice.

She picked up the bottle with a malicious gleam in her eyes.

'Oh, all sorts of things,' said Justine. 'A clever woman against a strong man, for instance. Or a petty cause against a grand ideal. Or a five-pound bomb against a hundred-and-fifty-pound man. Or a loud-mouthed mediocrity against an unsung genius.'

'Talk sense, will you!' he shouted, the fear giving way to anger.

She put the bottle down with a thud and looked Murphy in the eyes, revealing for the first time the intense, implacable anger that she had been concealing for too long.

'You want me to spell it out to you? I'm talking about people who think their causes count for more than their neighbours' lives! It's time someone stood up to you.'

She held up her full glass in front of Murphy, reminding him by the gesture that she had drunk none of the tequila that she had brought along.

'Well, now we're fighting back.'

She picked up the bottle with her free hand and inverted it, along with the glass, emptying the glass and pouring away most of the contents of the bottle. Then she slammed them both down. Still uncertain of the implications of her outburst and thoroughly confused by her latest action, he picked up the bottle and looked at it while she walked back into the house.

Suddenly the recollection of the last hour all flooded back to him, and he realized what had subconsciously been puzzling him about her behaviour. *She had brought the tequila to drink with the meal. But she hadn't drunk any herself.*

He heard the sound of the front door slamming, and all of a sudden the realization hit him with full force.

'The bitch poisoned me!' he wailed.

How much time? he asked himself. *How much fucking time?*

He knew that she had deliberately given the game away and let him know that she had poisoned him. It was part of her cruel and vicious game. She wanted him to know that she was killing him. She hadn't said why. He wondered if she was a Unionist . . . or a British intelligence agent. But he knew that it wasn't just anger in the end. She was a cold, hard, calculating bitch who had set him up from the beginning. If she had made it clear to him at this stage that she had poisoned him then it must already be too late, he reasoned.

Still, where there's life there's hope.

Grabbing the bottle from the table and screwing the lid back on, he rushed out to his car. With any luck he could still make it to the hospital. He wasn't feeling any effects yet, apart from sweating hands and a pounding heart and a dry throat.

I'm going to get over this, he told himself. *And then I'm going to get the bitch.*

28

After the salvaging of his case with the smooth passage of Lieutenant Hogarth's testimony, Abrams was beginning to think that it would be plain sailing from now. He had established most of what Justine had done, and barring a sympathy verdict for her, was more or less sure of getting a conviction. The sympathy vote would probably merely mean a lower category of homicide. He could live with second-degree manslaughter, although he thought that technically at least first-degree manslaughter was indicated.

The trouble was that the faces of the jury told another story. They didn't look convinced. He had learned through many years of courtroom experience to read the jurors' eyes. Sometimes you could tell things from their postures or the way they held their heads, especially if they were bored or afraid to look at the defendant. But it was the eyes which really betrayed their feelings. The jurors were looking at Justine with quiet respect, more so than before her cross-examination of Ostrovsky. One juror in particular was looking at her with obvious approval bordering on admiration. He decided to have the jurors checked out again. Especially as the one who seemed so captivated by Justine was a hard-headed businessman who had voted for guilty on his previous jury service and looked until now as if he had all the emotions of an eighteen-wheel truck.

Abrams's next witness was a girl who worked as a sales assistant at the drug-store. She had taken a lot of effort to track down. The police had checked around the drug-stores near where Justine lived in ever-increasing circles until they got a positive answer. But Abrams was convinced that it was worth it. He didn't want any loose ends in his case. One minor humiliation had been quite enough. He had to hammer his facts home so forcefully that there could be no doubt as to those facts. If Justine wanted to play silly games, quibbling about the elements of homicide, he would give her a lesson in the law when the time came . . . as long the jury didn't go overboard with their misguided sympathy.

Someone must have given the girl instructions in how to dress so as to tantalize the male members of the jury, thought Abrams.

On second thoughts, he realized that these days most girls didn't *need* any instruction.

She was wearing a print-patterned, knotted shirt and a pair of tight-fitting jeans that could easily have been mistaken for her skin, but for the fact that they were a faded blue. Her hair was cut in an early Beatles/Donny Osmond fringe, the bangs covering her forehead and almost reaching her eyes. But if the haircut was boyish, the bare midriff, the well-rounded buttocks and the long eyelashes all emphasized her femininity in much the same way as Justine's eyes underscored hers.

'Have you ever seen the defendant before?' asked Abrams after dispensing quickly with the preliminaries.

'Yes.'

'When?'

'On September the sixth of last year,' said the girl.

'How can you be sure of the date so accurately?'

If Parker had been conducting the defence Abrams wouldn't have asked this question. He would have waited for Parker to try to discredit the witness and given him the opportunity to fall flat on his face. But with Justine in control and offering no more than a minimalistic defence there was no certainty that she would rise to the bait. It was important that the jury should know that the witness wasn't exaggerating or worming her way into a case for the sake of enjoying a moment of glory, as some eagerly volunteering witnesses had done at the expense of the credibility of the DA's office.

'It was the week after I came back from my vacation in Florida.'

'And where did you see the defendant?'

'At the drug-store where I work.'

'What was she doing there?'

'She bought insecticide.'

'How come you remember so accurately?'

'Well she bought about three ca . . . I mean she bought three cans.'

Abrams almost winced at the slip, the small slip that would not have undermined the credibility of this lovely well-rehearsed witness, even if emphasized under cross-examination, had she not emphasized it herself by correcting it. Now it was as if she were wearing a sign that read 'I've been coached'.

'Do you remember what brand it was?'

'Yes. DeBug.'

'Your Honour, I've brought along a can of DeBug and I would like to introduce it as an exhibit although it has no direct connection with the defendant, for the purpose of showing that it contains pyrethrum.'

Justine was on her feet.

'Your Honour, I'm ready to stipulate that DeBug contains pyrethrum,' she said quietly.

'Let the record so indicate,' said the judge as Justine sat down.

'That's really all I have to ask the witness,' said Abrams, returning to his seat.

'No questions,' said Justine, without waiting to be asked by the judge.

The next witness was the man who had sold Justine the tequila. It was the same story. He identified Justine and Justine let him pass without cross-examination. But there was much inter-departmental politics at work behind the scenes in this little episode. The Police Department had been resentful about having to do so much legwork to tie up the loose ends.

They thought their resources could be better spent elsewhere, solving other crimes and patrolling the streets, rather than chasing up the minor details of an open-and-shut case in which the main facts weren't even disputed. They would have preferred to have settled this case quietly with a plea bargain. Even the Irish-American contingent in the police bore no malice towards Justine, and thought that a lesser charge and a non-custodial sentence were justified. But once the press picked up on the word 'vigilante' the Irish-American community at large had come into open conflict with the Jews – the Irish-Americans clamouring for a conviction, the Jews speaking out for Justine. With demonstrations and counter-demonstrations outside the DA's office, they knew that they had to follow through on this one and let the law take its course.

'Have you ever seen the defendant before?'

'Yes.'

'Where?'

'In my liquor store.'

'Did she buy anything?'

'Yes.'

'What?'

'A bottle of tequila.'

'Thank you. Your witness, Miss Levy.'

'No questions.'

And that's that, Abrams told himself. *Maybe not one more nail in Justine Levy's coffin, but certainly one more bar on her cell.*

29

The pieces of the snub-nosed revolver lay before Declan, spread out on the folded white sheet like pieces of a jigsaw puzzle. It had taken him only four minutes to strip the gun down, and he could probably have done it blindfold. Such was the thoroughness of his training. But putting the pieces back together again would be harder. Not that he lacked the skill or training to reassemble the gun, or even the manual dexterity. But when it came to reassembling he would be operating under different conditions. Instead of the flat, rigid surface of a solid oak kitchen table, he'd be sitting on a toilet in the court building with the sheet spread across his knees, struggling to keep it steady, while others would probably be queuing up outside waiting to use the toilet. But he knew that he would be able to assemble it if he had to, even under those conditions.

The question was how many of the pieces could he smuggle in past the metal detectors at the courthouse in one trip? The metal detectors were calibrated to respond only to large metal objects, so as not to be set off by keys or belt buckles. So merely carrying the parts of the gun in different pockets would enable him to get several parts through and thus reduce the number of trips he'd have to make. But on the other hand, if one of the pieces *did* set off the metal detectors, he'd have a lot of explaining to do. And if any lynx-eyed bailiff then noticed the shape of the objects and figured out what they were, he'd be back in jail on another gun charge, this time more serious than mere possession.

The kid who sold him the gun for two hundred dollars assured him that it had no history. But he couldn't be sure of that, and if it turned out the gun had been used for another crime he'd be forced to rely on the dubious alibi of having entered the country under a false name for a purpose that he could hardly disclose without digging a deeper pit for himself. So from every point of view he had to get the parts of the gun into the courthouse undetected. There was no margin for error.

Then an idea hit him. The parts of the gun could be glued on to the chain of his key-ring with superglue and then removed with glue solvent. If they stopped and searched him, it would look like an ordinary key-ring with an unusual metal tag. Swiftly recognizing the potential of this scheme, he went out and bought a kit containing a tube of cyanoacrylate and its solvent.

Half an hour later he arrived at the Hall of Justice and walked through the metal detector at the entrance with the barrel of the gun attached to his key-ring. It set off no alarm and as he reached the elevator he knew that he was home and dry. If he could get the gun barrel through the metal detector he would have no trouble with the other parts.

He made his way to the toilet on the same level as Courtroom Number 1, where the Levy trial was taking place. Once inside the toilet booth, he quickly closed the toilet cover and sat down. In short order he proceeded to dissolve the glue holding the gun barrel on to the key-chain and placed the barrel in a plastic bag that he had brought with him. Next, he hastily unscrewed and removed the top of the toilet tank.

The plastic bag had a wide piece of tape stuck to it, extending from the top. The extension was folded over double and stuck to itself, except for a cardboard tab. He pulled at the tab, opened out the extension of the tape and stuck it to the inside top of the toilet tank. He realized that the bag would dangle into the water and might be jerked loose by the emptying of the tank during a flush or the refilling thereafter. He regretted not having brought along a second piece of tape with which to stick the other end of the bag to the lid of the tank, thereby keeping it out of the water completely. But it was too late for that now. He'd just have to hope for the best. As long as water didn't permeate the plastic bag and rust the ferrous parts of the gun, he shouldn't have any problems. Now all he had to do was smuggle in the remaining parts over the next few days.

Declan felt a twinge of nervousness when he stepped out of the courthouse. It was not the prospect of killing that frightened him. He had killed before. Nor was it the fear of IRA retribution. After this he would probably disappear to South America with the money he had brought for operational expenses from the INLA's bank robbery-funded war chest. It would be too hot for him back in Ireland. When the heat died down he'd probably go back to the Republic. But it might be two years or more before he could go back to the North.

30

'My next witness,' said Daniel Abrams, 'is Nancy Cullen.'

As she walked into the courtroom she gave Justine a quick, nervous, apologetic glance and then she looked away. In Justine's eyes there was no sign of anger or resentment. Even the granite-like hardness that normally graced her face seemed to have mellowed as she watched Nancy walk nervously up to the witness stand and take the oath. It was almost as if Justine felt sorry for her.

But she was avoiding Justine's eyes.

She sat down after swearing the oath and the clerk withdrew. She met Parker's eyes briefly, and she seemed to be trying to say 'I'm sorry.'

But whatever she wanted to say was lost as Abrams rose and walked towards her.

'Miss Cullen, would you tell the jury about your relationship with the defendant.'

'We studied together . . .' There was hesitation in her voice. 'We're also . . . friends.'

Justine gave her an encouraging look.

'Would you tell us please about the events of September the fifth of last year?'

'Well, it was a pretty usual sort of day. I mean I studied as usual, so did Justine. I think it was surface anatomy in the morning—'

'Your Honour,' interrupted Abrams, 'this witness had to be subpoenaed. In view of this and in view of her friendship with the defendant, I ask the court's permission to treat her as hostile.'

'Any objection from the defence?'

'No, Your Honour,' said Justine. 'As long as he doesn't use it as a pretext to badger his own witness.' There was nothing else she could say. But she gave Nancy another encouraging look when Nancy appeared to take it badly.

'So ordered.'

'Miss Cullen,' Abrams continued, 'did you see Justine taking or removing anything from the premises of the medical school when she left that day?'

'Well, she had some books with her . . . and a notebook. I mean, yes, she took things with her . . . sure.'

'Anything else?'

'Like what?'

'Come on now, Miss Cullen, stop playing games!'

Now Justine was on her feet, and looking angry.

'Your Honour, for an experienced lawyer Mr Abrams has some very strange ideas about what it means to treat a witness as hostile. The fact the witness is hostile merely entitles the prosecutor to ask her leading questions. It doesn't entitle him to intimidate the witness.'

'Your Honour, the witness is a friend of the defendant and she was being particularly evasive—'

'Strike that,' said the judge. 'The jury will disregard the prosecutor's last remark.' He turned to Nancy. 'You must understand, Miss Cullen, that the prosecutor has the right to ask these questions and you are obliged to answer them fully and truthfully. Now, without putting any interpretation on your motives, you were forcing the prosecutor to go to unnecessarily great lengths to clarify his questions. In the end all the relevant evidence *will be heard.* It will save us all a lot of time if you would answer the questions without requiring the prosecutor to dot the I's and cross the T's.'

He turned to Abrams and nodded for him to continue.

'Well, Miss Cullen?'

'I saw her removing a Rotavapour and putting it into—'

'Just a moment, Miss Cullen. What exactly is a Rotavapour?'

'It's a piece of laboratory equipment.'

'What is it used for?'

'It's used to extract a substrate from a solution by means of a combination of creating a vacuum above the solution, immersing the flask with the solvent in a warm bath and agitating the flask containing the substrate in order to increase the surface-to-volume ratio of the solution.'

'And what does that mean in layman's terms?'

'I'm not good at putting things in layman's terms.'

'Could it be used to separate pyrethrum from insecticide?'

She sighed and hesitated. She looked over at Justine, again with that apologetic look. It was only when Justine gave her another encouraging nod that Nancy finally broke her silence.

'Yes.'

A gasp went through the courtroom. It was another of those quiet gasps that seemed to indicate a milestone in the People's case.

'No further questions.'

'No questions,' said Justine.

The judge looked over at the clock.

'As I see that the hour is drawing close for the lunchtime adjournment, I'll adjourn now. This court will reconvene at two thirty.'

31

When the court reconvened after lunch Abrams called his final witness: Sergeant Kent. He was the leader of the police team that had conducted the search of Justine's home. He wasn't altogether sure why he was being called considering that the search had failed to turn up anything of substance, or at least no poison substance.

But Abrams had chosen to call him and he must have had his reasons.

'Did you, on the morning of September the eighth, conduct a search of the home of the defendant, Justine Levy?'

'I did.'

'Did you have a search warrant?'

'Yes, sir, I did.'

Abrams produced a document.

'I am now going to show you an item marked exhibit seven for the State and ask you if you recognize it.'

He handed the search warrant over to the clerk of the court, who in turn handed it over to Sergeant Kent. The police officer perused it for a moment.

'Do you recognize it, Sergeant?' asked Abrams.

'Yes,' replied Kent.

'And did it authorize you to remove anything from the premises?'

Kent smiled as if he were about to burst out laughing at the inanity of it all. He pulled out a handkerchief and coughed into it in a not particularly successful attempt to conceal his amusement.

'Yes, sir, it did.'

'Could you tell the jury *what* it authorized you to remove?' asked Abrams, exasperated by Kent's minimalistic response to his question.

'I was authorized to remove any poisons or suspected poisons that might be on the premises.'

There was a hustle of movement at the back of the courtroom. One of the spectators who had been sitting in the front row had been very disconcerted to find that the place where he had been sitting was now occupied by a man who, to the best of his knowledge, had previously been sitting in the back row. But he didn't want to argue. The man looked angry, and not the sort to pick a fight with.

'Mr Abrams,' said the judge, 'I must confess that I'm somewhat confused. If this witness didn't find anything, then for what purpose has he been called?'

'I wish to show that while he was conducting the search he saw the Rotavapour in Miss Levy's home.'

Parker was looking furious. He started arguing quietly but frantically with Justine, begging, pleading, badgering her to let him speak. But in any case the judge was way ahead of him on this one.

'That seems rather like an attempt to introduce evidence not listed in the search warrant by the back door, doesn't it, Mr Abrams?'

'Well, Your Honour, what the witness saw is relevant and I know of no formal rule that excludes it.'

'This is a matter that should have been dealt with at the pre-trial hearing. But if it's going to be dealt with now then I'll have to hear it in the absence of the jury.'

The jurors were led out and Abrams was invited to speak.

'Your Honour,' the ADA explained, 'although this witness didn't find any poison he did see a device that could have been used to extract pyrethrum from insecticide. Furthermore we have already heard evidence that the defendant bought the insecticide. There is clear foundation for these questions and their relevance is obvious.'

'Miss Levy, do you have any arguments to present on this point?'

'No, Your Honour.'

Parker was on his feet.

'Your Honour, I know that a hybrid defence isn't normally allowed. But as the defendant has no preference one way or the other and as this is in the absence of the jury, I would like to ask the court's permission to present a legal counter-argument.'

'You didn't bother to ask the court's permission *last* time you assumed the role of acting defence counsel. However, as there was no objection then or now, and in the light of the sensitivity of the point at issue, that would be desirable.'

'Thank you, Your Honour. First of all I would concede that the Rotavapour may be relevant to this case. But it is clearly inadmissible because of the way in which the discovery came about. Evidence obtained in an illegal search is always inadmissible—'

'By that I presume you mean *physical* evidence, Mr Parker. If a person witnesses a crime with his own eyes while conducting an illegal search, the eyewitness testimony is not excluded simply because of the circumstances in which the witness came to see the events.'

'That may be, Your Honour, but in this case we're not talking about witnessing a crime. We're talking about a police officer who conducted a search for one piece of evidence, a legal search admittedly, testifying to the fact that he *saw* another piece of physical evidence *not* mentioned in the warrant. This was evidence which could not have been introduced in its physical form. That is, to use your own words, Your Honour, an attempt to smuggle illegal evidence into these proceedings through the back door.'

'Mr Abrams?' the judge invited.

'Well, Your Honour, I take the position that this witness's eyewitness testimony on this point is just as admissible as that of the previous witness. She saw the defendant taking the Rotavapour, this witness saw her with it at her home.

If the search had been illegal, then stand-by counsel for the defence *might* have a point. But as the search was legal he really has no valid point at all. The witness saw something relevant; the People have the right to present his eyewitness testimony. How much weight to attribute to it is up to the jury.'

'I am inclined to agree with you, Mr Abrams. However, this is a matter that should have been raised at the pre-trial. Nevertheless, I'll allow the testimony. Mr Clerk, bring the jury back.'

The door to the jury room was opened and the jurors were led back.

In the spectators' section another man had just arrived. It was Tom, the man whom the IRA had sent to stop Declan McNutt from killing Justine. He had stayed away from the court for a few days because his presence there had not been necessary. But he had decided to come in today to see how the trial was going. While killing Justine was out of the question, he wanted to see her convicted as much as everyone in Ireland who supported the nationalist cause. In fact, if she were branded a murderess it would certainly benefit their cause.

But when Tom entered the courtroom and took his place he got a shock that felt like a kick in the ribs. Sitting on the other side of the spectators' section was Declan McNutt. Incredibly, he had made bail.

32

'She poisoned me! The goddamn bitch poisoned me!'

Sean Murphy was muttering to himself as he swung the steering wheel first one way then the other, broadsiding other cars and scraping against them. He paid no heed to the scraping of metal on metal as he recklessly overtook one car after another.

Like so many of his brothers in the cause, it was an article of faith that he was ready to die for his country, and not just to kill for it. He had always thought that he belonged to that élite tiny minority like the hunger strikers who gave their lives by starving themselves to death in British prisons and in the process put the Republican cause on the international map through their courage and dedication.

But now, when the possibility loomed, real and recognizable, he was frightened by the vision of oblivion that he saw awaiting him. He had thought that he had escaped from all this turbulence and found peace at last. He had done his bit for the liberation of the Six Counties and now he wanted to be free, to enjoy the good life. He felt that he had earned the privilege. He had paid his dues to the cause by risking his liberty and even his life for it. Now he wanted to get away from the conflict in which he had received and inflicted so much pain and live out his remaining years in the country in which so many of his compatriots had found refuge.

Yet now he was set on a collision course with the grim reaper. He wouldn't even have the dignity of dying in the pursuit of his cause. He was the victim of a vengeful woman who didn't even understand the dispute.

Why me? he thought. *And why her? What did she have to do with it? What did she want from me? She didn't even know what the dispute was about. Why should she care about some Indian professor or someone else's child?*

Not all bullies are cowards. But a great many are. And there are as many forms of cowardice as there are of courage. Murphy had brushed with death many times before in the course of his INLA operations. But in the past, the danger had been camouflaged by the excitement of the mission and the smouldering remnants of anger that drove him to it. But here, for the first time, he was staring death in the face, without the usual distractions.

So now, when he found himself looking out at a nameless void and an eternity of oblivion, the fear welled up in the pit of his stomach and he realized how futile it had all been.

The hospital parking lot was reserved for hospital staff, with the area for ambulances round the back. But Murphy was so totally engulfed in fear that he didn't care. Nothing was going to stand in the way of his pursuit of survival now, just as he had let nothing stand in the way of his pursuit of the liberation of the Six Counties.

He drove straight into the parking lot, nearly hitting a doctor who was opening the door to his car. As Murphy's vehicle screeched to a halt by the hospital entrance he dived out and sprinted into the building.

'She poisoned me!' he said frantically to the girl at the reception desk. 'The slag poisoned me!'

People were staring at him openly and mothers were shielding their children from the angry intruder as if they sensed that this hysterical man was capable of violence.

'Your name, sir,' said the girl with deliberate calm.

'What the fuck does it matter?' he exploded. 'Didn't you hear what I just said?'

His face was white with fear. The girl, realizing that rules of procedure hadn't prepared her for this sort of situation, reached for the telephone.

'Dr Stern, please,' she said.

While she waited for Dr Stern to come to the phone, the receptionist felt a tinge of sympathy for Murphy as she saw the look of desperation in his eyes.

33

'Look, I need that reference!' said Parker belligerently.

'I'm sorry, young man. But that volume is in use by someone else.'

He was standing at the desk of a law library, facing the librarian, a stern-looking woman. She reminded him of one of his elementary schoolteachers, a formidable, elderly spinster, a sort of archetypal Miss Thistlebottom. He could almost hear her priggish voice correcting his English grammar.

'But this is an emergency!' he almost shouted.

'We can't just go up to someone who's looking at a law volume and take it away because someone else wants to look at it. You'll just have to wait until it's free.'

'But that could be hours!'

'That may be. But there's nothing I can do. And I would be grateful, young man, if you would refrain from shouting. This is a library.'

'All right, *I'll* do it. Just point out who's got it.'

'Don't be absurd,' said the librarian, stiffly. 'That sort of information cannot *possibly* be given out.'

'Look, I've got a client who's facing a murder rap . . .'

He trailed off, seeing a look in the librarian's eyes.

'Is this what you're looking for?' asked a familiar voice behind him.

He turned round to see Abrams standing there with a large volume.

'Is that . . .?'

'The Murphy extradition case,' Abrams confirmed.

Half an hour later the concrete grid of the Big Apple was spread out before them a hundred storeys below as they sat at a corner table of the restaurant at the World Trade Center.

'And you mean to say that some bastard of a judge wouldn't extradite Murphy because his crime was politically motivated?' asked Parker incredulously.

'That's what the man said,' replied Abrams, not entirely blasé, but tempered by bitter professional experience and numb to this kind of judicial perversity.

'Planting a bomb that killed two people, including a three-year-old child!'

'Judges are recruited from the legal profession. And we both know there are more than a few assholes in our mutual profession.'

Abrams's apparent agreement had a pacifying effect on Parker. As he sat in this luxurious restaurant, he looked out through the sheet of glass at the concrete network of roads and buildings of New York City. As the image before him changed continuously in a succession of undulating waves, he experienced a sensation that was almost like flying. But the thought of a three-year-old child lying torn and twisted in the debris and rubble of a man-made tragedy and a murderer walking away from a courtroom laughing at the system of justice that he had cheated was still playing on his mind.

'I wouldn't mind betting that the judge secretly sympathized with their cause.'

'You're right there, kid,' said Abrams. 'He even made a few anti-British remarks just to make sure everyone knew where he was coming from. He threw in a speech about Irish people who were accused of planting bombs and turned out to be innocent after spending years in prison, but when it came to the formal ruling, he covered his ass against an Appeal Court reversal by saying that it was because of the so-called political nature of the crime, not the weakness of the evidence.

It's not the first time this has happened. Can you imagine if it was the other way round? But that still doesn't justify what your client did.'

'Judging by the way she demolished Ostrovsky I'd say it's not too clear at this stage what she did do.'

Parker looked away from the window and polished off his Ogen melon filled with prawns.

'Tell me something, Rick. If you thought your client was ready to plea-bargain, would you advise her to make a deal?'

'Why? Are you offering one?'

'I'd be ready to give you negligent homicide and five years' probation.'

'You think the judge would go along with that?'

'Hal? Sure he would. I think he's quite taken by your client. At any rate he recognizes that she doesn't belong in prison. And I recognize it too. I don't know what drove her to do what she did. Maybe hearing those reports about a three-year-old child blown to pieces by a bomb made some sort of impression on her. She had a rough childhood with her father. Maybe it was because the other victim was a doctor. I've had people turning the case upside down and we still haven't come up with an answer to the question of motive. But whatever the reason, she isn't evil and she's not likely to do it again. She doesn't belong in prison. But she does need help, counselling.'

'So why aren't you offering to accept an insanity plea?'

'Then she'd have to be committed to a secure psychiatric institution for a fixed minimum period of one year. That's why I'm offering a nickel's probation on a Section 125.10.'

Parker hesitated for a few seconds, flipping through the pages of the New York Penal Code in his mind's eye as he considered the offer. If Justine pleaded guilty to criminally negligent homicide, the ADA would agree to five years' probation. But then he shook his head, remembering the critical flaw in the whole idea.

'She'd never go for it.'

'She could be looking at a lot longer.'

'You know juries better than she does. I know *her* better than you do. She'd rather die than compromise.'

'Work on her. The way things are going now she might have to serve hard time. Even if I can't make murder stick it's beginning to look like first-degree manslaughter.'

'I'll put it to her. But I don't hold out much hope.'

Parker lowered his head regretfully.

'Let's put the case on the side, Rick. Tell me something about yourself.'

'Like . . . what do you want to know?'

'Like, for instance, why did you decide to become a lawyer? And why legal aid?'

Parker swallowed the final mouthful of his hors d'oeuvre and put the silver cutlery down on the elegant bone china plate. He had been asked this question before, and it wasn't an easy one to answer. He could tell people why he wanted to become a lawyer easily enough. But the legal aid question was a tough one. He had a well-rehearsed answer. But the trouble was he didn't really believe it himself.

'I grew up in a typical black home in the urban ghetto. Lots of kids, lots of noise. No privacy or solitude. We took a lot of shit from both sides. We were more likely to be accused of a crime than middle-class kids and more likely to be the victim of one, only not many people know about that side of the coin.'

'And you saw a lot of injustice because you were black and poor and you decided to do something about it.'

'Not just because we were black and poor but also because we were ignorant. I mean, we had street smarts, but it took a long time to get them. You don't read about those things in books so you have to learn everything for yourself. We couldn't get taken for a ride by con men the way a white doctor might get suckered into a bum investment by a smart ass yuppie stockbroker. But when one of us got into trouble with the law, ignorance was usually our downfall. One of my brothers copped a plea for a crime he didn't do because he didn't think he could beat the rap and a shark hanging around the night court offered him an out. I was only eight at the time. It was round about then that I learned what they mean when they say knowledge is power.'

Abrams was smiling.

'You remind me a bit of myself when I was your age.'

'But you—'

'I don't mean I was poor,' the ADA explained. 'I grew up in a well-to-do Jewish household. But I was also a crusading young idealist out to change the world. I had that same spark of fire in my eyes.'

'What extinguished it?' asked Parker. There was no immediate reaction from Abrams. But Parker realized that he shouldn't have said it. Just because this man was on the other side was no reason to question his sincerity.

'I'm sorry,' he said, genuinely apologetic. 'I was out of line with that.'

'No, you're right,' said Abrams wearily. 'It *was* extinguished. Or maybe it burnt itself out. I used to tell myself that it was still alive. But now I think the only thing left is a few smouldering embers. The last faintly glowing traces of an enthusiasm that was once going to set the world on fire. Now I just keep plodding on, trying to do the right thing. But I don't kid myself that the forces of evil are going to fall before my ringing oratory. I guess it all started when I discovered that justice isn't so easy to identify, let alone achieve.'

'An elusive butterfly?' asked Parker, trying gingerly to figure out the right metaphor.

'More like a team of horses pulling in two directions. Procedural justice goes one way and substantive justice usually goes the other.'

'How do you mean?'

Abrams leaned back and inclined his head slightly.

'I had a case . . . oh, quite a while back. A *pro bono* case. An indigent client accused of a series of brutal rapes and one murder. The case against him was open and shut in terms of the facts. But the police had taken a few short cuts to get the evidence. There was a faulty warrant with the wrong address and instead of rushing back to get a new one they went ahead with the search and found the evidence.'

'You got the physical evidence thrown out at the pre-trial, presumably.'

'Exactly. I mean it was standard defence procedure, and the prosecutor was furious. But there was nothing he could do.'

'I bet he hated your guts after that,' said Parker, knowing the feeling.

'As a matter of fact he didn't. And he didn't blame the police either. He hated the Supreme Court judges who interpreted the Constitution in that asinine way. He knew that I only did what any lawyer would have done.'

'Still . . . he couldn't have been very happy.'

'Oh, he wasn't.' Abrams hesitated. 'But neither was I when I heard two days later that my client had raped and killed again. This time the police cornered him and shot him when he resisted arrest. At least that was *their* story. But it was too late to save the girl he murdered. So there I was, a smartass defence lawyer who had scored one more for my résumé. That's when I learned that prosecuting the guilty is every bit as idealistic as defending the innocent.'

'And that's when you threw in the towel and became a prosecutor?'

'I didn't throw in the towel,' Abrams corrected. 'I just changed corners.'

'How did you get on with your former opponent?'

'He's the one who held out the olive branch and invited me in. I was his protégé. I rose through the department with Jerry.'

'Jerry Wilkins? The DA?'

'That's the one,' said Abrams, with a smile.

34

White . . . the room was all white . . . the men and women gathered around him were all in white. White was the colour of good. Murphy's mind grappled with the situation, trying to figure out where he was. He remembered Justine, remembered her beautiful face turning to one of anger as she revealed to him what she had done. But now there was no sign of her. Now there was only peace and tranquillity.

He wondered about the figures in white, especially the beautiful woman in her early twenties attaching a bag to a pole beside the bed.

'Am I in heaven?' he asked.

'You're in a hospital,' said one of the men in white. 'I'm a doctor.'

For the first time since the death of his wife Murphy showed an emotion that was neither fear nor anger. It was sorrow . . . he felt himself crying.

'I feel worse now than I did before you gave me that injection. What was it?'

'It was the antidote to the poison you swallowed.'

'Then why isn't it working?' asked Murphy, the pain mounting.

'I . . . I don't know,' said the doctor.

He had been about to lie. But he realized that he couldn't carry it off.

'Is the priest here?'

'I'll just go and check.'

He moved a few feet away from the bed and sent one of the nurses to bring in the priest who was waiting outside.

In the moment of silence, Murphy started brooding again and reminded himself of what had brought him here, the poisoning by Justine, an act of revenge by someone who seemed to have no motive for vengeance.

'Have they arrested the bitch?'

'I don't know,' the doctor replied, embarrassed by the language of the pathetic specimen before him.

The nurse returned, leading the priest into the room. The priest began the last rites, inquiring if Murphy accepted that Jesus was the only begotten son of God who had died on the Cross and been resurrected that his sins might be forgiven. While Sean Murphy confessed his sins and prepared to meet his maker, Dr Stern signalled Professor Ostrovsky to join him in the far corner of the room. Ostrovsky had come rushing down when Stern called him. But Stern was still the physician in attendance.

'Do you have any idea why he isn't responding?' asked Stern nervously, already fearing a malpractice suit.

'I don't have a clue,' replied Ostrovsky, his mind going into overdrive in a desperate search for the solution to the riddle. 'We *must* have given the antidote in time. The pyrethrum hadn't even been absorbed into the bloodstream when we gave him the atropine.'

A stab of doubt hit Dr Stern. In fact, it wasn't so much doubt, as outright realization.

'Are you sure it was pyrethrum in the bottle?'

'I checked and double-checked.'

'What about the quantities?'

'The proportion matched both times. If he was right about how much he drank then we got the quantity right too.'

'Didn't you cross-check the amount he said he'd drunk against the amount that was actually missing from the bottle?'

'I thought you said he told you she poured the contents of the bottle away,' said Ostrovsky.

'Oh yes, that's right,' said Stern, remembering. He had been on the verge of trying to shift the blame to Ostrovsky, and they both knew it.

'At any rate I based my recommendation on what you told me he said,' the professor continued.

Stern was getting increasingly nervous.

'Maybe we should up the dosage. Maybe he drank more than he thought.'

'Not a good idea,' said Ostrovsky, casting a quick glance at the screen readout from the equipment monitoring the patient's vital signs. 'Specially in view of the readings we're getting.'

'What do you mean?' asked Stern, a tinge of terror creeping into his voice.

'Those are strange readings for pyrethrum poisoning,' said Ostrovsky. 'They look more like . . .'

He trailed off into silence, allowing the dreaded words to go unstated.

'*In nomine patris, et fili, et spiritus sancti . . .*' the priest was saying.

Dr Stern was pacing up and down helplessly, cursing the twist of fate that had put him on duty today, that had dropped this potential fireball in his lap. It wasn't the pain of watching a patient die that was tormenting, it was the thought that he might be in some way responsible, and worse still that others might discover this fact and use it against him, embarrassing him professionally and sending his malpractice liability insurance rates through the roof.

The equipment monitoring Murphy's vital signs gave off a long, continuous whine. Stern and Ostrovsky looked round to see the priest rising, his own work done, hopefully with more success than theirs.

35

The office was illuminated not by any lamps of its own, but by the myriad lights of New York City beyond the window, the static lights of the apartments and the moving lights of the cars as they swept along the roads, carrying people to their homes, their nightclubs and their nocturnal assignations. Abrams sat behind his desk, trying to put some semblance of order into his thoughts in the darkened room.

He had rested his case that afternoon. Tomorrow was Justine's turn ... unless she pulled another surprise and let Parker take over, which was not beyond her even at this stage. She seemed to make a speciality out of wrong-footing the opposition, and sometimes even her own stand-by counsel. Abrams liked Parker, especially after their lunchtime meeting, when he had made what Jerry would have called the psychological error of dropping his guard and gaining a glimpse of the human side of this opponent. Of course, Jerry regarded showing one's *own* human side as even more of a strategic error. But to Abrams it was the human side that was his *raison d'être* for being there, for doing the job that he did. As he had told Parker, it was the human factor that had brought him to the practice of law, that had caused him to switch from defence to prosecution, and that drove him on through hopeless cases when all seemed lost, fighting with as much tenacity as someone brought up in a quiet upper-middle class neighbourhood was capable of. He was glad that he had dropped his guard and opened up to Parker, if only because it had given him a clearer insight into himself. He had seen a lot of himself in Parker, perhaps even more than he had admitted over lunch. But for the time being at least they were adversaries. He couldn't escape that piece of logic that Jerry would have been only too quick to hammer home if he ever forgot it.

Papers and law books were liberally scattered across Abrams's desk. But he paid no attention to them. Nor even to the panoramic view of the city behind him. His eyes were focused inward, on to himself, as he tried to understand his feelings about the case, his feelings towards Justine, in fact, although he couldn't quite admit to himself that this was what it was all about.

He barely looked up when the door opened and the DA entered.

'Burning the midnight oil?' asked Jerry, looking over at the desk where Abrams sat.

'Racking my brain over a mystery inside a puzzle.'

'The Levy case?' asked the DA, doubtfully.

'The Levy case.'

'I thought it was open and shut,' said the DA, walking further into the room.

'I'm talking about the why and wherefore. You're only talking about *what*, and even *that's* not too clear any more.'

Jerry sat down on the corner of Abrams's desk.

'What's the problem?' asked the DA, more out of curiosity than sympathy.

'A vicious murderer cheats justice because of a judicial ruling that isn't even legally or constitutionally correct. So a girl with no previous record decides to take the law into her own hands. And now she finds herself looking at twenty to life for doing what the courts should've done.'

'I never thought I'd live to hear you defending a vigilante.'

'I'm not defending her. It's just that I'm not sure I can

defend the system either. How can I defend a system that punishes people for fighting back, but lets the hoods slip through the net?'

'You're not defending the system. You're prosecuting a defendant.'

'That's *working* the system.'

'Correction,' the DA shot back hard, 'that's *making* the system work. It's up to the defence to work the other side of the equation. Besides, you're talking in stale old redneck clichés. That's not like the Daniel Abrams I know, the Daniel Abrams who presented this case to the grand jury, the Daniel Abrams who once said that vigilante justice is a classic example of throwing out the baby with the bathwater.'

'That's when I was talking to a middle-class jury. They're not on the front line in the war that's raging out there. They're separated from the combat zone by a thick blue line, manning the trenches. And the same goes for us. We sit behind our mahogany desks and get all the facts in nicely sanitized form. We don't have to look down the barrel of a Saturday-night special like a cop on the street. We just read a report about it afterwards, a load of neatly typed words on clean white paper.'

'And how does the jury get the facts?' asked Jerry Wilkins. 'Words in a courtroom flowing from the lips of a well-rehearsed orator. Juries are drawn from the voting register, the half of the population who choose to participate in the political process, perhaps with a few more thrown in from the driver's licence records. They're as sheltered as we are.'

'Not this jury,' said Abrams. 'You should see the collection of down-to-earth hard-heads she's put together. Even the businessman on the jury. A self-made millionaire who worked his way up from the gutter. He's seen the sleazy side of town and he knows what it's like living on the battlefield. I'm not getting through to them . . . I can see it in their faces.'

'Maybe you're reading them wrong. If they're from the gutter you should appeal to sentiment. The rich bitch who killed a working man for revenge. The heartless vigilante—'

'Uh-uh, no way, Jerry!' Abrams interrupted, putting a hand on the desk for support as he rose abruptly. 'For all your blue-collar background that you like to brag about at election time you sit here so high on Olympus you're more out of touch than I am. The Liberal Hour has come and gone. And the plebs are the most conservative of the lot!'

'So play it the other way,' Jerry shot back. 'Give 'em the old law-and-order line.'

'You still don't see it do you?' asked Abrams, disillusioned by Jerry's lack of helpfulness. 'Your average Joe American is no more into law and order than he is social reform. What the people are crying out for is *justice*, and there's a growing perception that we're not delivering the goods.'

'Are you sure you're speaking for *them*, Dan?'

The words seemed to hit their target. A painful smile crossed Abrams's face and he fell silent. He went to the window and turned his back on the DA. For almost half a minute, he looked out at the lights of the city, a tableau of black velvet stretching as far as the eye could see, with a smattering of iridescent diamonds sprinkled liberally across it. He drew a warm touch of comfort from its lights.

'Maybe you're right. I guess I'm just projecting my own doubts. But it's not just moral doubt. I still don't see why an innocent girl from a good home, without a blemish on her record, should suddenly become a murderess, and what's the connection with Murphy?'

The DA rose and slid into a nearby armchair at right angles to the desk and the window.

'OK, try this for size. She was born in 1973. Her father was in the ROTC programme, and when Justine is two Daddy gets sent off to do his tour of duty in 'Nam as an "adviser", just in time for the fall of Saigon and the descent of the city into a fear-crazed hell-hole. All clear so far?'

'It's in the book.'

'He comes back battle-scarred and shell-shocked and is diagnosed as a schizophrenic. That's before they had sound-bite terms like post-traumatic stress disorder. The next seven years are hell, with her father's angry spells becoming more frequent and more violent. Her mother had postponed having more children before he was sent to Vietnam and now she decides that she can't afford to bring another child into this troubled environment. So

Justine is destined to grow up an only child. How am I doing so far?'

'A little speculative, but still on track,' said Abrams.

'OK. In that time her mother assumes the mantle of the strong figure, keeping her husband at bay and protecting the child. She wasn't born to wear the mantle but she grows into it. Finally the old man blows his brains out with his old service revolver and Justine enters the room just in time to see it.'

'I see you've read the report.'

'Now her mother no longer has to deal with the violent fits of a deranged husband, but she still has to deal with the big rough world outside, and even though he was just dead weight in his last seven years it's still harder without a man around, in some respects. Are you still with me?'

'Just about,' said Abrams, deprecatingly.

'Her mother doesn't remarry,' the DA continued. 'She's just got over the trauma of one man and she isn't about to go look for another. Also she's turned into quite a tough cookie and that probably intimidates most guys and keeps them at a distance.'

'Tempered by war, disciplined by a harsh and bitter peace . . .' Abrams's voice rang out in stinging mockery.

But the DA was past hearing. He was launched on a voyage of his own rhetoric – as he had so often been in his courtroom days.

'OK, you've got the picture. So now mother and daughter live for each other and fill each other's worlds. The daughter may even develop a bit of an Oedipus complex—'

The DA's legal skill had not suffered from his childhood poverty. But he lacked the broad, liberal, middle-class education that Abrams had received, and sometimes it showed.

'That's what sons have for their mothers.'

'Well, an Electra complex—'

'Daughters for their fathers.'

'All right, but whatever you call it maybe there was some sort of incestuous lesbian attraction—'

Abrams wheeled round abruptly.

'Now you're really going off on a flight of fancy.'

'All right, forget the dyke bit. But you know what I mean.'

'OK, let's say that they grew closer together so that the maternal–filial bond strengthened rather than weakened when the girl entered adolescence.'

'All right, let's say that.'

Abrams turned back to look out at the city. The DA continued.

'The girl learns, in that time, that she could always count on her mother to supply the strength and wisdom. Her mother became the pillar of support. Any complaints so far?'

'I'll take the Fifth,' said Abrams mockingly. 'Go on.'

'OK. Then the mother gets hit by the Big C and the girl sees her tower of strength beginning to crumble. Being a medical student she also knows there's precious little she can do about it. Now the roles are reversed. She has to become the strong figure to give what little encouragement and support she can to her ailing mother. Reasonable?'

'Plausible.'

'As her mother loses her grip on life, Justine gets tougher from within – tougher and more bitter about the injustice in the world. She develops a nameless, undefined anger. Finally her mother dies and the aloof, friendless Justine is left alone in a world in which her mother had once been her only companion.'

'OK, so she's bitter about the world. Why doesn't she just become a junkie? Or hit the bottle.'

'Or take up shoplifting,' the DA added.

'Exactly.'

'Wait a minute, I'm coming to that. This is where we get to the interesting part.'

Abrams made a gesture towards the ceiling as if to say 'Thank God'.

'While all this has been going on, she also hears about the professor and the child being murdered in England, and, worse than that, the murderer managed to get his tail over to this country and avoid extradition. *Now* she's ready to commit murder. Her sense of anger in the face of injustice has built up to breaking point and here she sees a murderer slipping off the hook on a very dubious legal technicality.'

'But why Murphy?' asked Abrams.

'Maybe because of the tear-jerking image of that three-year-old child blown to pieces by a terrorist's bomb. Maybe because the professor Murphy killed had given a course that she took and she happened to remember him. Maybe she and the professor even had an affair. Or maybe that's another flight of fancy. But the point is, whatever it was, that's the incident that finally set her off. Not the terrorism itself, but the abuse of law and the misinterpretation of the Constitution by the judge. The perversion of the course of justice and the denial of justice to the victim for political reasons. The same sort of thing that provoked such a public backlash against the exclusionary rule and all those other technicalities that defence lawyers loved using. Murphy's the one who just happened to cross her path when she finally got tired of being a passive spectator to the world's injustice. So even if she has no personal axe to grind she picks Murphy as a symbol of—'

'That's it!' yelled Abrams, spinning round.

The DA leaned forward, bewildered.

'What?'

'I've got it.'

Abrams rushed over to the door and grabbed his hat and coat.

'Got what?'

Abrams opened the door and turned.

'Half the answer.'

The ADA left the office, closing the door behind him.

'Half the answer?' said the DA to thin air.

36

The aftermath of the prosecution's case brought a new awareness of the trial to the general public. Interest in the case, which had been declining with the prosecution's later witnesses, was picking up again. Thus the courtroom was once again packed with spectators. Extra bailiffs had to be called in to prevent people without tickets from entering the courtroom. The press benches were full, while ordinary, curious members of the public flocked to the court building to hear Justine open her defence.

Many of the would-be spectators had to be turned away disappointed, but some of them hung around the building in the hope of hearing some flash of news that would satisfy their appetite. Many of them could have watched it at home on cable TV, but they wanted to be near the courtroom when it happened, in case any exciting news broke, like a change of plea or a sudden dismissal of the charges.

There was a strong Irish contingent, not all of them hostile to Justine, and many Jews. There were girls too. To some Justine was a role model to be glimpsed at, if only for a moment in the hope that some of the radiance would shine into their drab lives as receptionists and waitresses. To others she was a cold-blooded, scheming, heartless she-devil, a new incarnation of Lilith, one of those rare specimens of evil female who is deadlier than the male. This was the old polarized perception of women in the public eye. Whereas men who are accused of crime are 'permitted' by the public at large to belong almost anywhere on a wide moral spectrum, alleged murderesses, and often women in general, are neatly slotted into one of two categories: the virtuous victims and the most evil creatures who ever lived.

It was against this backdrop of polarized public opinion that Justine Levy faced the judge as he addressed her.

'Miss Levy, are you ready to proceed with your defence?'

'Yes, Your Honour,' said Justine, rising to her feet.

'Proceed,' said the judge perfunctorily, nodding in her direction.

'My first and only witness is myself,' said Justine, sending a shock wave through the courtroom.

It was as if the entire press section sucked in its collective breath. Justine's unusual qualities had already stood out, but most people were surprised at this development. Many defendants conduct their own defence for an unstated purpose to which they dare not admit: that of being able to influence the jury by their demeanour and put questions to prosecution witnesses without the risk of taking the witness stand and giving a particular account of events, thereby being exposed to the perils of cross-examination and a direct challenge to their version of events. Yet Justine was now submitting to this very risk, inviting the prosecution to challenge her testimony or find fault with her account of events. And now, for the first time, the public were about to hear that account. As far as the press and public were concerned, the drama had climbed a few rungs on the ladder of excitement.

Justine was led by a bailiff to the witness stand. When asked her religion by the clerk of the court she stated not 'Jewish' but 'atheist'. Thus it was not the oath but the affirmation that the clerk of the court recited to her and to which he asked for her response.

'Do you solemnly affirm that the evidence you shall give shall be the truth, the whole truth and nothing but the truth?'

'I do,' replied Justine, with the quiet firmness that had been her hallmark throughout this trial.

The clerk withdrew as Justine took the witness stand.

'State your name for the record,' said the judge.

'I am Justine Deborah Levy.'

The judge nodded gently to her and added quietly, 'Go ahead.'

'Members of the jury, I won't bore you by repeating the facts of the case. You all know by now that Sean Murphy died of the atropine that they gave him in the hospital as the antidote to pyrethrum poisoning, and not from pyrethrum itself. Just to clarify the issue, let me add that I hadn't given Murphy any pyrethrum. There was no pyrethrum in the tequila that he drank.'

A gasp went through the courtroom. Declan leaned forward angrily. On the other side of the same row of spectators' seats, Thomas leaned forward too, as if poised to restrain him. In practice it would be very hard for him to do so. There were several other spectators in between them, and even if Declan rose, Thomas couldn't be sure of getting a clear shot. He doubted that Declan was going to make his move now, or even that he was able to make it. He couldn't possibly have got his gun into the courtroom or even into the building. The security was far too good. Of course, Tom himself had beaten the security with his polymer composite pistol. But then the IRA had access to the larger terrorist network comprised of such diverse groups as Hamas, the German Red Army Faction, the Italian Red Brigades and the French Direct Action, as well as neo-Nazi groups who were only too happy to work with the Left on the grounds that national socialism and international socialism were not really so different as to require a complete separation of interests, when all too often their anti-individual causes overlapped.

It was unlikely, thought Tom, that Declan or any of his INLA co-conspirators would have access to such sophisticated weapons as polymer pistols which could not be detected by metal detectors. The question was when and where was Declan planning to make his move? If Justine was acquitted, it would be no problem. He could shoot her in the street or even go to her home and shoot her there. But all the evidence suggested that she would be convicted, especially now that she had effectively admitted to the crime. If she was convicted, bail would be revoked and she would be taken into immediate custody. How could he hope to get her when she was in custody? He had to have a contingency plan and it must involve making his move in court.

Tom couldn't figure out what Declan was planning, but he resolved to sit closer to him from now on, and preferably in the row behind him, even if it meant paying money to the person who occupied that seat now. In fact both Declan and Tom had paid more than a thousand dollars to buy their tickets on the black market from ticket touts. The touts had effectively offered money to people who weren't interested in the trial to persuade them to enter the lottery for the tickets with the promise that those who won tickets would be offered even more money to part with them. It was ironic that a criminal trial should have given rise to such corruption on the very doorstep of the Hall of Justice, and typical of New York City that nothing was done about it.

Several yards away, Abrams was smiling to himself. He had been right. He knew it for sure now. His belated theory was about to be vindicated. He had figured out her motive yesterday, after his talk with Jerry. Now, in a few minutes at most, the jury would hear what he already knew. The realization that he had solved this part of the mystery filled him with pride. Parker noticed the prosecutor's reaction, and looked tense.

'I put the pyrethrum into the bottle after Murphy had drunk from it, in order to make him think that he had been poisoned, knowing that when the contents were analysed the doctors would also assume that he'd been poisoned with pyrethrum and give him atropine which would kill him.'

She paused to let the full meaning of her words sink in. She had now told them that she had set out to cause Murphy to die and had effectively done so. Many legal scholars would have said that, in the formal sense of the law, the prosecution's case had now been made and that any defence other than diminished capacity or insanity was no longer possible. But Justine hadn't finished yet.

'The question you're probably asking yourselves is *why*. Some of you may know that Murphy was wanted by the British police for planting a bomb in a shopping centre in Britain. He killed two people: a three-year-old child and a professor of radiology.

'The British police arrested one of Murphy's accomplices shortly after the incident. But Murphy got away and slipped out of Britain to the United States.

'The British government applied for his extradition pursuant to the same extradition treaty under which two British women were recently extradited to this country to face trial for murder, based almost entirely on the testimony of alleged co-conspirators. In spite of the weak evidence against them to begin with and the unlikelihood of a fair trial, they were sent here by the British and convicted. The British government made no effort to hide behind technical formalities, but simply handed them over to trial before a judicial system that is no better than theirs, and in some cases worse.

'But when the British applied for Sean Murphy's extradition, expecting reciprocity and the same measure of cooperation that they had given us, and with a much stronger case to begin with, a judge here refused to extradite him, ruling that because Murphy had acted in the pursuit of a *political* cause, he was wanted, in effect, for a *political* offence. That wasn't the first time this sort of thing has happened. In other cases, IRA terrorists have not been extradited from the US for killing British soldiers. This, in a country in which Lynette Fromme and Sarah Jane More were imprisoned for trying to kill president Gerald Ford for political reasons! Apparently, murdering a private in the British army is a *political* crime for which one can't be extradited from the US or prosecuted within it. But trying to assassinate the Commander-in-Chief of the United States armed forces is a conventional crime for which one can be prosecuted in the normal way.

'But with the refusal to extradite a man who murdered a doctor and a toddler, American justice sank to an all-time low. I wonder if that judge would apply the same logic to the Weathermen of the sixties or the Symbionese Liberation

Army of the seventies. I wonder what that judge would think if someone were to kill an American *judge* in the pursuit of a political cause.'

Her anger was showing now. She had wanted to keep it hidden and present nothing but the raw facts. However, it wasn't easy. The rage against injustice and hypocrisy that had prompted her to act as she did in the first place, was now erupting to the surface like a volcano and pouring down on all around her like a torrent of molten lava. They could either be swept away or immersed in it. But there was no way they were going to get away from it, just as there was no way for Justine to contain it.

'Whatever that corrupt judge's morally depraved position may have been,' Justine continued, 'Murphy's was equally perverted. He believed that he had the right to take the life of a fellow human being who had done no wrong, in the pursuit of his *cause*. As if a political cause is an all-embracing excuse for any human action. Well, if there's one thing worse than a thug it's a sanctimonious thug. They think that they are the only people with causes.

'But you see Professor Shankar also had a cause. His cause was saving lives. Like so many other unknown and forgotten people, he was one of the unsung heroes, one of the victims of terrorism. Whenever a terrorist commits a crime the press dig up every trivial fact they can find about the perpetrator. But they forget the victims. They never take the trouble to find out who they were or what they did or stood for, and they soon fade from human memory. It was these unsung heroes who had to be avenged.

'But the question you're probably asking is why did I pick Murphy?'

She paused and took a deep breath.

'Shortly before I killed Murphy, my mother died of breast cancer that metastasized before it was detected. As I watched her wasting away, knowing what fate had in store for her, it occurred to me that Professor Shankar could perhaps have saved her – her and hundreds of others. These were the *invisible* victims of Sean Murphy's terrorism.'

Tears were now streaming down her cheeks. But her voice didn't break or falter.

'And if you think that vigilante justice usurps the role of the courts, then ask yourselves which is worse, for a citizen to *appropriate* the function of the courts or for the courts to *abandon* the responsibility which was theirs. And if you think that what I did was a threat to law and order, then consider the fact that a judge, who was sworn to uphold the law, refused to extradite a man against whom there was a prima facie case of murder . . . and ask yourselves if there was any law left to uphold.'

She wiped the tears from her cheeks. A stunned silence settled over the courtroom. Abrams nodded slowly, his suspicions confirmed.

Again Declan leaned forward. But this time Tom remained stationary. He knew that it was just plain interest, no more than that, which prompted Declan's movement. He clearly wasn't ready to act just yet.

'Cross-examine, Mr Abrams?' asked the judge.

Abrams rose, looking confident but unsmiling.

'Miss Levy, there's just one point I'd like to clear up. Why did you kill Murphy in the way that you did?'

'The way that I did?' repeated Justine, confused.

'Yes. Was it because you thought that by not touching him physically you could beat the rap?'

'Not at all. I admit that I acted with malice aforethought – if you consider a desire for justice to be malicious.'

'And with prior intent?'

'Yes.'

'Then I return to my original question. Why did you kill him in that way? Why not simply poison him? Or shoot him?'

She paused for a moment, looking puzzled.

'Murphy was a man of muscle. He lived by the code of brute force. His was the philosophy of the thug. That was the code I wanted to refute. My code is the code of the mind, the philosophy of reason and logic. When I was growing up, my heroes weren't cowboys or detectives or soldiers or singers or actors or athletes. My heroes were scientists and businessmen.

'Murphy believed, like Mao Tse-Tung before him, that

political power comes from the barrel of a gun. I believe that political revolution is the end result of a long process starting in the ivory tower of the philosophy departments of the academies, working its way down through the print media and then the broadcast media until it reaches the minds of the masses.

'Murphy believed that whatever your philosophy the gun is the final argument. That was what I had to disprove. I had to show him that the mind alone was supreme – him and all of the men of violence. I had to show them that the human mind, the distilled, undiluted essence of human intellect, is invincible. That's why I had to kill him without a gun, without poison, without a weapon of any kind. I had to kill him with my mind.'

Abrams nodded his head slowly and wearily, as if complete understanding had finally dawned on him for the first time. After a few seconds he slumped into his seat.

'You may step down,' the judge told Justine.

She stepped down and returned to her place, but remained standing.

'The defence rests.'

Pandemonium broke out in the courtroom. The judge rapped with his gavel to restore order. After almost half a minute some semblance of quiet returned to the courtroom.

'Mr Abrams, will you be ready to begin your closing argument by Monday morning?'

'Yes, Your Honour.'

'Court is adjourned until ten o'clock Monday morning.'

There was a stampede of journalists towards the exits.

37

Parker was sitting alone at the same corner table at the same deli where he and Justine had had their first real conversation. He sat facing the wall with his back to the other patrons, as if he were trying to shut out the world and not share his standards or values with the rest of humanity. He knew that there was a bitter look on his face, and he didn't want to share his bitterness with others, nor accept the casual abandon with which they continued their lives oblivious to the suffering of someone who had suffered too much already and was now destined to be penalized for fighting back.

He was finishing off his cheeseburger when a shadow cut across the table, disturbing his fragile peace and denying him the escape from the world that he had sought. At first he thought that it was just another customer, looking for a free table. But he could tell from the stationary image, from the shape of the shadow, from its resolute lack of motion, that it could only belong to one person: the only person who had the right to be there, or perhaps the person who had the *least* right.

He looked round to see Justine standing there looking both implacable and sympathetic, as only she could.

'Is this place taken?' she asked.

He didn't reply. She sat down.

All through the trial it had been possible, as far as he knew, that she could have been innocent. Now he knew that she was guilty. She had let him down by being guilty, and betraying his trust in her innocence. She had let him down by confessing and by not giving him a chance to convince the jury of her innocence. She had let him down by embarking upon a suicidal course that would put her behind bars for many years to come and destroy any prospect of the two of them spending their lives together.

She had let him down.

And yet he couldn't escape the feeling that he should have seen it coming all the way, should have seen it looming on the horizon, both the truth and the way it would play out in court. In retrospect it all seemed obvious. All the facts were there. He just hadn't seen them. Just as Abrams hadn't. Just as the press hadn't.

Perhaps that was why Justine had to tell them. Perhaps therefore she was right all along to conduct her own defence and he had been wrong. As she alone had known the truth, it followed that only she could have revealed it to others. Just as she had revealed to others the deficiencies in the legal system and the erosion of the integrity of judges, by her brazen act of taking the law into her own hands.

'You look glum,' she said, picking up a French fry from his plate. There were plenty of French fries left. He always left them until last, telling himself that he wasn't going to eat all of them. It was all part of his diet, which was always due to start tomorrow.

'You could at least have let me make a fight of it.'

She spoke softly.

'You know, I've been thinking a lot about you, Rick. From some of the things you whispered to me in court about objections and points of law and all that, I get the impression that you're a good lawyer.'

He said nothing, not knowing if this was going to be a put-down or a pep talk.

'And you graduated first from your class at Harvard?'

He nodded, forced to give some sign of confirmation by Justine's silence and inquisitive look.

'So why are you working as an underpaid lackey at the legal aid office?'

He was jarred by this question. It was something he had often been asked by other lawyers. But never by a client. Most of his clients assumed that he was just a not-too-skilful young lawyer at the beginning of his career, taking whatever jobs he could get. And most of his clients were pathetic low lifes who were grateful to have a lawyer at all.

'Why should you ask me that?' he replied defensively, knowing by now that with Justine no question was ever just casual small talk. She was economical with her words and every statement or question had a purpose.

'Just answer,' she said with quiet firmness.

He hesitated, searching the back of his mind not so much for the answer as for the best way to express it. He knew the answer by instinct, by feeling. But he had never really put it into words, and he suspected that the reason for this was that it wouldn't stand up to scrutiny, especially his own.

'Would you believe because of dedication?' he asked tentatively.

'Then why should you want to stop me offering the only defence I've wanted to offer, that is, the truth?'

Now he found himself searching his soul for the *real* answer, the one he had buried at the back of his consciousness. When it came to him, he realized how much of his professional life had been a lie. He knew now how Abrams must have felt when he had watched one of his clients walk only to see him commit a violent crime again. The ADA had been right when he had suggested that they were kindred spirits despite their different backgrounds. They were both ambitious men who had hidden behind a wall of bogus ideals. And now it was time for Rick Parker to bear his soul to a passer-by who had thrown a spotlight on it.

'Do you really want to know? I'm not as dedicated as I liked to kid myself. Dedication was just my excuse. I really wanted to be a big-time, hot-shot defence lawyer. When I was growing up in Harlem I used to dream about being another Clarence Darrow. I used to imagine myself carrying on in the footsteps of Earl Rogers and Sam Liebowitz. But it wasn't the rights of the defendant I was after, it was the glory, and the money.'

'I thought there wasn't so much money in criminal law.'

'Not in the practice of criminal itself. But if you get a high-profile case that hijacks the media and you win it, or even if you lose it, you can write a book about it afterwards, or have a ghost writer do it. Then you can write a fiction book with a legal background. Then you can sell the movie rights. Then before you know it you're churning out a whole string of books and selling the movie rights and doing the lecture circuit and appearing on the talk shows and living in a fifty-room mansion or duplex penthouse and maybe even going into politics.'

'But with your qualifications you could have landed a job with a top law firm and made the same progress that way. You could have had the pick of the law firms from coast to coast.'

'And done what? Sat at the back of a team of lawyers three tables deep, looking up precedents while some big-shot wearing the old school tie stood out at the front taking the credit? Worked my way up through a long apprenticeship while being put on show as silent proof of ethnic equality?

'This was supposed to have been my short cut: take a low-paying job with the legal aid office, plea-bargain for the muggers and rapists while waiting for a case like this to come along – a high-publicity case with at least *some* chance of winning. The idea was that I'd milk the case for all it was worth, then cash in on the publicity to open my own office and watch the clients come pouring in, along with their money.'

'Why are you telling me this?'

'You asked me.'

'You didn't have to admit it. You could have just brushed me off, the way I've been brushing you off since you came on board.'

She had said it without a trace of guilt, but without malice either.

'Because I've discovered that I've been lying to myself about other things too.'

'Like what?' asked Justine, gently.

'Like my *ability*,' he said weakly. 'I've had my nose rubbed in the fact that I'm not as good as I thought I was. I know all the legal technicalities all right, but I lack courtroom experience. If I'd been defending you I would have hurt your case. I saw how you let the evidence build up against you unchallenged, and I thought it was suicide. But when I think of it I realize that one way or another the evidence would have come out anyway. By letting it come out without objection and sometimes with obvious cooperation, you took the sting out of it and debunked it.'

'That's not what I was trying to do. I just wanted the jury to know the facts . . . and the reasons behind them. That was all I ever wanted out of this trial.'

'You know it's not too late for an insanity defence,' he said, perking up. 'After what you said in court . . .'

Justine was shaking her head slowly but firmly and he saw that it was hopeless, saw also that it was wrong.

'I guess you're right. It's a *good* defence, but it isn't *your* defence.'

She looked at her watch.

'We've got another five minutes,' she said.

38

Daniel Abrams stood facing the jury, looking as implacable as ever, as he addressed them at the close of the People of the State of New York versus Justine Levy.

'Members of the jury, you have heard both from the evidence which I have presented, and from the defendant's own lips, that the defendant wilfully and deliberately embarked upon a course of action which had as its consequence the death of Sean Murphy.'

He began walking towards the jury, as if closing in on them as his arguments closed in on the truth.

'That Sean Murphy was or may have been a murderer is irrelevant. That the actions of the defendant might not have led to the death of the deceased if others had acted differently is irrelevant. Those others, the staff at the hospital, acted reasonably, given that they genuinely thought that Sean Murphy had been poisoned with pyrethrum. This belief was *wilfully and deliberately* propagated and fostered by the defendant as part of a *premeditated* plan to cause Sean Murphy's death.'

In the spectators' section, Declan McNutt sat forward keenly. He realized now that there was going to be no acquittal. There couldn't possibly be. She had admitted to the crime. Of course, she could still quibble over the fact that the method she used was indirect, but the fact remained that she had killed him and she had done so with premeditation and, more importantly, that she had admitted to it. It was all over, bar the shouting, and the only thing the jury would have to decide was whether she was guilty of murder or manslaughter or one of those other offences that American law seemed to create to deal with all manner of fine distinctions.

But whatever the verdict, she would not be walking out of the courtroom a free woman, that was certain. She would be taken into immediate custody. He knew that much about the American legal system. So the hit would have to be made here today, or not at all. And it had to be done when there was already confusion in the courtroom.

Declan continued to watch every move very carefully. But he was no longer listening to Abrams's words. He was looking at the jurors, studying the impact of the lawyer's oratory upon them.

In the seat directly behind Declan, Thomas noticed Declan's slight movement, the body language that spoke of arousal of interest as the INLA assassin listened to the prosecutor's words. But unlike Declan he heard something in those words which suggested a different interpretation of the situation. He heard an element of uncertainty in that voice, or even a faint trace of indifference. Was it doubt as to the verdict? Or ambivalence as to how the cause of justice would be better served? The almost perfunctory tone of the prosecutor suggested the latter, a hint of doubt as to the morality of his case. Unless it was just a kind of professional cynicism, as if the practice of law were no different from the random roll of the dice in an Atlantic City casino, or the planting of a bomb in a shopping centre in England.

'The defendant, Justine Levy, clearly knew that the remnants of poison in the bottle would be detected by the doctors,' Abrams continued. 'She has admitted this herself.'

He was now standing at one end of the jury box, leaning on

the rail, alternating his attention between the jury and Justine, trying to get them to look at her and see her as an embittered murderess rather than some sort of lofty idealist.

'But doctors do not just stand around idly and do nothing when they know or have reason to believe that a man has been poisoned; they render assistance and give treatment. The defendant, as an intelligent woman, let alone a medical student, must have known this. The antidote for pyrethrum poisoning is atropine, and the defendant as a medical student must have known this, and indeed she admitted as much. But atropine is poison and when administered in sufficient quantity can kill a man. The defendant, again, as a medical student *must have known this*. And in case there was any doubt on the subject, the defendant, again, has confirmed this herself in her own testimony.'

He paused to let the facts as summarized thus far sink in. Now he drew back slightly to look at all the jurors together. Now came the next phase in his carefully structured closing statement. It was the phase in which, having displayed the strands of his case one by one to the jury, he quickly wove those strands together in a finished tapestry. This was a technique he had learned from Jerry, the technique of moving from the particular to the general. It was like the method of all good novelists: present the specific factors that add up to a particular conclusion and then add them up into a final sum, instead of presenting a conclusion divorced from the facts on which it is based.

All too many lawyers instead use the technique of good journalism: present the conclusion in the first sentence and then cite the facts on which that conclusion is based. This is fine for an *opening* statement, where the lawyers summarize what they *intend* to prove. But it is wholly inappropriate for the closing, where the lawyers draw the strands of their case together. The underlying logic behind this technique is that different jurors will attribute different weight to different pieces of evidence and it is therefore wrong to close the case on any one piece of factual evidence. Rather, the last thing the jury should hear should be the *logical conclusion*: the sum of all the parts they have heard and seen before.

'If we take all this together we get a picture of the defendant deliberately *and with prior intent* implementing a carefully worked-out and meticulous plan to cause Sean Murphy to die of atropine poisoning, and in case there was any doubt, the defendant confirmed this version of the facts *in her own testimony*. Indeed, I could not have put the case against Justine Levy better than she has put it herself when she took the stand and testified freely and of her own volition. Whatever *moral* significance Miss Levy may attach to her actions, you must understand that from the point of view of the law she is guilty of murder, and *premeditated* murder at that.'

He paused again. He knew that he had presented all the elements of his case and summed them up as eloquently as anyone could. But his long years of courtroom practice had taught him to read faces and he could tell that some of the jurors were not convinced. Just as the act of covering one's mouth with one's hand during cross-examination tended to indicate lying, or a desire not to speak about the current subject, so a slight opening of a juror's mouth during a closing statement indicated that the juror was unconvinced, revealed a desire to blurt out 'You're wrong' to the lawyer who was currently speaking. Abrams noticed that several of the jurors had open mouths, and it filled him with dread. This was not going to be the open-and-shut case that he had anticipated after Justine's obligingly straightforward confession from the witness stand. There were going to be several hours if not days of tough, angry arguing and negotiating in the jury room over the degree of homicide.

He decided to depart from his prepared structure and branch off into some philosophizing. He knew that any remaining doubts that the jury had must be about the *morality* of his case, not the *legality*. It was *these* doubts that he had to address, these fears that he had to allay. The trouble was, these were the very doubts that had plagued him throughout the case, and more so after Justine's testimony. He realized that in challenging the jurors' moral uncertainties on this score he was going to have to confront his own. And this was a prospect that at some deep-seated level of his consciousness he had always been dreading.

He took a step back towards the jury rail.

'In a way, members of the jury, the defendant is condemned

not only by her testimony but also by her rhetoric. She has told you that Sean Murphy should not have been allowed to escape justice and that a murderer should be punished even if he committed murder for the sake of a cause. Yet she then proceeds to invoke her *own* cause as her excuse for murdering Murphy.

'I'm sure she genuinely believed that Murphy deserved to die. Perhaps some of you do too. I try not to think in these terms myself, but I certainly wouldn't have lost any sleep if he'd slipped on a banana peel or fallen down a flight of stairs, as long as no one was in the way at the time.'

He was greeted by the nervous laughter that he had hoped for. He was carrying them with him.

'But private thought is one thing, unlawful *action* is quite another. *Who* decided that Sean Murphy should die? Was it God? A judge? A jury? A legal tribunal?'

He slammed his fist down on the jury rail.

'No!' he thundered. 'It was decided by a young lady who set herself up as judge, jury and executioner! A young lady who decided, in fact, to play God!'

Some of the jurors winced at this and he wondered if he had gone too far. But he realized that it was the sheer force and power of his voice which had frightened them, not his words.

'If you let her get away with what she did then you'll be doing the very thing that she claims to object to: *subverting justice for the sake of someone else's cause.*'

He started walking away from the jury, towards Justine.

'Whatever sympathy you feel towards the defendant, and I too feel some sympathy for her, you must not let it blind you to your duty as jurors and to the public trust that has been placed in you. The fine balance that makes it possible to sleep in our homes in safety is so easily rocked and shaken. The fragile fabric of law and order that makes it possible for us to walk in the sunlight and hold our heads up high without fear is so easily ripped to shreds. We must preserve this sensitive balance and shield this delicate fabric with every measure of protection that our great institutions of justice are capable of providing, and the public are counting on you faithfully to discharge your duties as members of the jury, that most precious and sacred of those institutions.

'If we allow a criminal such as Justine Levy to escape justice because we sympathize with what she did, then we may as well pack up our law courts and police forces and go back to the jungle.'

He stood for a moment more in silence and then sat down.

39

Justine's decision not to offer a closing statement had thrown everything into confusion. Abrams had half expected it, because her testimony had said everything that she needed and wanted to say. But he had still been caught by surprise when the judge gave him the go-ahead to start his. And now, in the twenty-minute recess before the judge began his summation, Abrams wondered if he had presented it as well as he could. He was brooding about his performance when a tall, burly man barged past him on the way to the washroom. He was angered by this, and considered remonstrating with the man. But the stony look on the other's face gave him pause. He looked like the kind of man who wouldn't mind having to do a few hours of community service for the pleasure of punching an assistant district attorney on the nose.

He took his anger out, instead, on the short man who followed the big one, deliberately not moving as the other man edged around him, apparently in a hurry to get to the washroom too.

Court hearings are a curse on people who have weak bladders, he thought with wry amusement.

*   *   *

In the washroom, Declan, who had just barged past Daniel Abrams, closed the door to the water closet where he had stashed the gun. He opened the tank and took out the plastic bag containing the pieces. He knew that he had to act quickly. The judge was taking advantage of Justine's cooperation to expedite the proceedings and clear the backlog on his docket. So he had decided to give his summation after a short twenty-minute recess, rather than the following day. Declan realized that the judge had probably prepared it in advance. More to the point, he also realized that he didn't have long to assemble the gun.

He closed the tank and rested the bag on top of it. Then he took out the pieces and, using his small screwdriver, began to assemble them quickly. He was an expert at stripping a gun and reassembling it, despite his size and somewhat pudgy fingers. But the flow of adrenalin was pumping his heart to a frenzy of excitement – he could almost smell the bitch's blood, and he couldn't keep his hands steady.

The presence of someone else at the urinal outside also made him nervous. He heard several people come and go, but one man was still there, he could sense it. It wasn't that he could hear him; the man seemed rather quiet in fact. But there is a kind of sensation one gets, when another person is there. And Declan had this feeling now. Only it wasn't just the feeling of another human presence, it was the feeling that this man wasn't actually doing anything. There was no sound of flowing water, nor of any other kind. And for some reason Declan had the feeling that the man had been the first to enter after him.

At first he had assumed that the man was waiting to use the WC. But there were other cubicles that he could have used, and they couldn't all be out of order, although some of them looked decidedly unsanitary.

Perhaps someone had found the parts of the gun in the tank, he thought. But he realized that it was highly unlikely that they opened the tanks unless they actually became clogged up.

He couldn't be sure. There was always the possibility that he would step out and find himself facing a whole posse of armed law enforcement officials. But the eerie silence outside the cubicle didn't testify to the presence of an army. It spoke of one man, and the man was still there. Years of survival in the war zones of Belfast and Derry had taught Declan to sense danger, to smell it. And right now the odour was overwhelming.

He fitted the silencer and now all that remained was the moment of truth. He transferred the gun to his left hand and slid it inside his partially unbuttoned jacket. Then he reached for the door latch.

Suddenly he realized that he had forgotten something, something that would arouse immediate suspicion if he didn't correct it. Leaning back and twisting his upper body slightly, he reached back to the toilet handle and flushed it. As the water came cascading down, he quickly unlatched the door and stepped out.

He saw himself facing a small man with his hand in his pocket who was looking straight at him and appeared to be smiling. He knew in an instant that he had been right, that this man had been waiting for him, that this man was his enemy. In that same instant he noticed the bulge in the man's pocket, a bulge too big to be explained by the presence of a diminutive hand there. He saw a movement in the pocket and knew that he was looking death in the face. But he had one thing going for him. In his escape plan, he had allowed for the possibility that he might come under fire after executing the Levy bitch. So he had taken the small precaution of availing himself of the rich culture of self-defence that America has to offer and bought himself what used to be called a 'bullet-proof vest' but was now known more commonly as 'soft body armour'. It was, in essence, a waistcoat made of aramid fibre, a composite polymer sold by Du Pont under the proprietary name of Kevlar. And although light, it could stop the bullets of most handguns, certainly the bullet from a light .22 of the kind Thomas was wielding.

Thomas was a pro and he aimed for the chest, to maximize the chance of hitting something if the target moved as he fired and to give himself the chance to fire a second time to finish the job. With Thomas, executions were always a two-shot affair, unless the subject was already a captive, and it was always the second shot that was fatal. But this time the first shot did not have the desired effect. In truth Declan had recoiled slightly, but it was more in shock than anything else, and a fraction of a second later he turned his body to improve his firing position, pulled out the silenced handgun and squeezed the trigger.

Thomas saw something happening, saw a movement of some kind under the jacket as the gun came out and Declan fired off the fatal shot. But his body failed to react as quickly as his mind would have liked. By the time he realized that he had to realign his aim for Declan's head, he felt a bullet from Declan's gun rip into his guts and another into his heart. It was as if the breath within him were let out of a huge puncture hole. And then the lights faded.

Declan dragged the body into the cubicle from which he had emerged and held it up in such a way that as soon as he let go and slipped out, the body would fall against the door, holding it closed. Of course, if anyone looked underneath they would see the body. But in the Big Apple the golden rule was to mind one's own business.

He looked at his watch and realized that it was time to go back to the courtroom. He had another meeting, this one scheduled by appointment. And he had every intention of keeping it.

40

The judge had decided early in this case to take advantage of Justine's refusal to engage in legal wrangling to assist in expediting the case and clearing up the backlog in judges' dockets which tends to build up in the crime-ridden cities of the United States. Accordingly he resolved not to postpone his summation until the following day. It was still only three o'clock and he felt confident that he could summarize the legal issues clearly and concisely. When the court reconvened after the twenty-minute recess that followed the prosecutor's closing argument, he turned to the jury and addressed them in a slow but commanding and authoritative voice.

'Ladies and gentlemen of the jury, you have heard the People's case and you have heard the evidence presented by the defendant. It is not my task to repeat or to summarize the evidence already presented to you, nor to help you to identify which parts of the evidence are most important or most relevant. It is my function to direct you as to the *law*. You and you alone are the judges of the facts.

'I must caution you, however, that on matters of law you must take your directions from me and from no other source. You must not be guided in any way by preconceived notions that you may have got from books or movies or TV shows or friends. Whatever prior assumptions you may hold on matters of law you must put completely out of your minds, just as you were admonished at the outset of this trial to put aside any preconceived notions you may have inadvertently acquired as to the facts of this case.

'After I have given you directions as to the law you will retire to consider the facts and then apply the law as I have explained it to you to the facts as you determine them to be.

'The defendant is charged with murder in the second degree. First-degree murder, which has since been ruled an unconstitutional category, concerns the murder of police and peace officers and need not concern you. But second-degree murder is only one of a number of four categories of homicide which you must consider, the others being criminally negligent homicide, second-degree manslaughter and first-degree manslaughter.'

Abrams looked visibly frustrated. The judge knew that by stating the articles in the order in which they appeared in the state penal law he was, in effect, encouraging the jury to convict on a lesser charge. In other murder cases that came before him, he invariably worked his way along the list in the other direction, from murder to negligent homicide. Sometimes he even neglected to give a preliminary list and simply defined them one by one, starting with murder. He knew that he was telling them to convict on a negligent homicide charge, and he knew that Abrams also knew. What was harder to admit to himself was his motive.

'Under Section 125.10 of the New York Penal Law, "A person is guilty of criminally negligent homicide, when with criminal negligence he causes the death of another person." I will explain the legal definition of criminal negligence in due course.

'Under Section 125.15, "A person is guilty of manslaughter in the second degree when he recklessly causes the death of another person", or "when he intentionally causes or aids another person to commit suicide".

'Under Section 125.20, "A person is guilty of manslaughter in the first degree when with intent to cause serious physical injury to another person he causes the death of such person or of a third person; or, with intent to cause death to another person, he causes the death of such person or a third person under circumstances which do not constitute murder because he acts under the influence of extreme emotional disturbance as defined in paragraph (a) of subdivision one of Section 125.25."

'I shall explain this further in due course. But first I must continue the relevant paragraph. "The fact that homicide was committed under the influence of extreme emotional disturbance constitutes a mitigating circumstance reducing murder to manslaughter in the first degree."

'Under subdivision one of Section 125.25, "A person is guilty of murder in the second degree when with intent to cause the death of another person he causes the death of such person or of a third person."

'We now come to the affirmative defence provided for in paragraph (a) that I mentioned earlier. According to this paragraph, murder is reduced to manslaughter if "The defendant acted under the influence of extreme emotional disturbance for which there was a reasonable explanation or excuse, the reasonableness of which is to be determined from the viewpoint of a person in the defendant's situation under the circumstances as the defendant believed them to be."

'Under subdivision two of Section 125.25, a person is guilty of second-degree murder when "Under circumstances evincing a depraved indifference to human life, he recklessly engages in conduct which creates a grave risk of death to another person, and thereby causes the death of another person."

'These, then, are the four categories of homicide which you are charged to consider.'

The judge then went into detail, describing the meaning of criminal negligence and the elements of homicide in general.

'. . . for example, in the People versus Jarvis Stewart it was held that "the prosecutor must, at least, prove that the defendant's conduct was an actual cause of death, in that it forged a link in the chain of causes which actually brought about the death".'

Abrams smiled.

'But there is a further requirement, as stated in People versus Kibbe, that "the defendant's actions must be a *sufficiently direct cause* of the ensuing death before there can be any imposition of criminal liability."

'However, as the Stewart decision pointed out, "direct" does not mean the same as "unaided". Indeed, it was held in People versus Kane that if "felonious assault is operative as a cause of death, the causal cooperation of erroneous surgical or medical treatment does not relieve the assailant from liability for homicide". It is for you to decide whether the defendant's actions constituted felonious assault.

'Similarly in the case of the Commonwealth of Pennsylvania versus Eisenhower, a persuasive analogy which the New York Court of Appeals cited approvingly in both the Stewart and Kane decisions, "the prisoner cannot escape by showing that death was the result of an accident occurring in an operation which his felonious act made necessary". Again it is for you to decide whether or not the defendant's original actions constituted such a felonious act.

'Also note that the wording there is "made necessary" not "caused". It is for you to decide whether the defendant's actions made the events at the hospital *necessary*.'

The smile had all but vanished from Abrams's face. The judge was coming as close as he dared to telling the jury that Justine might not be guilty of homicide at all.

'If in the light of the foregoing you are satisfied that the defendant is *legally* responsible for causing the death of Sean Murphy then you must proceed to consider the question of intent. Specifically, you must, if you get to this stage, consider whether it was the intent of the accused to kill Sean Murphy, to cause him serious injury, to cause him simple injury or to frighten him . . .'

'. . . and now, ladies and gentlemen of the jury, you will retire to consider your verdict.'

41

Justine sat calmly as she watched the jury filing out. There was no tension left in her now. Throughout the trial she had been like a coiled spring, the force holding her together being her story, her truth and her desire to tell it. But now that she had released it and let it unwind the tension inside her was gone. Awaiting her fate held no fear for her. It was waiting to be heard that had been her only jail.

The bailiff led Justine away, to await the verdict in a holding cell a few storeys below. She was silent, almost catatonic, as the door slammed behind her, leaving her alone in a cold room of stone walls and iron bars.

But when she closed her eyes she was no longer in a grey cell but in a warm carpeted corridor, a nine-year-old girl walking towards her father's bedroom. He had just been through one of his violent rages, but it had burnt itself out and he was now in that mood of sombre depression when he could safely be approached. There was nothing he liked more than the gentle hand of his daughter stroking the back of his head at these moments, and in a perverse way it gave Justine pleasure to give him this comfort, knowing that she was close to him and that he loved her.

He was sitting on the edge of the bed when she entered the room, holding a gun in his hand. He raised the gun to his right temple, not seeing her. She wanted to cry out, to scream at him to stop. But she just stood there frozen, as if she were watching the playback of something that had already happened seven years ago, something that was impossible to stop.

He squeezed the trigger. The explosion merged with Justine's wail of anguish as blood and brain tissue splattered her dress.

For Declan, it was a time of great tension. The body in the washroom could be found at any minute. Even now, Declan didn't know who it was. It could have been an IRA hit-man, but it could also have been an agent of the British. Whoever it was, they would send others. But more to the point, he knew that if the body were found, everyone who had been at the trial would be a suspect. And he already had that arrest record and the scheduled court appearance.

He never really knew who had set him up for the arrest. It was obviously a set-up. But he couldn't figure out the purpose. If it had been to get him into jail so he could be killed, then why was no effort to kill him made when he was in custody? It could be because he made bail so quickly. But he had been free for a while. Why had the attempt been made only less than an hour ago?

He wondered how long it would be before the jury came back. He had heard of cases where the jury reached a verdict on the initial vote, and cases where they had deliberated for hours or even days before telling the judge that they were deadlocked.

Justine sat unmoving in her cell. There wasn't a trace of fear on her face, just a quiet sense of regret at what might have been if the twists and turns of fate had been different. Only it wasn't fate, it was man-made destruction. She was in a white hospital room, looking down at a frail skeleton of a woman whose once-full hair was now no more than a few sporadic patches on an otherwise bald head.

As she looked down at what little was left of her mother she remembered the shocking pictures she had once seen of the concentration camp survivors. Her mother wasn't a victim of the Nazi holocaust. But there was in some way a parallel between her mother's fate and the millions of Jews, half a million gypsies, and tens of thousands of homosexuals and suspected communists who had perished in that genocidal atrocity. Her mother was a victim of the philosophy that made Nazism possible, the philosophy that treats the individual as the property of the group to be used as a human sacrifice, the philosophy that holds that force may be *initiated* against one's neighbours, as opposed to merely used in self-defence or defence of the innocent.

'The ripple bed wasn't ready when we brought her in,' the head nurse explained. 'I'll have it brought up by Maintenance as soon as possible.'

The ripple bed was supposed to make the patient more comfortable and reduce the risk of bedsores, by undulating slowly under the control of a motor, thereby changing the patient's position periodically.

'Is it all right if I stay for a few minutes?'

'All right, but try not to wake her. She needs her rest.'

The nurse left. Justine knew that there was nothing that her mother needed now, nothing that anyone could give her. She had been deprived of that a long time ago. In the past few months Justine's psychological strength had waxed as her mother's physical strength had waned. But now, in a last-minute return to the way it had once been, it was the girl who had a full life ahead of her who wept profusely while the woman whose life was almost over remained like a dry rock, trying to give her daughter some hope.

'That's not what I want to see,' said Justine's mother in a voice so strong that it seemed to defy the presence of death that hovered over her.

'I can't help it,' said Justine, burying her head in her hands.

'I know I haven't got long. Let me use what little time I have left to explain a few things that I want you to understand.'

Justine forced herself to contain her tears. Her hand slid down from her face and she nodded.

'I'm ready,' she said.

'Justine, you once said that medicine for you is a hobby

and a profession all rolled into one. There aren't many people who can say that about their work. Most people, even people who do jobs that most people regard as interesting, think of it as just a job. In time you may become like that too. I've heard that medicine is a job with a lot of stress of its own, and most doctors would be quite happy to go home and put their feet up at the end of the day, even though they very seldom can. But as long as you've got your youthful enthusiasm, make the most of it. Don't throw it away on something less important.'

'I won't give up my career for marriage—'

'You know that it's not marriage I'm talking about.' Her mother paused, as if challenging Justine to admit or deny the unstated accusation. Justine remained silent. 'Don't waste your time on regrets, Justine.'

'You had a chance to live . . . and someone took it away from you.'

'That's all in the past.'

'You once told me never to accept injustice as the final word, to challenge it at every turn. You said that it isn't normal to try to live in a house that's on fire, so why try to live in an unjust society. The house is still on fire. Why shouldn't I try to extinguish the fire?'

'There's nothing wrong with trying to *extinguish* the fire. But don't fight fire with fire. You fight fire with water. Use your desire for revenge constructively, as the psychological fuel to propel you forward, not as an incendiary bomb that burns itself into destruction along with its surroundings. Murphy is a terrorist, a murderer who takes lives. You're going to be a doctor, someone who *saves* lives.'

'It wasn't just your chance to live that was stolen, it was others', and all the good that *they* could have done.'

'You mean Srini Shankar.'

'How did you know?' asked Justine, tearfully.

'I was tidying up your room and saw the reprints of his papers from medical journals. I found the letter you got back from University College in London telling you he'd been killed.'

'I read up every paper on cancer I could get my hands on and discovered that he was the world's foremost expert on breast cancer. I wanted you to go to Britain to have him as a consultant,' said Justine.

'You must have been shattered when they told you he was dead.'

'It was as if someone cut the last supporting girder beneath me.'

'Then I guess you'll just have to learn to fly.' The voice was still firm even through her pain.

'You're not making this any easier for me,' Justine said defensively.

'I never said it would be easy. But you're going to face life after I'm gone, and without self-pity.'

'Shankar was unrivalled in his field,' said Justine. 'I heard one of the doctors say he wished he could consult him. And the other one nodded. Shankar might have saved you if that bastard hadn't blown him away! Well, now he's got to pay!'

'You can't waste time on what might have been. You must concentrate on what you do best. Shankar is dead, but think of all the lives *you'll* be able to save! Don't blow it all on petty revenge. Otherwise you'll be doing something worse than Murphy. You'll be destroying *your* ability to help others in the future.'

'But *who's* going to make him pay?' she whined like a small child. 'The authorities have already had their say. *Who* is going to give us justice?'

Justine's mother was shaking her head slowly.

'All right, I see I can't dissuade you, but at least let me make one request: whatever you do, do it well.'

Justine's mother closed her eyes and the equipment beside her gave off a high-pitched tone.

The door to the cell was opened abruptly, shattering her daydream.

'The jury's back,' said the bailiff.

She wiped the tears from her eyes as she was led down the corridor and into the elevator. From there it was a short walk down another corridor back to the courtroom. Abrams was approaching the entrance from the opposite direction. He reached the door first but he paused for a moment. He appeared to be playing the gentleman and waiting for her to enter first. As she walked past him their eyes met for a couple of seconds and she thought she saw something there that she hadn't noticed before. Was it sympathy? Solidarity? Regret? Whatever it had been, it was gone in a moment.

He didn't look at her again when they both took up their places inside. It was as if he had said too much with his eyes already and didn't want to reveal any more of himself. It was one thing for a defendant to take the stand and let her own blood before the jury, it was quite another for the prosecutor to bare his soul before the defendant.

The jurors were filing back one by one, taking up their places. Leading them in was James Lawson, the businessman and self-made millionaire whom Justine had indicated was to be her advocate in the jury room.

Parker wasn't so sure. Lawson was a man who had made it within the system and seemed to believe in the rules as a common guide rail to keep people on the right track. He had set up his computer services company in the seventies, when mini-computers were beginning to get into the smaller departments of businesses and external services no longer seemed like the cash cow they had been a decade earlier. But he specialized in a lucrative niche market: matching price quotes from suppliers to the needs of companies using dummy applications. He became so strong in the field that suppliers lowered their quotes when his consultancy applied for them and his clients began paying him commissions to make the applications for them.

He was a firm believer in the consistency of iron discipline, whether it be the discipline of computers or the discipline of the law: a set of rules to be drawn up with careful forethought and then rigidly adhered to thereafter, until the rules were formally changed. It was easy to see Lawson voting for guilty even while sympathizing with the accused. The last time he had served on a jury he had voted guilty and there was nothing in his background to suggest that he would be any more willing to compromise the law on this occasion. He had made it in his chosen field without breaking the rules and he had no sympathy for those who took short cuts. Was it possible that he would make an exception now, in Justine's case?

Parker was trying to read their faces. Conventional wisdom held that in serious cases such as murder, when jurors are going to convict they avoid looking at the defendant, especially if the defendant is looking at them, forcing those who look to make eye contact. They were looking at Justine openly. This was a good sign. If the conventional wisdom was correct then it boded well for her. But when there was such a wide range of verdicts open to the jury, such as three possible lower categories of homicide, one couldn't really tell. The jury might have been planning to convict on a charge of negligent homicide or second-degree manslaughter. In their eyes that would be an act of kindness and a favour, not a reason to look down at the ground as if they were finding the defendant guilty of murder.

In any case the eye-contact rule only applied rigidly in states where they had capital punishment.

Next to Lawson, sat the housewife whom Justine had first antagonized and then befriended in that strange sequence of questions during the *voir dire*. She looked at Justine with a look of encouragement that Parker couldn't decipher. Was it the encouragement one gives to a person who is about to face an ordeal or the encouragement one gives to a person who has already been through one? It was a small but significant difference. And the difference was between a verdict of innocent and one of guilty.

Parker knew that this woman had daughters too. Her children were talented like Justine. Did she see Justine as someone who had been victimized by life, or someone who had squandered her opportunities on something as petty as revenge?

Abrams was straightening out his papers, in preparation for any post-verdict motions that he might have to make, or to respond to any that Parker might make. There was a kind of false briskness to his actions as he quickly extracted the papers, tapped them straight on the desk, closed the case and put it on the floor beside his chair.

There was a truck driver on the jury. He was called Mulligan and was probably Irish himself. But Justine had not challenged him, and there was nothing in the look on his face to indicate hostility to her. On the other hand there was nothing to indicate his thoughts at all.

Whatever those thoughts might be, he had kept them well hidden throughout the trial. The only thing that was clear was that he was a hard man who had no patience for weakness. Did he see Justine's actions as a sign of weakness or of strength?

The jurors were all in place and only the judge remained absent.

'All rise!' the bailiff's voice rang out.

The judge re-entered and sat down. The rest of the courtroom followed suit, but the tension hung in the air as they waited while a piece of paper was passed from the foreman of the jury to the judge via the clerk of the court. The judge opened it and perused it briefly.

'Proceed, Mr Clerk,' said the judge.

'The prisoner will rise and face the jury.'

Justine rose and looked at the man whom she had singled out to represent her in the jury room.

'The foreman of the jury will rise and face the prisoner.'

The foreman rose with firm dignity.

'Mr Foreman, in the case of the People of the State of New York versus Justine Levy have you reached a verdict on which you are all agreed?'

'We have.'

'What say you?'

The foreman of the jury stated the verdict. But before doing so, at least according to a reporter from the *New York Post*, he winked at Justine.

42

Declan heard it, incredulously. The bitch had openly admitted the whole story from the witness stand, positively bragged about it, and this jury was letting her out on to the streets.

By now the court had descended into pandemonium, after the initial gasp and then the pause of pregnant silence. The judge rapped with his gavel to restore order.

'Miss Levy, you are an extremely fortunate young woman. You are free to go.' Then, turning to the jury, he added: 'Members of the jury, I thank you for your services. You are hereby discharged. Court is adjourned.'

The judge rose and the court again erupted into pandemonium. In the ensuing chaos, Declan jumped over the railing that separated the spectators' section from the front of the courtroom.

'Now you're going to die, you fascist bitch!' he screamed, pulling the Colt .45 from his pocket.

He swung the gun towards her, looking around to see where the bailiffs were. In the split second that he wasted, Parker leapt up and dived at him, deflecting the gun upwards just as the Irishman squeezed the trigger. The gun barked, its lethal projectile harming no one, but bringing splinters of plaster down from the ceiling as journalists and spectators ducked for cover. While Parker struggled with Declan and several more shots were fired into the air, a bailiff pulled out his handgun and managed to squeeze off a clear shot at Declan, hitting his body armour and leaving him unharmed.

In shock at having come so close to being hit himself, Parker reeled backwards, off balance. The bailiff was trying to calm a frantic middle-aged matron while Declan staggered over to Justine and met her eye to eye, holding the gun aimed at her head. She clawed at the gun in a frantic effort to deflect it upward as Declan fired. She fell backward with a red spot on her temple and cried out in pain as Parker spun round with a look of horror on his face.

For what seemed like an eternity Declan and Parker eyeballed each other, Parker with fury, Declan with what seemed to Parker like the indifference of an android. Parker knew that there was no way he could get across the space that separated them without being shot. But Abrams, who was crouched on the ground behind Declan, had seen what had happened and he was ideally poised to act. Drawing on the collegiate boxing skills that had never deserted him, he dived at Declan, spun him round with his left hand and knocked him backwards with a single, ferocious right hook. The gun fell from his hand. Without pausing Declan dived on to it, but by now he had lost the initiative. As his hand scooped up the gun a shot rang out from one of bailiffs. A spot of blood appeared in the centre of Declan's forehead, and the INLA terrorist fell dead with a powerful thud on the courtroom floor.

The panic continued all around them, but Parker looked at Abrams for a few seconds and Abrams saw the gratitude in his eyes, forcing its way through the young man's tears. A few yards away, the judge was having a word with the clerk of the court.

43

'I thought it might be better for you to leave this way,' the judge told Parker. He was still wearing his robes, having huddled Parker out of the room and led him to his chambers by a long and tortuous route to avoid the more tenacious members of the press corps.

'Let the police get the situation under control,' he continued. 'And let the press deal with the public chaos, not with your private feelings. You've earned the right to peace and quiet.'

Parker knew that the judge was being gentle with him. After what he had been through it was not unreasonable. But Parker was grateful, and relieved.

'Is there any way of getting out without the press noticing?'

'There's a rear exit where they make deliveries.'

'Thank you.'

'You know, Rick, as you're a lawyer, and may be a judge some day, I think there's something you ought to know. It's not a judge's job to preach. But—' He jerked his finger towards the door. '— *that's* what happens when people start taking the law into their own hands.'

Parker nodded in quiet understanding.

'You know . . . it's funny,' he said.

'What is?'

'Justine told me that her mother once said to her: "Whatever you do – do it well." And you know what? She did. She did it so damn well, she made the rest of us look like fools.'

The judge put a comforting hand on his shoulder.

It was ten minutes later when the rear door opened. Parker stepped out and looked around. He held his head up to the fresh air and breathed deeply.

He looked around again. There was no one about. He glanced back at the door and gave the signal. Justine stepped out, her head bandaged where the bullet had grazed her, and looked around. They exchanged conspiratorial glances and walked down the street.

'I'm glad I was of some use to you in the end,' he said.

'You were great, Rick.'

'You know, it looked like you weren't even afraid.'

'I was more frightened than I looked. I just didn't show it. I guess my trouble always was I didn't like to show my emotions.'

'Were you frightened during the trial?'

'I don't know. I suppose I always knew that I might end up behind bars for life. But it was overshadowed by the image of my mother wasting away in that hospital bed and the smug face of Murphy telling me that he had the right to kill the man who could have saved her.'

'You know you could have killed Murphy without exposing your identity.'

'I know . . . but then I wouldn't have been true to myself.'

They reached an intersection. There was no one else about. Parker pointed right.

'I left my car back there. Can I give you a ride anywhere?'

'I need to be alone for a while . . . just for a few hours . . . maybe a few days.'

'I understand,' he said, looking sad but not hurt. He realized that this was it, the parting of the ways. He felt a tinge of regret, anticipating the emptiness in his life that would follow, wondering how long it would take to get over her.

He walked off in one direction, she in the other. When a distance had opened up between them Justine turned.

'Hey, Rick!' she called out. She saw him turn and look at her across the distance. Without a trace of pity in her voice she added: 'I'll call you tonight!'